A self-employed forester, Steven Wray spends most of his time in the woods since retirement from a career in the NHS. Married for forty years to Sally and a father of three.

This first novel was written before the Covid pandemic. Steven was inspired to publish after both his sons had their books published.

To Sally who puts up with me and my sons who inspired me to finish.

Steven Wray

ALEXANDRA

AUSTIN MACAULEY PUBLISHERS™
LONDON • CAMBRIDGE • NEW YORK • SHARJAH

Copyright © Steven Wray 2023

The right of Steven Wray to be identified as author of this work has been asserted by the author in accordance with sections 77 and 78 of the Copyright, Designs and Patents Act 1988.

All rights reserved. No part of this publication may be reproduced, stored in a retrieval system, or transmitted in any form or by any means, electronic, mechanical, photocopying, recording, or otherwise, without the prior permission of the publishers.

Any person who commits any unauthorised act in relation to this publication may be liable to criminal prosecution and civil claims for damages.

This is a work of fiction. Names, characters, businesses, places, events, locales, and incidents are either the products of the author's imagination or used in a fictitious manner. Any resemblance to actual persons, living or dead, or actual events is purely coincidental.

A CIP catalogue record for this title is available from the British Library.

ISBN 9781035835829 (Paperback)
ISBN 9781035835836 (ePub e-book)

www.austinmacauley.com

First Published 2023
Austin Macauley Publishers Ltd®
1 Canada Square
Canary Wharf
London
E14 5AA

Chapter One

This is the story of a journey. A story of how some people survived where most did not.

Natalie was very young when the old world ended. Although that world died a long time ago, the memory of it clung to her like a bad smell. No matter how far she travelled, no matter how strong she had been within this new world, she kept the aroma of the old world. Natalie learnt to accept this; she knew it would not change, no matter how hard she tried. The old world was a fact of her existence; she had been there, had experienced it in a way that was inaccessible to most others in her community.

People looked at her and saw with all their senses the old world. In truth, the memories she was prevailed upon to share were mostly those of her mother, or things learnt from the old books she so treasured.

Today, her thoughts are so full of the past, she is finding it hard to stay focused on the chores that are an everyday part of her life. As she pulls a comb through the hair of a wriggling, complaining grandchild, she can see herself in a mirror. She will be eighty-five years old if she lives the few days to her next birthday. Although she still feels young in her mind, the mirror tells her what her body already knows—that she is old.

Her hair is grey and flat, and her wrinkled skin has seen too much sunshine. Her body sags at the shoulders no matter how much she tries to straighten her back; her breasts, once full, are now empty sacks. Only her eyes and her smile retain the youthfulness she still feels on the inside.

As Newtown's "Community Mother", Natalie is responsible for the well-being of those that call Newtown home. It is Natalie who must make the final decisions about how to use resources, and Natalie who must be the final arbiter of the many and various arguments between Newtown's people.

Still looking into the mirror, Natalie released the child with a kiss to the top of its head, suddenly feeling lighter and more carefree than she had for years.

'I'm too old for all this,' she confides quietly to the mirror. 'It's time for Newtown to elect another "mother".'

She didn't take time to reflect on this decision to let go of her status as community mother. Gazing into the mirror, comb in her lap, her thoughts moved, with an agility her body lacked, to how she would manage the resignation. Her emotions could be dealt with later. There had been many endings in her life, but few of them had been in her own gift.

Rising up from the little seat in front of the mirror to make her morning tea, she pondered on how and when to reveal her decision. By the time she had lit the little gas stove kept in the corner of her room, it came to her that the day of her eighty-fifth birthday would be the ideal occasion to announce her retirement to the people of Newtown. It was meant to be a surprise, but she knew that the community was planning a birthday celebration for her.

The preparations had got to the ears of the children, who lacked the guile to hide their illicit knowledge from Granny Natalie. She had even overheard the children whispering excitedly about Alexandra coming to Newtown. Natalie thought that unlikely, as she and Alexandra had not spoken properly for more than thirty years. Natalie thought it more likely that the children's imaginations had added an extra detail to their eavesdropping on parental conversations.

Apart from the hated and much feared Nathaniel, Alexandra was the most famous of the old worlders, so what was more natural than that the children should come up with the name of Alexandra in their conspiratorial gossiping? Carrying the steaming tea back to the little chair in front of the mirror, she felt both a delight and a little fear at the thought of Alexandra breaking her silence on the night of her birthday. Despite the rationalisation that it was simply the imagining of children, she allowed her mind to create the scene.

Alexandra moving through a packed community hall and taking her into a fulsome hug. She knew that Alexandra would behave as if they had spoken only yesterday rather than the stony silence she had maintained for so long. Sipping at her tea, Natalie sighed to herself for she knew that she would forgive Alexandra for her intolerant silence, as she had forgiven her so much else in their long lives. She had always loved Alexandra and could never stay angry with her for very long, no matter how much she deserved it.

Her thoughts turned back to her resignation. *My little announcement means I'll be surprising the people of Newtown, more than they will surprise me.* This thought brought a smile to her face, which she caught in the mirror's reflection. The smile for a moment resurrecting the youthfulness in her face.

"Natalie, Natalie, where are you?" The impatient voice of Kenny came, the far too young "Father" of Newtown community. The sound of the impatient young man chased the smile from her reflection and drained the carefree feeling she had so enjoyed.

Chapter Two

"Community mothers" were elected, but by the adult males only. The women of a community elected the "Community father". Some of the larger communities also had elected councils of both men and women, but small communities like Newtown made do with a mother and a father. The role of the Community "mother" and "father" was to provide leadership and order within their communities.

Though in law, the roles were equal in status and power almost exclusively, it was the mothers who the communities looked to for leadership in most matters. Community "mothers" were elected for life, but community "fathers" had to stand down after a maximum of five years. The community mother could only be removed by a majority of adult females in a community. How the mother and fathers of communities divided their responsibilities was entirely a matter between them. As in any family, a good relationship between the "mother" and "father" was important for the well-being of a community.

As Community mothers were elected for life, Newtown was not unusual in having an older mother and younger father, but the degree of disparity was something remarked on by many. The difference in age had not stopped them being a good team over the last three years. Newtown had been stable and prosperous in that time, and so its inhabitants thought well of their "parents" despite the lifetimes that separated them in age.

However, frustrations existed in their relationship. Kenny used his status as Newtown's "father" to spend much of his time organising football games between the communities that spread along the Lammermoor shore line. Natalie resented this obsession with football, and had argued with him that he should be spending his time persuading the other communities to work together to improve the tracks and patchwork of old world roads that served as communications between them.

Kenny argued that the football was developing good relations between the communities, and out of that would come the cooperation needed to improve the links. A point she reminded him of when a game with nearby Garvally had resulted in numerous injuries amongst the rival supporters. Natalie suspected that he was so keen on the football because it elevated his status amongst the other young men. He was a compact, strongly built young man who excelled at all things physical.

The football was an excuse to visit the other communities socially, and the male players had the opportunity to flaunt their prowess in front of the women of other communities. Even now, seventy-five years after the end of the old world, men still outnumbered women by two to one. Kenny, too plain to be handsome, and too practical in his thinking to be charming, relied on his physicality to attract feminine attention. A task he was not unsuccessful in, although he remained un-partnered.

Today, it was not football, or women, that was on Kenny's mind. There had been a report that a thirty strong party of raiders were seen passing the village of Carfree. Kenny was keen to ride out to see if the reports were true, but Newtown could not hope to deal with thirty raiders on their own. He would have to raise the alarm and gather in fighting men from along the Lammermoor's to deal with such a force.

Kenny could have taken the decisions needed to deal with this reported threat on his own, but it was custom for "father" and "mother" to consult about mobilising the defences of a community and particularly in calling upon other communities for support.

Natalie trusted Kenny to deal with such situations, which regularly disrupted the normal flow of life in Newtown. She would always listen quietly to his plan of action and agree where he seemed to need agreement or gently advise where he seemed to need advice. Kenny normally left such sessions confident in his ability to deal with the situation at hand, just as Natalie wanted him to. She knew that what Kenny needed most of all was the confidence to believe in himself and his abilities.

Although Kenny appeared to have too much confidence to many, she knew that this was mostly a young man's bravado. In fact, he experienced the responsibilities of being Newtown's "father" as no small burden.

Today, as on all the other occasions Natalie would make a point of thanking Kenny for his courtesy in sharing his plans, and praising him for taking the time to think where many "fathers" might just react. She would praise him as if his consultation came as an act of consideration and strength, and hoped that in the future this is how it would be. Yet even as this thought was in her mind, she realised with a small pang of regret that if she were to see this transition, it would not be as the mother of Newtown.

In all probability, this would be the last time that Kenny came to her for advice and support. Today, Kenny lingered longer than usual as if he hadn't quite got something that he had come to Natalie for. She knew and shared his dilemma; for if he discovered that the threat from the raiders was real, the plans for her birthday would be disrupted. Travel between the communities would hold dangers, many men would be away, and the communities would be both excited and oppressed by the possibility of violence.

Natalie could feel the tension in Kenny who wanted to apologise for disrupting the celebration, but couldn't because she wasn't meant to know about it. She decided to let him wriggle on that hook.

Kenny took his leave to make the necessary arrangement in a rush of excitement, mixed with fear and concern for the safety of his community, and for the personal danger that may lie ahead of him. But nagging away on the surface of his mind was how he could deal with the raiders, if they be real, without disrupting the "old birds" birthday party. It would not improve his popularity if the much planned celebrations were cancelled because he had raised the alarm, especially if it proved that there were no raiders.

However, he trusted the old man from whom the news of raiders had come. He had sent a boy with a message on a strip of leather, for as he had written, he "trusted the boy's legs but not his tongue". He decided that he must put concerns from the celebration from his mind and concentrate only on the raiders.

The raiders were bands of men who scavenging from both the old and new world, lived in neither. Most of the bands that still roamed the country were made up of violent and shiftless men who had fallen out with their communities, or had been expelled for crimes. The most dangerous bands were descendants of groups of men who had made their homes in the ruins of the old cities. After the cities had been picked clean of preserved food and resources, these men had learnt to survive by stealing from each other and the settled communities.

They raided the emerging communities that grew on the outskirts of cities, or the older rural communities, some of which had coped better with the chaos of the death of the old world better than the towns and cities. One of the strongest motivators for the raiders was the hope of capturing women.

As Kenny used Newtown's short wave radio to call the fathers of the nearest communities, he hoped that it was not a band of city raiders that they would have to deal with.

The very worst thought in Kenny's mind was that it might be the raiders led by Nathan, who with his father of the same name, had terrorised Scotland from his base in Glasgow for over fifty years. To the children of Lammermoor, the bogeyman had a name, and it was Nathan.

Chapter Three

Kenny had fought with raiders before, in fact it was his reputation as a fighter that got him elected as "father of Newtown". He was the youngest father of the Lammermoor communities. He had good reasons for his hatred of all raiders. It had been a band of them that had killed his family—mother, father, and older brother. Kenny was twelve years old when the thriving community of East Lowtown was overwhelmed.

Natalie had known his parents well, as they had been "father" and "mother" to the community of East Lowtown. At the time of the raid, Natalie had not long left her own community of Stainton to establish a new community only five or six miles from East Lowtown. So she had on many occasions called upon the advice and support of Kenny parents. East Lowtown was by then a large, relatively stable, and prosperous community with much trade passing through its streets.

The nearby and older market town of Haddington had been all but deserted by repeated flooding and violence. After the collapse of the old world, Kenny's father had used his engineering skills to develop a trade in machines from tractors to computers, mending or adapting machines then selling them on throughout the Lothian's and Fife. His mother was an expert on small scale wind turbines, both repairing them and building them from scratch.

It had been largely their dynamism and partnership that had brought the community of East Lowtown out of the chaos of the old world, to a place where they could bring up children. The town had given Kenny the protection of a community forged in mutual hardship, the freedom to roam and explore relished by all energetic children, and above all the space to enjoy the love of family. All that was lost to him along with the rest of his childhood the night the raiders came.

The raiders came early in the morning taking advantage of a spring tide to manoeuvre their small, fast moving boats to the very edge of the town's defences. East Lowtown, once a small inland commuter town, now had direct access to the Forth Estuary at high tide, so much had sea levels and flooding changed the map since the old world had collapsed. Awoken, by the screams of people he had known all his life, Kenny emerged from his home to find his father's half-dressed body slumped by the gate.

Not understanding what was happening he called out and ran to his father. Getting no response, he had bent down to look into his father's face, finding only a swollen mass of flesh and blood matted hair. Still not able to understand what had happened or what was taking place in the village, he persevered in attempting to rouse his father. The next thing he was aware of was being roughly manhandled into a group of crying women, girls and boys mostly younger than himself.

The raiders were roaring abuse, pushing and kicking at the confused and terrified group of East Lowtown women and children as they herded them through the village towards the river's edge. Many were lavishly spattered in the blood of those they had taken life from, adding authentic horror to their garish armoured costume assembled from scrap metal, chain and leather. Each one carried an array of weaponry almost as accessories to their macabre costumes.

The miserable and despairing human remnants of the village of East Lowtown were driven like animals to the jetty that extended from the town's defences into the estuary, where they were loaded onto small boats to be taken to large open barges, waiting in the deeper water.

On the barge, his mother had pulled Kenny to her, and taking his head into her hands so firmly that it hurt, she stared deep into his eyes. Speaking very slowly, she made him understand that he must take the chance to escape she was going to give him. Seeing that he understood and wasn't afraid, she loosened her hold on his face and gave him a message that she said would bring help for them if he could carry it to their friends in the other communities.

After he had repeated the message to her twice, she hugged him and told him to move discreetly to the side of the barge. Each word of the message was already burnt into his memory so deeply that he would never be able to forget them. Kenny didn't see what happened, but suddenly, there was a terrible scream and a rush of movement followed by an explosion that he would later be able to recognise as the sound of a shotgun firing close by. Knowing this was his time to act, he slipped quietly into the water and submerged himself until his lungs were about to burst.

The estuary tide caught him and when he surfaced, he was twenty or thirty metres away from the barge. Despite his hands being tied, he swam to the shore by floating on his back and kicking his legs like a tadpole.

Once ashore, he hid, as instructed, until friendly men from the other Lammermoor communities arrived in response to the alarm someone in the village had managed to send in the midst of the assault. The information in the message from Kenny's mother led the Lammermoor men to an oil tanker that had become lodged on what was now the island of North Berwick Law.

The men had wanted to leave Kenny at East Lowtown, but he created such a row, they agreed to take him with them on the condition that he was to stay in the boat. During the fight at the oil tanker, he had at first obeyed his elders, but the sound of the battle within the tanker fanned the rage he had felt growing within him for those that had killed his father and taken his mother. He could see small dinghies, one with an outboard motor tethered to the side of the tankers hull, which must be the boats of the raiders.

Making sure he had his knife, he swam to the raiders' boats thinking that he could untie or cut their tethers and prevent the raiders from escaping. Just as he had managed to pull himself from the freezing water into the nearest dinghy, a young man appeared at a hole in the side of the tanker and started to climb down a rope to get to the boats. Too late to untether the boats, and unsure whether he had been seen or not, Kenny let the anger and hate he felt overwhelm the fear that came to him at the sight of the raider.

He waited until the young raider was engaged in the tricky transfer from rope to dinghy, and then threw his knife with all the might he possessed. He was confident it would strike home for he practised long and hard with his brother the skill of throwing a knife at targets far smaller than a man. It struck home in the man's unprotected lower back, who then fell with a grunt on to the side of the dinghy. Although the knife had struck well, it was probably the blow to the head on the hard wooden prow of the dinghy that was the end of the man, who slipped into the water face down and unmoving.

Kenny was quick to retrieve his knife before the man began to sink below the surface of the water. Despite the hate he felt for all raiders, a sickness rose in his stomach as he pulled the bloody knife from the back of the raider he had killed.

The battle went badly for the raiders. The Lammermoor men were all carrying shotguns, and more importantly, they had an ample supply of home-made cartridges. The anarchic raiders relied almost exclusively on scavenging, and ammunition was one of the old world items that became exhausted quickly after the collapse. Many of the raider gangs had all kinds of 21st century weapons but few had a reliable sources of ammunition, nor the know-how and organisation needed to produce their own. So in the sustained fighting that was taking place in the torch lit darkness of the oil tanker, the Lammermoor men had an advantage in having plentiful ammunition.

They played on this, pushing forward as a group and never allowing the raiders to close for hand-to-hand fighting.

After retrieving his knife from the body of the young raider, the twelve-year-old Kenny calmly set about untethering the boats. For good measure, he used his knife to puncture the two boats that were inflatables, as he did so, he was constantly looking over his shoulder at the opening that he expected any fleeing raiders to emerge from. As he worked on the last dinghy, he heard a roar from above him, and not even looking, he used both feet to push at the side of the tanker causing the dinghy to begin to move away.

Hearing a large splash followed by another, he knew the raiders had dispensed with the rope and jumped into the water to get to the now slowly drifting boats. One of the men scrabbled at the side of his dinghy, but being heavy with the weight of weapons and his armoured costume, he struggled to pull himself on board. As the man heaved at the side of the dinghy, he tipped the light boat, causing Kenny to grip tightly with feet and hands on the opposite side of the dinghy to stop himself from sliding towards the struggling raider, or being thrown out of a capsizing boat.

It looked like the man was going to be successful in getting over the side so Kenny launched himself at him with his knife aiming to stab at his hands to loosen his grip on the boat. Missing his aim, Kenny found himself holding the hilt of a knife that was sticking from a thick and dirty neck. The raider grabbed for Kenny, who jerked away pulling his knife from the man's neck. The movement caused a bright jet of blood to erupt from the injured neck, the pulse faded and then pulsed again.

The raider opening his mouth to scream only managed a bloody gurgling noise. He clawed at the wound in his neck, which was squirting blood all over the deck of the dinghy. Kenny flew from the boat to splash into the water.

Surfacing, he tried to swim away from the boats not knowing where the other raiders were. He managed to cover only a few metres in the water when he felt strong hands clutch at his clothes and begin to pull him out of the water.

He kicked and flailed with his arms feeling a panic rise up him and take hold of his mind, which until that moment had been cold and clear. His knife was lost in the sea, so he kicked and punched blindly, as he tried like a hooked fish to get back to the safety of the water. It was to no avail; he found himself floundering in the bottom of the dinghy, hands pinning him down, the world a blur as he gasped for the air he needed to fuel his struggles.

Suddenly, he was scooped from the floor of the boat and held so tightly that it was all but useless to keep struggling. Only then did his adrenaline fevered brain cool enough to hear the voices that were shouting his name, or allow his eyes to focus on faces that smiled. As his brain struggled to understand what his eyes and ears were reporting to him, his struggles came to an end, his breathing began to calm.

Only then was it clear that it was over, that they had won, and that these were his friends. This realisation created a rushing, unstoppable wave of feeling through his body, which spewed out of him in a gush and then a torrent of tears. Curling into the arms of the man who held him, he sobbed like the child he was, but could no longer be.

The community of East Lowtown took a very long time to recover from the carnage of that night despite the rescue of the women and children. Kenny's parents had been its life and soul and their death were almost the death of the community. It was decided that Natalie would take in Kenny and some of the other survivors of East Lowtown that could not face returning to the devastated community. So Newtown became Kenny's new home.

Chapter Four

People still argue over when the collapse of the old world started. Many argue that its roots were in the 1980's when the first signs of global warming were detected and ignored, others are more exact and say it was Friday, 11 September 2031. This was the date when the first woman died from what became known simply as the "death".

The first decades of the 21st century had seen a rising number of communicable diseases, created by the disturbance of ecological systems, caused by a warming planet. Most of these diseases started in the poor countries, then known as the third world, and were transmitted around the world by international travellers, be they human or animal. The better resourced public health systems of the rich countries had kept the worst of these diseases from taking hold in the west.

This changed with the advent of the "death", which started in a now forgotten small town in Florida, America. The 'death' was different from any communicable illness previously encountered by humans. Many speculated that it had been engineered, though nobody could agree on who the designers were; some said "terrorists", others scientists, or the security agency of one country or another. For males, the illness was usually a severe flu like illness, but for adult females, it was fatal in two thirds of cases.

One in ten young girls who had not yet gone through puberty had also died from the "death". It was transmitted through airborne particles in same way as the common cold, and spread virulently from Florida through America and Europe borne by holidaymakers returning from the Disney pleasure worlds. In females, the course of the illness from first sneeze to the complete collapse of lungs could be as long as three months—perhaps six months if you got the best of care and treatment.

Health systems were completely overwhelmed. From the international travel centres in London, New York, and Paris, it reached every corner of the planet within two months. At best, it was only slowed down by the increasingly strident and repressive public health measures instituted by governments around the world. A few countries held out against the disease for a year to eighteen months by trying to completely close their borders to travel and trade.

The early 21st century world was so internationalised that these measures proved futile and eventually, the disease penetrated every human community worldwide.

The world's scientific community desperately searched for the means to tackle the disease, and were eventually successful. But by the time an effective treatment was found, the epidemic had all but burnt itself out. By the end of 2035, there were very few new cases, but the world was yet to come to terms with the loss of two thirds of the worldwide adult female population. Although nobody counted, it is probable that more than two billion adult women died from the "death".

The world's human population, which had grown to over seven billion, was probably halved by the end of the pandemic. The social, political, and environmental chaos that followed the end of the pandemic must have resulted in as many human deaths as the disease itself.

The national governments of the world at the same time as trying to cope with the deadliest pandemic in human history, had also to cope with the other environmental problems created by a warming planet. At the beginning of the 21st century, the scientific and political world knew that the effect of global warming could not be completely prevented, and some believed that it was already too late for humans to prevent catastrophic climate change.

The planet wide industrial revolution had doubled the levels of carbon dioxide in the atmosphere by 2005, a level not seen for millions of years. By the time the epidemic had burnt out in 2035, patterns of wind and rainfall were disrupted planet wide, and extreme weather events became common.

However, it was the inexorable rise of sea levels, combined with extreme rain in most of the northern hemisphere, and extreme drought in most of the southern hemisphere which was the final nail in the coffin of the old world. The complete collapse of social systems worldwide. In this period, the physical map of the world changed more than in the previous 10,000 years. The scientific and political community were as unprepared for the catastrophic rises in water levels as they were for the pandemics.

Change was expected but the presumption always was that it could be managed. It was understood that there would be winners and losers as the planet warmed, but the unspoken assumption was that human society would somehow be able to swim against the tide of change and toemerge from the other end essentially unchanged. Alternative views were seen as prophets of doom, marginalised and ignored.

Populations weakened by the pandemic had also to face changes forced on them by climate change. Rising sea levels began to inundate low lying land, disrupted weather patterns brought frequent flooding in some areas and droughts where once rain had been dependable. In northern Europe, summer flooding frequently washed out crops and winter floods, combined with high tides, regularly displaced tens of thousands.

However, it was countries in more southerly latitudes that were first to succumb. Bangladesh was the first of the nation states to collapse under the strain caused by the "death" and the rising water levels. In 2034, after a particularly long lasting rainy season, all public order broke down in what remained of the country. Its neighbours refused to allow any males to move across their borders; the rest of their world chastised Bangladesh's immediate neighbours but made only token efforts to help the displaced people of Bangladesh.

Many African states, which had already suffered the devastation of an AIDS epidemic, simply failed during the years of the death, and were totally unable to address the problems created by an increasingly arid climate in most of Africa. The world's media pre-occupied with disaster and social upheaval across the globe simply forgot about most of Africa, which after an orgy of civil strife and violence, quietly returned to a pre-industrial world based on subsistence agriculture, and political boundaries determined by kinship and ethnicity.

By 2035, the only African states that remained viable were the oil rich North African-Arab states.

In the midst of the "death", the year of 2035AD was the point in time when the scales tipped towards the collapse of an industrial and technological human society. The southern coastal states of America and the islands of the West Indies were devastated by tidal floods caused by hurricanes and exacerbated by the Mississippi river system bursting out of its confines following an exceptionally wet summer. The exposure of the southern coastal states of America to flooding and rising sea levels had been well known and all those that could, had already left the area.

But millions of poor and predominantly black Americans had not been able to move. The sight of streams of poor black people, mostly male, moving along the highways of the richest country in the world, receiving a great deal of open and often violent hostility from frightened communities, set off an explosion of race riots in almost every American city.

In the last days of 2035, war broke out in the Middle East as America began to abandon its interest in the region to focus on its own internal strife. Israel joined forces with Saudi Arabia, Kuwait, and the United Arab emirates in an alliance inspired by their fear of the reaction of religious dictatorships to the American withdrawal. In a precisely timed action, they invaded neighbouring fundamentalist states. Quickly occupying Palestine, Jordan Egypt, and Syria, they stopped at the border to Iraq, which was continuing to tear itself apart in the civil war started after the American overthrow of Saddam Hussein.

Iran responded with a nuclear strike on Tel Aviv and Riyadh. Israel, India, and America and what remained of the Russian states responded within hours of Tel Aviv and Riyadh dissolving in a nuclear blast by launching over thirty warheads at targets in Iran—Tehran being hit twice within two hours.

The human world looked into the chasm of extinction. People around the world having survived the "death", and the social and political upheavals created by climate change, listened to the still functioning world media and knew that the world they had known was gone for ever. The nuclear exchange caused the complete collapse of order in the Middle East, bringing an end to organised warfare and replacing it with civil strife that ripped through the region like a forest fire.

War in the Middle East caused the old world's economy reeling from the catastrophic pandemic, and still heavily dependent on exploitation of fossil fuels, to go into complete meltdown. Banks collapsed like dominoes, credit cards were cancelled and paper money became increasingly worthless. Catastrophic inflation wiped out pensions leaving many older people completely destitute. Most international trade completely stopped as the dollar became worthless.

Within six months, multi-national companies were bartering products in an attempt to stay solvent. Millions and millions of people lost paid work as service based industries collapsed. Food shortages became an everyday occurrence in western nations that were used to prodigious excess. All of this mayhem and chaos was instantly communicated across the planet as the world's information infrastructure proved remarkably resilient.

One by one, the fracture lines within nations, regions and individual communities were exposed and deepened until they were torn apart and civil society unravelled to be replaced by barbarism. The rules of civil law were replaced by the law of "might is right". Laws of property were replaced by "mine is what I can defend or take". Human rights were replaced with the "survival of the fittest".

This process took less than ten years—no nation remained fully democratic after five years, no nation-wide power was left within ten years. By 2045, human society across the planet was reduced to squabbling bands trying to avoid death from starvation or violence. Cities imploded, as they could no longer rely on the enormous organisational effort it took to keep so many people so closely crowded together. People lost respect for authorities that could no longer ensure the order and safety that they had grown to expect.

The disproportionate death of so many women deepened the fracturing of social structures way beyond what was to be expected following environmental catastrophe and disease. The first obvious impact was the virtual collapse of education, as well as health and social care systems, which across the planet had been staffed and operated largely by women. However, it was the tension and competition between men for the attention of the remaining women that had the most devastating, if insidious, effect on the capacity of human society to recover from the devastation caused by a warming planet.

Women who survived the "death" quickly discovered that they were at risk in a world that now had three times as many men as women, and where social order was rapidly disappearing. Men whose wives and girlfriends survived were envied by those whose partners had not. Young men who had not formed partnerships despaired of ever realising the personal and biological imperatives that they were growing into.

Competition between men for women deepened the breakdown of trust within communities. So few women meant the vast majority of men wanted what another man already had. Those men with women feared they would lose them. Women had to be able to protect themselves or seek protection from men who were not subject to laws of a civil society but only to local and unaccountable sources of power.

Male violence, borne of frustration and fear, exploded into what was left of communities. As viable centralised authority dissolved, levels of violence rose in inverse proportion. Violence between men and rape and kidnapping of women grew to such an extent that people and communities locked themselves away or formed tight knit groups for mutual defence. This further undermined the remnants of central authority. The same process repeated around the globe.

As people increasingly spent energy, effort, and time protecting and caring for themselves and their immediate families, it eroded the level of organisation and cooperation needed to maintain the complex systems, which had for many so comfortably supported life before the "death". Across the globe, and at an accelerating rate, essential systems broke down never to be repaired.

In nation after nation, martial law was declared, but modern armies and police forces were small and technology dependent, and completely ineffective against the unprecedented scale of social and political disorder. Invariably, the men that formed armies gave way to the pressures evident in the rest of society, forming isolated bands pursuing their own goals rather than a central force enforcing the will of the state.

Despite the many, and sometimes heroic, efforts that were made to stem the tide of social breakdown, the process seemed unstoppable. However, not all effort to regain order and organisation were heroic. Governments and organisations of all description also used some of the worst methods that human history has made us familiar with. Victimisation was rife. Governments sought to explain what had happened by blaming some group or other.

A wave of anti-science feeling was whipped up by religious organisations, which saw a huge revival as a result of the "death". In an ultra-catholic France, all known "scientists" and their "followers" were herded into prison camps and forced to publicly repent for their sins against humanity. The Russian state embarked on a war with their European neighbours, blaming the scientists of the European Union for creating the "death".

The war lasted for four days and resulted in the collapse of the Russian, German, and Austrian states as soldiers refused to fight instead turning on anything that represented authority.

Throughout all this, temperatures continued to creep upwards, sea levels continued to rise, crops refused to grow where once they had prospered.

As the old world died, billions of individual humans across the planet struggled to continue their lives and come to terms with change as best they can.

At first, people watched on TV and computer screens as the world they knew unravelled in glorious technicolour. As the electrical power infrastructure started to fail, people turned to the radio for news. Radio became, in most of the world's developed countries, the last bastion of state authority—but gradually people stopped listening, as they realised that what they heard was not going to stop or change what was or had already happened.

Humans—the adaptable and social ape faced the kind of evolutionary challenge it had forced on thousands of other species since its spectacular rise to ecological dominance across the planet—adapt or die.

Chapter Five

Natalie is almost the last of the old world people. The three she knew still lived, were in communities along the shore. There was Barry at Updean who had repaired the turbine that provided power to Newtown, but was now so old, he spent most of the day sleeping. James, who lived in the Stainton community, was the youngest of the old worlders at sixty-seven, only a baby when the old world collapsed.

James was the son of Jim and Prisca who had started the community of Stainton, one of the first new world communities. He was still able enough to travel around the new world and was respected by all as a leader and protector. And, of course, there was Alexandra, of whom there was always news, brought mostly by the traders that moved from community to community.

Alexandra was a young girl of eleven years at the time of the collapse and had been fortunate that her and her mother had been found by Jim of Stainton and protected by his wife, Prisca. Jim and Prisca were one of the few couples whose families had survived intact.

Throughout the long years of chaos, Alexandra found shelter and protection within new and old communities along the Lammermoors. Throughout her teenage years, the little community led by Jim and Prisca was under a constant threat of being overwhelmed by the chaos that surrounded them. Mostly they lived in the village of Stainton, in what had been East Lothian in the South East of Scotland.

The village itself had been in existence for hundreds of years and at the time of the collapse consisted of fifty or so houses, a church, a school and an art gallery. Although many women of the village had died in the "death", the population of the village steadily grew with refugees from the towns and cities.

Jim had been a policeman and Prisca, a doctor before the "death". During the pandemic, Prisca had practically lived in the Edinburgh Royal Infirmary and Jim had been drafted into a unit whose task was to stop people moving around the country in an attempt to limit the spread of the disease. It wasn't until the pandemic started to burn itself out that they found that they were able to think about what was happening.

The news media was tightly controlled and governments, in their wisdom, had decided to try and limit information about the extent of the disaster caused by the pandemic, and the rising public disorder that followed in its wake.

In June 2033, Jim had been driving back to Stainton when he saw two women dart from the side of the road and try to hide. He pulled over and eventually, persuaded the women to reveal themselves. At this time, there was still some trust for a man wearing a police uniform. The women held two young girls close to them as if they were afraid of some immediate danger.

It took some time before the women trusted Jim enough to be able to say that they had to flee a gang of men roaming the streets of their hometown looking for women. They had taken shelter together in one of their homes, but somehow the men found them and tried to batter down the door of the house. They called for help from the police and from neighbours but nobody came. Fearing for their lives, they decided they had no choice but to leave.

They got into a car, kept in a garage with access from the house. Too afraid to open the garage door, they smashed the car through the doors, and the gang of men in the driveway. The men pursued the car, smashing the windows, before they had managed to accelerate away from them. They had driven about country roads afraid to stop, but not knowing where to go for safety. Eventually, the car had run out of fuel about a mile from where he had found them.

Knowing that there was little else he could do, James persuaded them to come to Stainton with him.

That night, at home in their bed, with their unasked for guests sleeping in spare rooms, Jim and Prisca spoke about what the future held for them and the world they had known and been so comfortable in. All night they debated with each other about what was the right thing to do. They both felt a strong sense of duty to go on performing the roles of doctor and policeman. In doing their duty, they had both suppressed their fears about the level of chaos and violence that was following in the wake of the "death".

The experience of the women he had found on the road opened the floodgates for their concerns about the future. If packs of men could roam about genteel North Berwick, apparently without fear of repercussion or consequence, what else did the future hold? Prisca asked who was going to protect their family whilst they were doing their duty.

In the morning, Alexandra and her friend, Brenda, came downstairs to find their parents in worried conversation with the people who had taken them in.

Chapter Six

Prisca and Jim sat on one side of the kitchen table facing Marina and Eleanor, the parents of Alexandra and Brenda. A tension hung in the room.

'We are talking about survival,' said Prisca. 'Believe us, the world we know has gone forever.'

Jim added, 'Prisca is right, it's not going to get any better; in fact I think it could get much worse, before it gets any better.'

'But on the radio the other day, it said that the schools would be re-opening soon and that travel restrictions would be lifted,' countered a tired and worried looking Marina.

Marina was Alexandra's mother, a single parent whose whole life had revolved around a string of relationships that never quite seemed to go anywhere. A successful accountant, she had lived a busy and comfortable life, and sought to work out her emotional and relationship difficulties through "therapy". Marina's lifelong friend, Eleanor, was a teacher, and married to a serving soldier whom she had not seen for the best part of a year, and had not heard from for more than three months.

'I don't know how they can open the schools, most of the teachers are dead,' said Eleanor, 'and they have stopped paying those that did survive.'

'It's just propaganda; the government is desperate to get us to believe that things will get back to normal,' said Jim, adding, 'I don't believe it will, anymore.'

Into the silence that followed, Jim said, 'I've seen a lot of terrible stuff over the last few years. I thought it was mostly a city thing, but what happened to you two shows it's starting to happen out with the cities. The police can't cope with it, not even with the army helping. It's the best we can do to protect factories, hospitals and distribution points from being looted by mobs. We can't do anything about ordinary people taking it into their heads to rape their neighbours in their own homes.

'We stopped responding at all to complaints of personal theft and robbery about a year ago. If you can't protect yourself then there is little the police can do to protect you. Oh yes, every now and again, somebody is made an example of, but that's just for propaganda purposes to make people feel that something is being done.' Jim shook his head, his mind had been fighting against the belief that chaos, disorder and hate were winning, and now he let the impact of the realisation that the battle was lost wash over him.

Prisca stood up, placing her hands on the kitchen table, she looked both Marina and Eleanor in the eye and said, 'We must protect ourselves and build a future for our kids. So we have to stick together; we want you and your kids to stay here with us.' Prisca paused long enough to see that Marina and Eleanor were not disagreeing with her before she continued, 'Jim and I are going to try and persuade as many of those in Stainton as we can that we have to build our own community, and be as independent as we can be.'

Prisca looked at the door behind which she knew that Brenda and Alexandra had been eavesdropping on their conversation and said, 'Today is the day we start to build a new world and stop trying to hold together the old one,' and then she added, 'and you two better come in and have some breakfast as its going to be a very busy day.'

Throughout the rest of the day, Prisca's kitchen became a hive of discussion and debate as they played host to any neighbour who was willing to join them in their kitchen. Some people were well known to them, some on nodding acquaintances only, and some absolute strangers. By the end of the day, they had spoken directly to twenty households, but the impact of their arguments had already reached throughout the village, and in some cases, further afield.

For the next two days, they didn't have to go out looking for people to talk to, people were constantly knocking at their door. Marina and Eleanor were introduced to everyone and asked to repeat their story, over and over again. Brenda and Alexandra were kept busy providing refreshments and keeping James or Jim Junior entertained.

Despite the chores, Brenda and Alexandra felt the excitement that had taken over the house, and this helped to exorcise the fear that had been with them since being chased from their homes. They could feel the hope that their parents were grasping at, and felt the strength in Prisca and Jim.

After three days, Jim and Prisca went to bed with their minds full of the many conversations and points of view they had encountered since making their decision. They had found that many people were thinking the same thoughts as themselves and preparing to defend their own homes and families and so welcomed allies. Others refused to believe that it was necessary; they still believed that the government could protect them.

These people doggedly repeated that things would eventually get back to normal. A few accepted the argument but felt that they were better looking after themselves.

They stayed awake into the small hours reviewing the last few days, and in doing so, convincing themselves that it was not only the right thing to do, but also the only option open to them. They needed to believe this so that they could let go of their guilt at not turning up for work as policeman and doctor. Before they allowed sleep to come, they had agreed that their next step was to get as many people together as possible and present them with a plan.

They went to sleep content that many people in the village would support them in trying to get Stainton not only to defend itself, but also to try and work together for a decent life.

In the morning, their plan was shared with Marina and Eleanor, who had been swept along by their hosts enthusiasm and generosity. A letter was produced on the family computer announcing a public meeting in the village hall. Brenda and Alexandra were dispatched with their mothers and bundles of letters to post it through all the doors in the village.

Fifty people turned up for the meeting, which was far more than actually lived in the village. The meeting lasted for over two hours, with Brenda and Alexandra providing a crèche for the village children. During it, the sleepy village of Stainton became the community of Stainton with Jim and Prisca as its unofficial, un-elected, but popular leaders.

The meeting decided on two groups. One to think about how to defend the village, the other to think about what was needed to survive the chaos. The next week was a maelstrom of discussion and activity. Jim and Prisca's enthusiasm and commitment for making Stainton a safe place to live and bring up children created a community spirit that hadn't really existed before. Many doubted the real need for all the deliberation, stocktaking, and stockpiling of resources.

Some few were openly critical of Jim and Prisca, declaring them as busy bodies who would be better off going back to their proper jobs. In particular, the local councillor who lived in Garvally started a campaign against them saying that they were misleading people and undermining efforts to restore civil society.

But mostly the world ignored Stainton and got on with its own efforts to survive the chaos.

Jim managed to collect together a range of weapons from shotguns to crossbows and cajoled a group of adults, nearly all of them men, to practise the use of arms and to drill for the defence of the village. An alarm was erected in the church tower, which had been without a bell for as long as anyone could remember. The villagers practised assembling in the village hall when the alarm was sounded and Jim's group practised rushing to pre-arranged positions weapons at the ready.

At first, people responded to the alarm because it was fun, but soon people began to tire and Jim found that he had trouble motivating more than a small band of the younger people in the village to take the need for defence seriously.

One of the first things Prisca's group, which included most of the Stainton women, had agreed needed to be done was to gather as much food as possible, and to begin to grow their own. By the time of the Haddington riot, they had started numerous vegetable gardens and some small scale animal husbandry on plots in and around the village. They had also managed to find enough preserved food to last them all for a week.

To get over the problem caused by worthless currency, the women had created their own local currency, which Marina developed an accounting system for. This local currency system had been around at the turn of the century and was known as Local Exchange Trading Systems. It had largely been the plaything of middle class families inspired by ecological and ethical ideals, and had never really caught on. But faced with a worthless national currency, the women of Stainton needed a more practical way to exchange goods and services than the straightforward barter that flourished in the village.

Prisca had started providing a medical service to any villager who wanted it and was prepared to pay into the community pot from which she was paid. Prisca made a note of all the time she was called upon as a doctor by the village, and gave it to Marina who credited her account with an agreed amount. This meant she could use this local currency to buy eggs or vegetables produced in the back gardens. A lot of the people of the village had no paid work and so took to using the local currency readily.

Eleanor started a community garden on some abandoned land close to the village. The garden was started with people paid in local currency for their labour and the produce sold for the local money, which attracted the name of

"Staintons". Eleanor was also instrumental in re-opening the village school, at first for three days a week and for the five under twelve's.

However, another teacher living in the village soon came forward. Roger organised a few of the village teenagers to come into the school in the mornings as helpers. This worked so well, the school opened for five days, with two afternoons for the teenagers to meet and study whatever they were interested in.

For the first six months, nothing happened to make all Jim and Prisca's preparation seem really necessary, people wearied of the practise alarms, and the attempts to get people to work together collectively. The world beyond Stainton continued its relentless slide into anarchy and chaos, but life went on. Then news came to the village of a riot in Haddington, in which young unemployed men had, to all intents and purposes, taken over the market town.

They had forced shopkeepers and householders to hand over food and alcohol, beating up anybody that resisted. A man from Stainton had returned to the village with stories of being beaten up after refusing to hand over food that he had bought. He claimed the young men were racing round the town in stolen cars—wasting precious and expensive fuel. He also brought back lurid stories of young women being taken by the men.

The news created much fear in Stainton, partly for relatives in the town, partly from concern that the youths might get tired of terrorising Haddington and move out to the villages. However, the more insidious fear was that Haddington was the main source of food for the village; the supermarket there had been taken over by the government and used to distribute the strictly rationed food that most people depended on. The supermarket had been protected by the local police force and access to it was strictly supervised.

If the youth had ransacked the supermarket, where were the people of Stainton to go to get food? It was very difficult to buy food. Money was practically worthless so the government run distribution points were the only place that you could use money to buy food if you had the right ration cards.

By the time of the Haddington riot, the village had turned from a collection of isolated and fearful individuals and families into a small community with a sense of hope and direction. The news of the riot and the threat to the ration food from the government caused consternation and fear but the response of the villagers was to come together and discuss how they should deal with this news. People converged on the church hall looking for news, support and direction.

It was soon agreed to send a party of a dozen men, discreetly armed, to find out what the situation was in Haddington. In the meantime, lookouts were to be posted around the village and everybody to be ready to assemble at the church at the sound of the alarm.

Chapter Seven

Many people in Stainton warmed easily to the new social life created in the village by its collective effort to survive. A level of social cohesion that hadn't existed before grew as most people learnt how much they depended on each other, and helped to ease the pain of the many losses they had to contend with. However, the pandemic that had taken so many, left people with personal psychological scars as well as a shared and general sense of isolation and fear.

A world with a preponderance of males also held many fears for women. The hope for the future being nurtured by Jim and Prisca's leadership, and all the activity in the village, created a space for the women to begin to think and talk about the gender imbalance and what it meant for them. Prisca was aware of the tension that was constantly bubbling under the surface of the women's conversation as they went about their life in the village. The news of the riot in Haddington turned the ever present tension felt by women into a palpable fear.

Marina and Eleanor were part of a very small group of unattached females in the village. Prisca was increasingly aware of the attention they received, and that the two women clung closely together. Prisca would like to speak to them and see if she could help, but felt it to be difficult.

As with all the other women, Prisca felt the implication of the gender imbalance as a kind of taboo subject; it was almost as if there was a kind of mass denial of the reality caused by the pandemic, that there were five adult males for every adult female.

The night before the mission to Haddington was planned Jim climbed into bed, and began to stroke her back in a way that she had come to know as his way of initiating sex, she turned to him and said, 'Jim, what do the men without wives say about,' she hesitated and then continued, 'you know about sex and there being so few women for them. I mean some of them must know that they haven't a hope in hell of having that kind of a relationship. At least not with a women.' She giggled.

'Aye, the sheep better watch out.' He laughed and continued stroking her back.

'No, I'm being serious, Jim,' she said, as she took hold of his hand to stop his advances.

'Oh, I don't know,' he said, somewhat in a huff as he rolled onto his back.

After a few moments silence, Jim realised that there would be no sleep or anything else unless Prisca got whatever was bothering her off her chest.

'Well, you know what men are like. They don't say much about it,' he paused. 'At least not in a serious way. The young men moan an awful lot, even more than before that is.'

'Yes,' said Prisca encouragingly, reinforcing this by resting her hand on his stomach.

'Well, there is a lot of talk about women who aren't attached, although maybe the talks different when I'm not there.'

'What do you mean?' Prisca said.

'Well, I'm one of the lucky ones—you lived,' said Jim suddenly sitting up, all carnal thoughts put to one side as he entered into the conversation Prisca had initiated.

'Yes, now you mention it, have you ever noticed how the widowers and the married men are slightly separate, as if they are not comfortable in each other's company? Never took much heed of it before this, but it's true—I suppose its…ehm, oh what do you call it, that psychobabble stuff your psychologist pal used to go on about.'

'You mean Jane,' said Prisca.

'Yes, she was always talking about it…oh what was it?' He said getting frustrated. 'You know, something to do with people who survive a disaster feeling bad because they survived when others didn't.'

'Survivor's guilt,' suggested Prisca.

'Yes, yes, that was it. Survivor's guilt,' repeated Jim and then quietly said, 'I suppose I've been feeling like that when I'm with men who lost their wives. It's like I feel bad because I've still got you where they have no one, and I can't help thinking that they must think, "lucky bastard, why does he deserve his wife living when mine died".'

'Do you really think that they think that still? It's been over three years,' said Prisca.

'Yes, I do,' said Jim firmly.

'Why?' Prisca asked gently.

Jim answered as if he was admitting a sin, 'Because that's what I would be thinking if it was the other way around.'

'Well, we can't change what happened, we just have to get on with it,' she said trying to prevent him from becoming too sombre. 'What else do the men think?' She prompted.

'Well, I do get a lot of leg pulling about having three women under my roof,' he said.

This was news to Prisca, and she injected a modicum of reproof into her tone when she said 'You've never mentioned that before, people in the village gossiping about what's going on under our roof, and you've never mentioned it.'

'I never gave it much thought—just blokes having a laugh, but I suppose now that I am thinking about it, there is a bit of an edge to it,' said Jim thoughtfully.

Chapter Eight

It was early morning, and yet it was warm enough for the gathered men to be taking off jackets and pullovers, as Jim called them to order. Ten men were gathered around two cars, all self-consciously holding an assortment of weapons. Some of them were talking excitedly, others were quiet and looked nervous, others lounged with an affected nonchalance that few, if any, possessed.

'Listen up,' shouted Jim. 'I'll go in the lead car with Dave driving. Paul, you'll drive the other car, okay?' When Paul nodded, he continued, 'Good; make sure you keep up, but don't get too close give yourself room to manoeuvre. If for any reason we are split up, you're to head straight back here, right.'

'Aye, right, I understand, Jim,' responded Paul.

'Now, the rest of you,' said Jim, and he slowly and purposively looked each one in the face before continuing, 'Nobody gets out of the cars until I do. We don't want to go frightening people or getting into any fight we don't have to. Most importantly, keep your weapons out of sight, but be ready! Remember, we are not going looking for a fight, we are going to see what the hell's going on in Haddington and whether it's safe for people to go there.

'If we find that these thugs have taken over the town, then we will come back here to plan what we can do, before we *do* anything.' Jim paused and looked around the group to make sure that each of them had taken in what he had said. Seeing that he had their attention, he finished by saying, 'I don't want anybody going off at half cock, so nobody does anything until I say. Is that clear?' There was a chorus of "Aye, Jim", and "That's fine" as he turned to get into the car.

They decided to head to the A1 expressway rather than take the more direct country road to avoid entering Haddington over a bridge where they could easily be stopped or trapped. The expressway gave them more options for entry, and as it had a view over Haddington, it also gave them the chance to stop and take a look from a distance. To the men in the car who had used this road frequently to travel in and out of Edinburgh, or between the main towns of East Lothian, the road almost seemed as if it was closed—only one vehicle passed them heading south.

Most strange was the complete lack of articulated lorries, which previously had thundered up and down this road day and night. The men knew that this was nothing to do with what may or may not be happening in Haddington, the traffic levels had plummeted during the "death" and steadily reduced as the economic impact of a global crisis took hold. Few people now had work to commute to, and any trade goods that moved on the roads now tended to go in convoys with army escorts.

Above Haddington, Jim asked Dave to pull the car on to the hard shoulder and got out with the binoculars he had brought with him. He was pleased to see that the other men made no move to get out of the car, and that the other car had pulled up about ten yards from his car. *Good*, he thought, *at least they are taking it seriously*. He quickly scanned across the visible parts of Haddington with the binoculars, not really expecting to see anything this early in the morning.

Seeing no obvious threat, he walked over to the car and leaning into the window, said to Dave, 'I think we will wait here for a bit, see if we can get a sense of anything out of place. Tell the guys they can get out of the car but not to wander off. Also tell them to leave the weapons in the car, we don't want to draw attention.' As Dave went to speak to the men in the other car, Jim resumed his surveillance of Haddington.

An hour later, he called his little band of Stainton men together and asked for their thoughts. The binoculars had been eagerly passed about and a lot of excited discussion had taken place initially which had subsided as nothing very much could be seen to be happening. Dave spoke first, saying, 'There's no dog walkers—this time in the morning, we should have seen a couple of dog walkers at the very least, but not a soul has stirred as far as I can see.'

There was a general consensus at this with a round of "Aye, he's right", and vigorous head nodding. Somebody else said, 'I think we should drive into the High Street and see what's what. We can't really see very much up here; if there has been any fighting, it will have been in the High Street.'

'Maybe you're right,' said Jim. 'Certainly not much point staying here any longer.' He looked around the group and seeing that nobody had anything else to say, he knew it was time to act.

'Okay, we drive down to the High Street from the Oakwood entrance. Same as before, Dave's car will lead, and nobody gets out of the car until I give the signal.'

Driving into Haddington, the tension in the car started to mount as the men's imagination had the benefit of the previous twenty-four hours to work on what they might find; but all seemed normal, except that there were no people in the street on a very fine summer morning. As they got to a pub called the Railway at the Pencaitland junction, they got their first sense that violence had taken place in the town. The pub's windows were all broken in and they had to pick their way through debris of pub furniture strewn on the street.

Onto the High Street and a car was smashed up against the Victorian waterfall and a JCB digger had been driven into the Sheriff court. The Royal Bank of Scotland building was in a similar condition to the Railway pub. As Dave drove slowly past the townhouse, they could see that the entire centre of Haddington had been trashed. All the shop windows were broken and debris from the stores and pubs littered the street, but still no people to be seen.

The two cars did a circuit of the town centre without seeing anybody they could speak to, or any sign of the people who had caused such devastation.

Jim decided that the next step was to go to the supermarket and see what state that was in. He debated with himself about stopping the cars and getting everybody on foot to approach the store through one of the many alleyways that led off the High Street, but decided against it and got Dave to drive slowly towards the supermarket entrance. Turning into the entrance road opposite the doctor's surgery, he could see that it was blocked with burnt out cars. He had Dave stop and checked that the other car had stopped and left them enough room for a quick exit if it was needed.

He gave the signal for everybody to get out. Dave and the other driver were to stay close to the vehicles and keep the engine of the cars running. The other men spread out, taking cover where they could. Jim had Dave pass the message that he was going to walk up to the burnt out cars and the men were to wait for his signal before approaching.

As he set off towards the burnt out cars that blocked the way to the store car park, he could feel the hair on the back of his neck rising. Years of policing in the city of Edinburgh had honed his sense of imminent trouble and now this street sense was telling him he was walking into bother. He was aware of a queasy feeling of unreality as he negotiated the ruined vehicles in broad daylight in the centre of a quiet market town he had known for years.

He slowed his pace and began to glance to the side taking note of where he could run for cover if needed. He edged towards the side of the store, moving out of the middle of the road. Although he had seen nobody and heard nothing, he had a strong sense that someone was either in or behind one of the burnt out cars ahead of him. He edged slowly forward towards the nearest car, still with no sign of any presence other than himself and the Stainton men whose eyes he could feel following his every movement.

As he thought about them all watching him edging up towards the car, he cursed himself quietly for not insisting that someone keep an eye to their rear. As he got to the first car, he let out the breath he had unconsciously been holding, as he felt less exposed with the car now blocking him from the line of sight of anybody in front. He was just about to call Dave's group to join him when he caught a movement from the corner of his eye.

He could now see to the main entrance of the store, and there swinging gently were two bodies suspended from the entrance pavilion. He found he could not take his eyes from the sight. He had come to this store with Prisca a thousand times for their grocery shopping; it had been the most mundane and normal place in the world and now it had bodies of what looked like young men hanging from its entrance. His mind raced through a series of emotions as he struggled to cope with this new reality.

Anger cut threw everything; he was furious that such public barbarism was taking place in his own backyard. As a policeman, Jim had seen and dealt with most human depravity and foulness, but it was always aberration motivated by greed or jealousy or some individual perversion and done covertly. The bodies swinging in the entrance of his local supermarket and the burnt out cars at its entrance seemed to announce that such aberration was now to be flaunted publicly, even paraded proudly.

Jim's life had been about law and order, about people living peacefully and playing by rules that applied to everyone the same. This above everything else he had witnessed since the "death" convinced him that what had been was gone, and that made him angry.

Standing up, forgetting his previous wariness, he called Dave and his group forward. His raised voice not only brought Dave and the other men in his group to run forward at a trot, it caused a scuffling under the car to his left. The anger he felt was still fresh in his veins and, knowing that Dave was approaching fast with his double barrelled shotgun at the ready, Jim reacted to the noise by dashing for the car and shouting at the top of his voice, 'Come out now, or you're dead.'

This was greeted with more scuffling and a pathetic whimpering that began to soften the edges of the anger that was still being fed by the hanging bodies.

Knowing he was taking a risk, Jim threw caution to the wind and himself to the ground by the side of the burnt out car. He could hear Dave shouting,' Jim! What is it? What's wrong?'

Beneath the car, Jim saw a young woman, almost naked, and curled into a tight ball that did nothing to improve her modesty. She was whimpering and snivelling in a way that said she was in a world of terror so consuming that she would not respond to reassurance or warm words.

The Stainton men gathered around the burnt out car beneath which the now silent young women lay.

'What the fuck has happened here?' Dave exploded. 'Where the bloody hell is everybody?' He exclaimed to nobody in particular.

Tersely, Jim snapped at Dave to get the men to spread out and take cover. He was conscious that they still didn't know what the threat to them here was. For all he knew, they might be in the middle of some kind of ambush, though increasingly he felt that what had happened here was over. There was little he could do for the young woman until he knew they were safe. Trying to pull her from underneath the car would simply traumatise her even more.

He set the oldest man with them to sit by the car and try and talk her out in the hope that he would be the least threatening. Then he signalled for the rest of the men to move towards the entrance of the store. All was in chaos—windows broken and the interior seemed to be a jumble of shelves. It looked as though somebody had driven a vehicle into the store, probably as part of the looting process.

From the entrance Jim shouted, 'Anybody in here has got two minutes to show themselves, after that we'll assume you are hostile and shoot to kill.'

Whilst the two minutes were passing, he split his little band in half. Half were to come with him, the others to stay around the entrance and protect their rear. Then he worried about the men looking after the cars being isolated and sent Dave to tell them to leave the cars as close to the store as they could get, lock them and join the group at the door. It took longer than two minutes to organise his forces, but when Dave returned with the two men from the cars, he shouted, 'We are coming in. This is your last chance to show yourself.'

There was no response, so he rushed forward towards the checkout and taking cover, signalled the others to move into the store. Ten minutes later, they had swept through the whole store without finding anybody. The men reported that the place had been picked clean with hardly a thing of any use left.

Dave asked if it was okay to organise cutting down the bodies of the two young men hanging from the entrance pavilion. Bizarrely, Jim had all but forgot about the grotesque sight of two young men swinging by the neck from the entrance pavilion of a supermarket. He nodded and went to see how Paul was getting on with coaxing the young women out from under the car. He reported that she seemed calmer, but hadn't moved at all.

In a whisper Paul said, 'I think it might take the rest of the day to talk her out, Jim. Either we find someone she trusts or we drag her out and I wouldn't volunteer for that.'

In a note of exasperation, Jim replied, 'Well, so far she is the only living thing we have seen in the whole of Haddington. God knows if there is anybody she can trust in the whole of this town. Even if there is, would they trust a bunch of armed men enough to show themselves.' After a pause, he added, 'Just keep trying to talk her out for now whilst I think about what to do next.'

'Don't leave her here, Jim. Poor sod has had a rough time and no mistake,' said Paul in a barely audible whisper an inch from Jim's ear.

'No, no, we won't do that,' said Jim, as he watched Dave cut down the second of the young men.

'Dave,' shouted Jim. 'Search them, see if you can find who they are and where they lived.'

'No need,' Dave replied. 'Ben knows, or I should say, knew, both of them.'

'Do you, Ben?' Jim asked when he had walked over to the little group. Ben was probably not much older than the young men he was now staring at. Of course Ben, although only twenty-five, was as familiar with death, even violent death as anybody in these times, but even so the shock of recognising people who had died in such a violent and publicly grotesque manner showed clearly in his expression.

Before Ben could answer his question, he followed it up with another, 'Did you know them well, lad?'

'Not really, used to play football with them occasionally,' he said not taking his eyes off the blue faces and protruding tongues. They had obviously been strangled by the rope and the weight of their own bodies rather than having had their necks broken by a sudden drop.

'Who could have done that to them, Jim?' Ben said looking away from the bodies for the first time since they had been cut down.

'I don't know, lad, but there's a lot of bad stuff happening in the world and it seems to be bringing the worst out in people,' he replied.

'Come on, Ben, tell me what you know about them, we still have a job to do here, son,' he said not unkindly, but he wanted to pull Ben back to the task at hand.

Ben spoke in a flat unemotional voice, which told Jim that the lad was on the edge of shock, and was obviously taking it hard. 'That one is Phil Heatherington and the other was Richard, but I don't know his second name. They both lived in Haddington and used to work at the "Fort" in one of the shops up there. That's about all I know, except that they would go for a drink in the Pheasant most weekends.'

'What about family? Do you know where they lived?' Jim pressed sensing that Ben might break down altogether if he was offered sympathy, and this wasn't the place for him or Ben to deal with that.

'No, sorry, like I said, I didn't know them very well,' said Ben and he turned his back to Jim as if to walk away.

'Wait a minute,' said Jim quietly. 'What about the girl?'

Still with his back to Jim, he said, 'What about her?'

'You might know who she is?' And Jim spoke with a note of hardness in his voice. 'She is about your age. I want you to go and see if you recognise her or can get her to talk.' Jim really wanted to keep him busy as he worried about how we could cope if he was left to ruminate on the hanging.

For a moment, Jim thought the lad was going to tell him to get stuffed, but without looking back or saying anything, he walked in the direction of the car and then bent down first to talk to Paul and then lying on his back, peered under the car at the girl.

Dave came over to Jim and said, 'What do you reckon we should do now, Jim?'

The other men were all looking towards them and Jim sensed that they were unsettled and needed direction. Quickly, he made up his mind and called them all over to him.

Once they were all gathered in a little knot around him, he began. 'I think we have learnt all we are going to from here. Whatever has happened here has been pretty bad and got the whole town scared shitless.' He paused and saw that they were all nodding and eager to hear what he was going to suggest next. 'I still want to find out what the fuck happened, and we can only do that if we speak to somebody. It's no use just to go and knock on the nearest door. All we will do is frighten people. So we need to go to someone who knows us. Any suggestions?'

Several hands shot up and a couple of names shouted out. It dawned on Jim that many of his little group would have friends and family in Haddington. He didn't have family in the area and his social life had been in Edinburgh associated with his work. He pointed to Dave. 'Okay, Dave, who do you suggest?'

Dave said, 'I know this bloke I used to work with; he lives just over there in Princess Mary Road. I reckon I could get him to come to the door if he is in.'

'Good,' said Jim. 'Take two men and see if you can get him to come here and help us make sense of this crap.' Looking to the group in general, he said, 'Everybody happy with that.' There was a round of nods and general assent.

Jim looked at Dave and said, 'Okay, Dave, if you're not back here in twenty minutes then I'll come looking for you.' Dave picked his two men and set off at a trot across the empty car park and disappeared through a gap in the wall that bounded the store.

Jim began to organise his men whilst they waited to see if Dave was successful. 'Okay, Paul, Ben, you keep working on that girl, we can't leave her here, so somehow she has to come out from under that car. Try some food and water. God knows how long she has been there. You two go and keep an eye on the cars, and the rest of you see what you can find in the store that we might be able to use in Stainton—we might as well get the use of it.'

This last was said with some guilt, and he thought how far things had gone that he, a policeman, was ordering the theft of property.

Jim stood in front of the dead bodies of the two young men and watched the Stainton men disperse to their respective tasks. To himself he said, 'What a bloody mess!' But deep in himself, there was a satisfaction that he and Prisca had made the right choice. He had occasionally doubted their decision to leave their jobs, effectively to abandon the civil society that he had known in favour of protecting himself, his family, and those he lived closest to.

Whatever had caused the madness that had happened here, he understood it as a further sign that society was breaking down. The systems and processes that had kept millions of people living cheek by jowl were no longer functioning properly and the result was the chaos and barbarism that he was surrounded by in the centre of Haddington, a small country town, close to the city of Edinburgh, in Scotland, part of the United Kingdom.

As he waited for the men to come back from their respective tasks, he wondered at what level things had sunk to in the inner cities and the peripheral estates which barely managed a civilised life even when the system was functioning normally.

Chapter Nine

Dave was successful in getting his friend to come and explain what had taken place in Haddington over the last few days. The men gathered around straining to hear as Dave's pal began to tell of what he knew. The story tumbled out as he was distracted by numerous questions and side tracked by stories of what had happened to particular individuals.

He told the Stainton men that there had been a riot of local youths who had broken into shops and stolen alcohol from pubs. Some of the older men and a couple of policemen in the town had fought with the youths who then holed up in the local supermarket. Even though people tried to reason with them, including some of their own family, they were all drunk and being egged on by their ringleader.

The ringleader was a lanky young man called Nathaniel, who had been known for getting into trouble even before his mother had died during the "death", but since then, he had become well known as a local troublemaker.

Anybody that went close to the supermarket was shot at with air rifles or catapults that they had got from somewhere. They stayed in the supermarket for two nights and then the army came. The youths who by this time, having drunk all the alcohol left in the store, had begun to sober up, and a few had drifted away. The rest were soon to wish that they had. The army drove an armoured vehicle straight to the store and quickly surrounded it, giving those inside one minute to leave or be shot.

The twenty or so lads still inside quickly came out with their hands up, looking very sheepish. Soldiers herded them into a group and made them kneel on the tarmac with their hands behind their heads. Any movement or noise brought a boot or fist in response, so they stayed very quiet and as still as they could. A jeep with a loudspeaker had gone round around almost every street in Haddington telling people to come out, that it was safe again and that they were all to gather at the store.

About two hours later, around about thousand people, mostly men, turned up to see what was to happen.

As they arrived and squeezed into the car park, soldiers marshalled them in front of the kneeling youths. When he was ready, the commanding officer gave the order to line up the very frightened and sorry looking bunch of young men. The officer then called on the crowd to identify the ringleaders. A few names were shouted out but most people remained quiet as they began to develop a bad feeling about the situation.

Those that were related to the offenders began to plead their cases. The officer turned his back on the crowd and picked three from the group in front of him seemingly at random. These three were roughly grabbed and pushed to the floor by the soldiers who then held guns to their heads. About a dozen soldiers quickly formed a double line, facing each other, between the remaining offenders and the crowd. The remaining soldiers turned to face the crowd raising their weapons in a way that said they were not going to brook any trouble.

A nervous rush of conversation passed through the crowd and many began to drift backwards and to leave. The officer then spoke to the frightened youths too quietly to be heard by anybody else. He blew a whistle and the youth at the front of the line ran towards the double line of soldiers who took great delight in beating him with fists, boots or weapons as he made his way along the line. As he staggered from the end of the line, the whistle blew again and the next youth in line, the lanky Nathaniel, ran between the soldiers as fast as he could.

The soldiers were ready for this and brought him to the ground to beat him before he was allowed to make his passage to the end of the line. The people of Haddington watching this scene became unsettled and restless, a few began to protest, particularly those related to the young men. An argument arose between those that supported the beating, probably the majority and those that were against either on moral grounds or because it was their kin that were being beaten.

Nathaniel quietly made his way to the back of the crowd and then managed to half jog, half stagger away as fast as he could. He probably had guessed what was to come and didn't want to be around when the soldiers left and the crowd was looking for someone to blame. People were still arguing when the last of the young men had staggered bloodily from between the two lines of soldiers.

The commanding officer, standing in the back of an open Landrover, raised his pistol and fired once into the air. Into the desired silence, he began immediately to talk at the crowd and even though his voice was unassisted, they all heard every word.

'I am Captain Peters, and I tell you that the United Kingdom Transitional Disaster Relief Authority has given the army authority to deal with looters and public disorder with ultimate force.'

After a pause he continued. 'The looting of public food distribution points is to be punished by death. Those caught are to be summarily tried and executed.' Again, he paused to let the crowd take in his words. Their effect on the crowd was to induce complete silence as they waited for him to continue.

Into the silence he said, 'Today, we are being lenient. These two only are to die. You have identified them as ringleaders and they will be hung from the neck until they are dead,' and with this, he signalled to men on the ground who hurried with the practical arrangements for the hanging.

Captain Peters, nipped the beginning of a hushed murmuring in the crowd by stating more loudly than previously, 'My men will shoot without warning anybody they believe is attempting to interfere in the carrying out of this punishment.'

The three boys were kept firmly held throughout the captain's short speech. On hearing that they were to be hung, one of them began to moan loudly and called for his father to help him. This was quickly stifled with a kick to the head that left the boy semi-conscious. Not until they were hauled up from the tarmac and turned towards where the ropes awaited them, did the other boy seem to take in what was about to happen to him.

The sight of the waiting rope was instantaneous on the still lucid boy, whose body simply locking into a rigid pose of resistance. It was almost as if he had turned into a child in a tantrum seeking to defy the parental will by arching his back and locking his knees. The soldiers, however, were strong and well trained in crowd control and arrest techniques, and it was the work of only a few moments to manoeuvre the boys to the ropes and to secure the ropes about their necks.

The boy who had called out for his father and had been kicked in the head offered the least resistance but had to be held up once his head was placed in the noose.

The crowd was now becoming very restive with people that knew those about to be hanged shouting and swearing at Captain Peters who remained on the back of the Landrover. Most of the crowd couldn't believe he was actually going to go through with it. Believing that it was simply a pantomime to scare the boys and give a warning to others. Two soldiers held the rope behind each boy and another continued to hold up the conscious but languid body of one of the boys.

One of the boys began loudly claiming his innocence, that he was not a ringleader, that it was Nathaniel who had started it all, and that it should be he that be hanged and not him. Some in the crowd caught the sense of this and began to look amongst the boys who had been beaten. Although they could not find Nathaniel, arguments began to break out in the crowd as people who knew the boys sensed a chance to influence the captain and the increasingly apparent course of events.

All arguments were ended when the captain gave the signal to his men to commence the hanging. The ropes were pulled and the boys were lifted by the neck from the ground in front of the store they had looted. The crowd looked on in a momentary silence of disbelief, and then a cacophony of pleas for mercy and boos cries of shame rose from the crowd. A few of the braver or more desperate began to push at the cordon of soldiers, but quickly desisted when the captain loosed another volley from his pistol into the air.

The boys took several minutes to die, initially struggling violently and then subsiding into decreasingly less vigorous twitches. They both lost control of their bladder and bowels before the life was gone from their bodies. The shocked crowd stared at the grotesquely blue and bloated face of the boys who had been strangled by the weight of their own bodies rather than dying from a broken neck.

Captain Peters waited for the silence to build and then spoke, 'Let everyone here know that this will be the fate of anybody that attempts to loot or steal from a transitional authority food distribution point. This event will be reported and guards for this distribution point will be posted with the next food delivery.' A few people began to shout names at the captain, but quietened when they saw that they were not being followed by the rest.

Finally, the captain said in a dismissive, wearied but strong tone, 'You will all now return to your homes. You will remain there for twenty-four hours. Anybody seen on the streets in that that time is liable to arrest; any protests will be dealt with by the utmost severity. Now go!'

The people of Haddington dispersed quickly; some were crying, some were angry, most were simply stunned and disbelieving about what they had seen.

Dave's pal confirmed that all this had happened the afternoon of the previous day, less than 16 hours ago. The Stainton Group had listened intently to the story realising that had they rushed to Haddington on first hearing the news, they would have pitched up at the same time as the soldiers. Each had their own thoughts as to what would have resulted from that.

'But what about the girl?' Dave asked. 'Where does she fit into the story?'

'What girl?' His friend asked.

'We found a girl, near naked under that burnt out car,' replied Dave, pointing towards the car where Paul and Ben were still sitting.

'Don't know anything about that,' said Dave's pal. 'Who is she?'

'We don't know. Poor lass must have been hiding under that car whilst all those people were watching the boys being hung,' replied Dave.

The men discussed what to do next about the girl under the car, and eventually agreed that one of the cars would go back to Stainton and bring back some women to see if that would make the difference. They thought the chance of getting women to come out of their homes in Haddington was unlikely and that it would be easier to get their own women to come out of the village. Jim was nervous about reducing his force and about hanging around in Haddington.

They had not seen any sign of the soldiers but that didn't mean they would not come back to make sure their curfew was being respected. Jim knew that there was no way his men could stand against a professional force, they would be as defenceless as the youths in the supermarket, and God alone knows what Captain Peters would make of a group of armed locals.

An hour later, the car returned with Alexandra and Prisca. Jim impressed upon Prisca the need for urgency, the soldiers could return at any time and probably would not wait for explanations as to why the curfew was being broken. He said they would have a half hour to talk her out and then the men would try and lift the car away so she could be pulled out safely.

As they went to the car, Alexandra caught sight of the uncovered dead bodies. The shock of it almost made her vomit, but she knew she had a task to do and was determined to be strong.

A female voice worked on the girl like magic, and she was out from under the car and into the arms of Prisca and Alexandra within moments of hearing their voices. In the car back to Stainton, she poured out her story to Prisca and Alexandra. Her name was Natalie and she was nearly fifteen years old. Natalie had lost her mother and sister to the "death", and her father had killed himself shortly after her sister had died. She lived on her own in Haddington, where her family had moved only a month or so before the start of the "death".

She had befriended her elderly neighbours helping with chores, and in turn, they kept her company when she needed it. She had got her rations from the store with her neighbour because she felt safe from the attentions of younger men when they were with her. On the day of the riot, she had been in the store with a neighbour when the boys arrived. They were all very drunk and although she tried to hide from them, they had grabbed her, and when her neighbour tried to help her, they beat him until he couldn't stand up.

She didn't know what had become of him and began to cry at the thought of him. Prisca stroked her hair and encouraged the tears, but prompted her to continue with the story. Prisca thought the more of it she could get out, the better chance of her finding a way of living with the trauma of what had happened to her.

Before they had got to Stainton, Natalie had told them that she had been raped. She didn't know how many of the boys had done this to her. Eventually, the rape stopped and they left her alone. Too weak to walk, she had crawled out of the store and hid as best she could under the cars the boys had destroyed whilst she was being raped inside the store. The metal of the car was still hot when she had crawled under and she had burnt her shoulder when she touched it.

Next, she described floating in and out of consciousness. Prisca thought this was probably the symptom of shock. She had been aware of a crowd in the store car park, and she had heard the loud bangs of somebody shooting, but her only concern was not to be discovered. She didn't know how long she had been under the car or how long had passed since the boys found her in the store, but her ordeal had probably lasted between twenty-four and thirty-six hours.

Chapter Ten

Following on from the "death", the effects of global warming drove the old social order to a chaotic disintegration. Stainton had to cope with the many natural and social disasters that followed the "death". At times, the community was completely overwhelmed by a tide of barbarism that was sweeping across the world, and had to pick up the pieces and start again. External threats were numerous, but internal tensions were, at times, even more of a threat to the fragile community.

From that night when they had lain in bed and talked over the tensions within their community, coping with the preponderance of males was to be the issue that they could not escape from. Of all the problems they had to deal with, this is the one for which they were least prepared. Attacks from outside could be fought off or run away from. The loss of a crop or the breakdown of a vital piece of equipment could be overcome with determination and hard work. Illness and disease could be isolated and treated with knowledge and whatever medicine they could access.

The gender imbalance generated persistent arguments and petty jealousies fired by the competition between men for the attention of women. This tension constantly ate away at the fabric of the community, disrupting efforts to foster cooperation and planning beyond the immediate. Over a period of twenty years, the answer that they arrived at made Stainton become a model for other communities that were grappling with the same issues across Scotland and the whole of the world. Coping with the imbalance of the sexes was ultimately the key to Stainton's ability to survive and sustain itself as a community.

Initially, one of the strongest impulses in response to the "death" was to try and shut the rest of the world out. Many surviving couples and men who had found or taken single women simply tried to survive on their own. To survive, people had to quickly learn that surviving on your own in a world where bands of men were willing to use any level of violence to take what they wanted was almost impossible. Many fortified themselves into homes they could not bear to leave, or attempted to become invisible.

Those strategies were based on the hope that the old world would somehow return before the last cartridge was fired or the last tin of beans was opened. Nobody could survive for more than a few years on their own or as small family groups. Eventually, they succumbed either to raiders or to the loss of a vital resource that forced to leave safe spaces and venture into a friendless world.

Some realised early that survival was not going to be an individual matter but would need the resources of a community to make it sustainable. Communities were formed all over the world that men could only enter if they had a female partner. Many even forced male offspring of a couple to leave the community once they had entered adulthood, only able to return once they had a partner. Such communities invariably had to hide behind walls or in geographical isolation in order to protect themselves from the jealousy and desire of those that did not belong.

The army officer who had hung the young rioters of Haddington, Captain Peters, formed one such community in Stirling. The ancient castle had been the base and barracks for his men. Initially, women entered the castle seeking protection from the army, or the soldiers brought female relatives in order that they could protect them. However, as the social structures he was sworn to protect crumbled around him, Captain Peters increasingly found that he was no longer commanding a military garrison but instead a small town.

As with every other newly forming community, Captain Peters found that his major problem in managing the day-to-day running of his garrison community was the tension between men with women and women-less men. Always pragmatic, he offered the unattached women who had sought safety in his community to choose one of his soldiers or leave. Most chose to stay. Once all his men had access to a women, he simply closed the gates. He would even turn away men who turned up with a female companion looking for shelter behind the castle walls, making exception only for those that could prove they were serving soldiers at the time of the "death".

Peters used a combination of 21st century technology and the ancient castle walls in an attempt to protect himself and his two hundred and fifty men from the chaos that raged around them. The men used their military training and access to weaponry to take what they needed from the surrounding communities and even forced women-less men to work on farms to produce food for the castle in a kind of 21st century serfdom. Captain Peter's community survived for many years and initially held a great influence across the central belt of Scotland.

Many people were willing to subject themselves to its influence in order to obtain protection from the random and barbaric violence that had replaced the rule of law. But like the ancient closed warrior community of Sparta, access to the community was so restricted that it had no way of quickly expanding its number or of replacing the trained men that were inevitably lost to fighting.

Although no force was able to withstand them in a pitched battle anywhere in Scotland or the North of England, they became increasingly conservative about exerting their influence beyond their immediate vicinity for fear of leaving their base exposed to attack, or to the inevitable attrition of its force. Even Colonel Peters realised that their community was an isolated outpost that could not survive in the long term. For many years, he clung to the hope that order would be restored, governments and chains of command will be re-established.

Eventually, Stainton became a model for the more open communities that evolved at the end of the old world. Many people have debated why Stainton became thought of as a model for other communities, when other communities across the globe were probably coming to similar conclusions at the same time. Nobody will ever know for sure, but it is true that Alexandra made great use of what remained of the World Wide Web to communicate or proselytise about Stainton.

Chapter Eleven

The web was one of the few technologies that managed to survive and adapt to the changing fate of the planet. Partly, this was because satellites continued to orbit and enterprising computer specialists could find ways to utilise a resource that was beyond the reach of angry crowds and rising water levels. It was also one area of infrastructure that was easy to patch and adapt and where necessary physically move.

The web became a simpler less energy intensive connection between computing resources rather than the mega information storage system it had become in the early part of the century. Other elements of infrastructure did not survive as long as the web. Power stations, roads, ports, airports, hospitals, sewage systems, etc. could not be easily adapted and moved as water levels rose or populations moved to avoid drought and civil disorder.

The economic collapse and the loss of so many skilled people meant that systems were not maintained or maintained poorly. As the people of Stainton organised to survive independent of old world systems, they saw them all fail and fade within the next three decades.

From the beginning, Jim and Prisca clung to the web technology ferociously as a means of interacting with the outside world. A satellite receiver was adapted to be able to link straight to the satellite network and powered by a bank of solar arrays. It helped them to shake off the claustrophobia of a small community, which made huge demands on them emotionally and mentally. However, they maintained their guard at all times and never gave away their physical location or their real identities—afraid that it might bring unwanted attention to their community.

From the first days of the Stainton community, Alexandra had talked about her experiences on the web. To her, it was like talking about family. Alexandra had not really known a father, and so Jim became everything she thought a father ought to be. Jim was strong and could not be bullied or shouted down easily by the other men. He was single-minded and able to focus on the job that needed done, but above all, he was always supportive of Prisca.

For this last alone, Alexandra loved him, for she worshipped Prisca. She loved her mother, but Prisca was the women who shone out to the teenage girl as the women she most wanted to be like. At first, the web was simply an exciting diversion for her, a relic of the comfortable world that she and everyone had lost. But it became a constant friend to whom she poured out her heart and worked out her understanding of what was happening in the new world that she and her generation were to inherit.

In this way, many thousands of people became aware of Alexandra and Stainton. Alexandra always followed the rules about security but eventually, her weblog was so popular, that her real identity and location began to leak out into the public domain.

As Alexandra worshipped Prisca, Natalie worshipped Alexandra. Although Natalie was the older in years, Alexandra filled the role of an older sister. Natalie dreamed of being as strong as Alexandra, and above all, to be as able to cope with the attentions of men. Alexandra tore through puberty, bursting into womanhood with a zeal and impatience that inspired and frightened the other girls of her age group. At this time, most young girls on the cusp of womanhood had to cope not only with their changing bodies and feelings but the keen interest of everybody in their community and far beyond.

Many faced these challenges without mothers and older sisters that would have been there to guide and support them. As their bodies changed, they felt the hopes and aspirations of others like a huge weight. It was not just the salacious comments of hopeful males, it was as if the new communities placed on the shoulders of these few emerging women the responsibility to reproduce all that had been lost to them. Most shrunk from this perceived responsibility as an intolerable burden.

Alexandra drunk it in; she loved the spotlight of attention that followed her femaleness wherever she went. By the time that her body was fully developed, she had learnt to radiate her femaleness and use it as a power. She was not flirtatious and did not lead on men in any kind of provocatively sexual way, she had no need to. It was male power that turned females into sexual objects. She had learnt from Prisca and the other adult women of Stainton and the Lammermoors that in this new world, femaleness was power.

More than any of the other girls, or women, Alexandra had grasped that female was powerful in this new world. It was women who held the communities together against the tide of chaos and barbarism. In Alexandra's mind, it was femaleness that would create order from disorder, and allow life to overcome death. To Alexandra, "Femaleness" was not about sex or even about gender, it was about the power to create, whether that be the incubation of a foetus, or the nurturing of children or the creation and nurturing of communities in which to raise those children.

As Alexandra blossomed into womanhood, she took all those that had discovered her web presence with her on an emotional and intellectual journey that was the zeitgeist of the post "death" world. Her weblog was feeding the minds of thousands, developing the ideas that would eventually begin to halt the tide of death and destruction that had swept so much and so many away.

Chapter Twelve

After the Haddington riots, the people of Stainton threw themselves into the work of making Stainton as independent and defended from the rest of the world as they could achieve. New people were welcomed as long as they had a sponsor from within the community. If somebody new turned up in the village that could not get an existing community member to sponsor them, then they were given half a loaf of bread and asked to leave. If they refused, they were manhandled, an act which some of the villagers felt as shameful, but was unanimously accepted as necessary.

After the sacking of the store by Nathaniel, no one could find out when supplies would be available again from Haddington. Jim worried that they would never be re-instated, but refused to join in any speculation, simply repeating his insistence that they could not rely on handouts and that they had to make do for themselves. Some had tried to get supplies from Dunbar but had faced a hostile welcome from the administrators there. They would not accept any amount of pleading; "If you don't have the right ration card, you don't get anything".

Power was another issue. The national grid was becoming increasingly erratic and Stainton had never had mains gas. It was still possible to buy bottled gas or to get deliveries of coal, but the suppliers charged whatever they wanted, and the main currency was now ration coupons. Haddington coupons were, of course, now pretty much worthless. A number of the houses in Stainton had solar water heaters and they were a couple of small wind turbines, but these didn't really make a great difference.

Many of the houses were old and still had open fires or at least had chimneys, so piles of firewood began to appear, and as the nights got colder and the power supply more erratic, the smell of wood smoke began to permeate the village. As the wood smoke drifted along the streets on a still evening, it was almost as if hundreds of years of history were peeling away from the village, revealing an older Stainton, where you were now as likely to see a horse in the High Street as a motorised vehicle.

Defence was always in Jim's mind. He knew what depths humans could descend to, and he knew more and more people would be desperate enough to leave behind whatever moral sense they possessed in order to survive. After the Haddington riot, there was a steady trickle of local people turning up in the village—looking for food—most wanted to get it honestly through trade or work, but reports of theft became steadily more frequent.

Although most of this was probably falsely blamed on outsiders, the thought of hungry men stealing into the village to take a loaf of bread or steal a chicken raised the anxiety of the whole village. The villagers knew they could not rely on the forces of the government, police or army. It might be different in a big town or city but in a small country village, they knew a call to the authorities would be ignored. After Haddington, most people were inclined to feel that calling the authorities for help didn't seem a good idea anyway.

After several village meetings, it was decided to raise a barricade around the village so that people could only enter at a guarded gate. Jim was sceptical that they could actually do this and was worried that the village might exhaust itself before anything useful was achieved leading to disappointment and disillusionment. However, once the decision was made, he threw himself into planning the task.

One of the men knew of a bulldozer that had been abandoned in a nearby gravel quarry when the company went bust. Dave led a small group to find out if it was still there and whether they could get it working. After an initial investigation and with a very little effort, they managed to turn its engine over. The next problem was to find a way of getting it to Stainton and then finding enough fuel to power it. It took much haranguing, pleading, and bartering to procure enough diesel to power the machine.

But try as they might, they could not get a transporter that would take the machine, so they had to drive it across increasingly wild and deserted countryside to get it to Stainton. On a dry spring day, it began the task of surrounding Stainton with a ditch and mound as if it were a medieval village. As the long ditch and mound was formed the villagers toiled up the mound to build a high fence strung with barbed wire. The construction work took every human and material resource that the community could spare.

To pay for the construction work, a tax was agreed on every adult male, payable in work or in the local currency developed by the community. They even paid for labour from outside the village with food bought from the community gardens with local currency raised by what became known as the "defence tax".

By late autumn, the work on the defences was finally completed with the raising of a set of massive gates at the entrance to the village. This event became the focus of a celebration and a party was planned for the whole community. For a brief time, happiness prevailed in Stainton whilst much of the rest of the world was overwhelmed with despair for what the future was to bring. Stainton was finding the resources to face that same future with some kind of optimism.

News of Stainton began to spread—a community that had food and was prepared to defend itself. News reporters came to the village and Stainton became known as the "community that turned away strangers with a handful of bread". Alexandra's weblog added to the village's fame as thousands followed her description of the daily struggle to survive and prosper, as well as her own teenage angst about the role of a girl in a world of men and boys.

For a few weeks, Stainton inspired a national media debate about the best way for people and communities to cope with the now unavoidable social and environmental catastrophe faced by all. However, news of food riots and storms that brought tidal surges into the centre of London soon displaced the doings of the people of Stainton. But, one way and another, Stainton began to inspire admiration and not a little jealousy among its neighbouring villages and towns, but also in places that had never heard of Stainton.

The winter of 2038 was the wettest anybody had known and massive flooding was reported from all over Scotland. Grangemouth's oil and chemical refinery, which was still working under military direction was swamped as were many other key remnants of the old world infrastructure such as water filtration stations and electricity substations. The prodigious rainfall combined with neglected drainage systems and flood defences during the preceding five years of chaos worked together to undermine what was left of much of the national infrastructure.

In the following spring, bands of armed men began to appear in the countryside around Scotland's cities. They would force their way into homes in search of food and women, and flee back to the city if faced with a force that threatened them. News of raids in the East Lothian area seeped into Stainton early in the spring, and once again, fear began to replace the everyday worries about food, heat, and the opinions of friends and neighbours. The gates of the community were closed before dark, and those that lived outside the moat were encouraged to sleep in the church until the situation improved.

Late in May, as the light faded on a particularly wet day, the bells of the village sounded an alarm. Running to the gate, Jim found Dave hollering about a bunch of men approaching along the Haddington Road. Taking hold of Dave by the shoulders, he calmed him down before panic spread through the whole community and set him to making sure that the wire fence on the mound had a man stationed at every twenty paces.

In the centre of the village, he found Prisca and Alexandra gathering the fighters who would act as the central force to counter any attempt to breach the village's defences. Satisfied that the defences were coming together as planned, he went again to the gate to find out if the threat was real or imagined.

Atop the gate, he took out his binoculars and inspected the knot of men forming a hundred metres or so along the road. After scanning the country to the side of the road, he decided that the forty or so men on the road were all there was, though he knew it would not be hard for many more to be hiding in trees and bushes around the perimeter of the village. Jim calculated that these men were unlikely to try and cross the moat around the village, which was deep with all the recent rain.

It was too wide to simply jump across, and besides, the sides were raw mud and very slippery; there was as yet little in the way of grass, or anything else to get a grip on to pull yourself out. So unless they had come prepared, they would find it very hard to get access to the village that way. The gates in and out of the village were the place they would attack, and since they all seemed to be armed, he was pretty sure that that's what was on their minds.

As he watched the men standing on the road, he saw one of the men walk forward. He was a tall thin young man, vaguely familiar thought Jim. He was wearing a long leather coat and carrying an automatic rifle casually over his shoulder. As he got to about fifty metres away from the gates, he held out the gun and deliberately made a show of placing it on the side of the road, before he walked slowly forward with his arms held open and wide.

Jim let him come to within ten metres and then shouted, 'That's far enough. Who are you, and what do you want?'

'I am Nathaniel and I want your food and your women,' came a chillingly calm and calculatedly confident reply. Pausing only for a few seconds, he continued, 'Send out the food and women, and we will leave you alone.'

'And if we don't?' Jim shouted.

'Well, we will have to take what we want and kill the rest of you,' he replied almost conversationally. Then he raised his hand and, with the raising of his hand, Jim heard the sound of a motor and along the road came a truck with a large calibre machine gun mounted on the top of the cab. Nathaniel calmly walked towards the truck. Afterwards, Jim cursed himself for not putting a round into his back, but his mind was fully occupied with the sight of the weapon on the truck.

He ordered everybody to take cover and to get away from the gate. He included himself in this advice, quickly jumping down from the palisade above the gate. He knew the gate was strong but wasn't confident that it would stop the bullets from that machine gun.

Five minutes of fevered silence passed, with the truck stopped about a hundred metres away at the same spot where Jim had seen the men gathered. Jim spoke to Prisca on the walkie talkie to tell her that it looked as though they had no option but to fight, and that they might well have casualties so she had better be prepared for them.

Their conversation was cut short by the percussive burst of the machine gun firing. It was only a fifteen second burst but already the gate, though still on its hinges, was badly damaged and unlikely to take too much more punishment. Nobody was hurt but everybody, including Jim, was pretty shaken up. Inside the gate they had set up what Jim thought of as a big "stinger". A "stinger" was a device he had used as a policemen for stopping stolen vehicles. This was a large version that would stop any vehicle on its spike if the gates were forced.

He heard the rattle of small arms fire coming from the top of the mound and shouts of "they're coming". Ensuring that the spikes were set and ready to hold anything that came through the gate, he unconsciously prayed that the thing would work. The heavy machine gun spat again, this time a shorter burst into the centre of the gate. The bullets soon ate a large hole in the heavy gate and ate away at the gate bar, which had seemed so strong and now appeared pathetically inadequate.

A few moments later, Nathaniel's men were springing from the roadside to rush the gate, whilst other laid down a suppressing fire against the men on the mound. For vital seconds, there was practically no return fire from the mound as Nathaniel's men rushed the door along the open road. Grenades exploded against the gate, which then swung uselessly open. A few bold men rushed inside but were immediately killed in the cross fire that Jim had carefully worked out with his defenders.

A rattle of return gunfire started from the men on the mound above the gate. Nathaniel's men were exposed as they hesitated at the gate and on the road, and took more casualties.

For a moment, it looked as though the Stainton defenders had repulsed the attack without a single casualty, other than the magnificent gates. Then the lorry accelerated forward smashing its way through the remnants of the gate. To Jim's relief, the stinger worked bringing the lorry to a metal wrenching stop. The heavy machine gun had been taken off the cab and was now mounted on the bed of the lorry, and was firing with devastating effect on the barricades of the defenders inside the gate.

The angle at which the lorry had stopped meant it could only fire in a limited area, but within its line of sight, it quickly tore the barricades sheltering the defenders to shreds. On the other side of the truck, men poured through the gates. A number of them fell but they managed to breach the barricades and were now fighting in close order with the villagers. Later, Jim would hear the overwhelming noise of the battle, people screaming in pain, the splintering of wood and that horrendous rattle of explosions as the machine gun fired.

His brain simply blocked out the noise and the sights around him as he ran and fired, ran and fired, ran and fired. He tried desperately to gain control over the Stainton forces, to get them to fall back and defend the hall where most of the women and children were. He did manage to get the men from the rear gate to reinforce the defences at the village hall. Fighting through the town streets, he made it to the hall and to his relief, he saw that it was as yet untouched by Nathaniel's raiders.

Outside the hall, he quickly gathered ten men armed mostly with shotguns and hunting rifles. As he refilled his revolver with yet another of the precious ammunition clips, he exhorted the frightened men to join him in a counter attack. 'We must throw them back. We must stop them from manoeuvring that fucking machine gun. If we don't we're all dead. Do you understand?' Looking at the assortment of nods and assents, he saw that though afraid, they understood what the stakes were and he knew they would follow him.

More gently he went on, 'We outnumber them two or three to one, and we will beat them, but we can't let them get that gun into a position where they can threaten the hall with it.' Once more he looked round the group of men, and said, 'Okay then, spread out and follow me.'

Crouching low, he ran from garden to garden in short bursts. He was heading back towards the gate, where there was still the sound of sporadic fire. Stainton consisted mostly of one long main street with houses on both sides, and a narrow road between. Each row of houses had large gardens to the rear and it was through the gardens that Jim was guiding his little force. They met no opposition on the way, though with each short spurt, he expected to hear shots ring out.

At the last garden before the gates, he paused to figure out the next step in his plan. He had a good view of the barricades they had set up to defend the gate, and tragically, he could see a number of bodies, one of which was undoubtedly Ben, the young man who had been with the group that had gone to Haddington after the riot. The barricades obscured his view of the gate but he could hear sporadic shots, probably from the Stainton side, as it was shotguns rather than the automatic weapons the raiders all seemed to have.

Quickly weighing options in his mind, he decided to gamble that they had not moved the heavy gun from the lorry yet. Signalling his men to follow quietly, he forced himself through a gap in the hedge that separated this garden from the gateway area. They reached the barricade undiscovered and Jim was beginning to feel this was too easy and that perhaps, he was walking them into a trap when a voice rang out calling his name. It came from the top of the mound and was responded to with a rattle of automatic fire from the gate.

'Jim,' the voice came again, and again was drowned out by gunfire. When the gunfire stopped, the disembodied voice came again, 'They're leaving, Jim.'

'That's Alexandra, I'm sure of it,' said one of the men behind him.

'Right, you three stay here and fire at that gate to give the rest of us time to get through the barricade and head for the gate.'

A few moments later, they were hurriedly stepping over, or on, the bodies of dead men at the gate. As he went through the gateway and onto the road, shots rattled around him. Blindly returning fire, he dived for cover. He felt something pull at his leg and looking down, he could see blood discolouring his trousers. When he tried to get up and run to a new position, he found that his leg crumpled beneath him and felt powerless. He dragged himself to the cover of the roadside ditch, and was losing consciousness as Dave landed heavily in the ditch next to him.

Chapter Thirteen

Jim's rise to consciousness was slow. As his hearing and then vision was restored, he became impatient with the confusion that still gripped his brain preventing him from making sense of his surroundings. He felt an urgent need to understand, to react but just couldn't put it all together.

Prisca had cried when Jim was carried in by two men with blood pouring from his leg. She had cursed them for not putting a ligature on the leg to stop the bleeding, and cursed herself for not having used her skills to plan for this. Doctoring in the village had been mostly been about minor injuries and management of long term medical conditions. The village hall had been transformed into a hospital with the sturdiest table becoming an operating theatre.

But she had no way of quickly matching people for blood transfusions and had to rely on people knowing their blood group. Already one boy, a raider, had died from blood loss which she could have prevented had she been able to give him a transfusion or even intravenous fluids.

Jim had a leg wound that had damaged an artery, and even though his men had brought him immediately, he had already lost a lot of blood. After stopping the bleeding, she quickly repaired the damaged artery, and then leaving the wound to be cleaned by Alexandra, who was proving to be a most able and stoic assistant, she set about transfusing blood from herself to her husband. She knew they had the same blood group. After a two litres of blood had passed between them, she could see from his colour and the beginning of a return of consciousness that he was going to survive.

She would worry later about possible infection from the clean but distinctly unsterilised and scarily "Heath-Robinson" arrangement for the operation and transfusion. Unhooking herself from the transfusion, she prepared a pain killing injection, that sent her husband back into the unconscious state he was starting to emerge from, and then closed up the wound Alexandra had so proficiently cleaned.

In the small hours of that night, Prisca was able to take a break from the makeshift hospital ward and take time to try and make sense of the snippets of information that she had picked up as the wounded, dying, and already dead were brought to the hall. She found Dave who reported that the community was secure again that there was no sign of the raiders, and that they had barricaded the broken gate. He had organised all the unwounded men into a rota to stand guard through the night. He had also "found" enough whisky to give all that wanted it a "decent nip", as he put it.

'How's Jim? Is he going to be alright?' He asked.

'He lost a lot of blood but I think he will be alright now. Thanks for asking, Dave.' She then added, 'Look, Dave, as soon as this is settled down, we need to make sure everybody knows the basics of first aid. Jim could have died because nobody thought to put a ligature on his leg to stop the bleeding.'

'Aye, there's a lot of new things we need to learn.' Dave paused and then coming back to the present, he asked, 'How many have we lost do you think?'

'There are three men from Stainton already dead—Ben, Jamie Kendrik and John Thurgood—and I'm not sure whether Peter or John Builder will make it through the night. There are another eight with fairly serious wounds but who should be okay. There are half a dozen of the raiders with serious wounds, there's also five or six bodies around the side of the hall,' she reported in a tired matter of fact voice. Then she added, 'My God, Dave, I still can't believe it. Who were those people?'

'I can tell you who the leader is—Nathaniel—the same guy that was involved in the Haddington riot. He was the ringleader but somehow escaped when the army came,' he replied. 'By the way, there are a couple more bodies at the gate or on the road that we haven't got round to clearing up yet.'

Prisca asked, 'Do you think they will come back?'

'Nope—I reckon we gave them a good beating, but it was bloody close. I thought they had us when they got into the village, then all of a sudden, they were breaking off from the fight and heading back to the gate, even before Jim got there with the reinforcements.'

Prisca began to feel a chill as it dawned on her that the raiders had left in an organised retreat rather than routed by the villagers.

'Dave, I want you to go and check the storehouse to see if they have taken anything from there,' said Prisca, as she felt yet another wave of adrenalin wash the weariness out of her system.

'You're thinking they left because they had got what they had come for rather than because we kicked their backsides.'

'I am, Dave, and we need to check that *all* the women are still with us. Do you understand?'

Without answering, Dave ran off towards the storehouse. Prisca spoke to Dorothy and together, they gathered together some of the women they most trusted telling them of their fears—asking them to check if anybody was missing.

Ten minutes later, Dave was back with a report that the storehouse was a mess with a lot of supplies gone. Then quietly, he said, 'Is anything else missing?'

Prisca already knew what was missing, Alexandra's mother and Brenda, a twenty year old, both had been fighting with the men and could not be found anywhere in the village. Alexandra was still in the village hall looking after the wounded and had no idea that her mother was missing.

A heaviness fell on the village as it remained on alert for any repeat of the attack. The success of the village community had been embedded in a sense of confidence that they were able to deal with what the future might hold for them. The attack had taken this confidence away as it had Alexandra's mother and her friend, Brenda, not to mention a significant part of the food supplies. Although the raiders had not been able to take all of the supplies in the store, they had taken the best of it.

For the rest of that long wet spring, food was in short supply and basic. They still had enough barley and oats, thanks to a good crop last year, so no one would starve. These crops coped better with the wetter conditions that global warming had brought to south east Scotland, so porridge and thick vegetable soups returned as the main staple of the diet of Stainton rather than the choice of the health conscious few.

For Alexandra, the taking of her mother turned her almost overnight from a young woman into a community leader focused on ensuring that Stainton and what it represented had a future. Within hours of being told by Prisca that her mother was missing, she had gathered to her many of the young men from Stainton and set out to look for her mother and Brenda. For the first time in her life, she refused to listen to Prisca's counsel, and Jim was still too unwell from his injury to be able to use his influence.

Prisca and Natalie watched as astride a quad bike and dressed in a bright red coat, she holstered the pistol that she had taken from Jim's bedside and harangued her young men to show greater haste. The ten young men who followed her out of the village gates were undoubtedly in awe of her. All but one hoping to win her affections. One young man left the village with a heavy heart, only going because he was afraid to be seen badly by his peers should he refuse to join this adventure.

Thomas' heart was already set on Natalie, who had recovered from her ordeal at the hands of the Haddington rioters to find the strength of character that was turning her into an essential member of the community. Thomas' patience and respect for her had already kindled in her some of the same feeling that he had for her. Older and wiser tongues in the village had noted that Natalie, usually so frosty towards men of any age, was warming to Thomas. Thomas felt for Alexandra's mother and Brenda, but was reluctant to leave the village when it needed protection most.

Chapter Fourteen

Of all the sadness in Natalie's long life, the greatest was that she and Alexandra had not spoken in thirty years. Alexandra was the reason that she and Thomas, her man partner, had started a new community at Newtown. When Alexandra had left to search for her mother, and taken with her a reluctant Thomas and nine other men, the only thing on her mind was to find her mother. Three months later, when she finally gave up the search and returned to Stainton, she was in love with Thomas and was sure in her mind that she wanted him as her partner.

For three months, Alexandra's band had roamed around the South East of Scotland in search of Nathaniel. Everywhere they went, they heard tales, and saw the evidence of the banditry that was sweeping through the country almost completely unopposed by the forces of law and order. It became obvious that Nathaniel's group were only one amongst many. Everywhere, surviving communities were organising their own hasty defences against the threat of groups of feral men who respected nothing and no one.

Returning from a harrowing but fruitless visit to Edinburgh, they came along the coast through Joppa to Musselburgh where they had found the bridges across the Esk barricaded. The bodies of two young men were hanging from lampposts with placards around them saying this is what looters can expect in Musselburgh. At first, they thought it was the handiwork of the army, but were proudly told that the people of Musselburgh had caught and strung up the young men as a warning to others who might come from Edinburgh in search of food or women.

Alexandra's little band had learnt that her bright red coat and youthful femineity easily allayed the fears of communities they came to, affording a hearing if not always access. Indeed, her little group became a curiosity; a young and beautiful woman who was the obvious leader of an armed group was sufficiently unusual to be news worthy. Alexandra, the red coat and quad bike soon became known in places they had never been to.

The notoriety also attracted negative interest, mostly from bored young men. The Stainton men had the benefit of being well armed and, thanks to Jim, all had had some training in the use of firearms. They easily kept at bay the individuals that sought them out with malice and went out of their way to avoid unnecessary trouble. As the weeks rolled by, their search seemed increasingly hopeless. There was no word of Nathaniel and his group seemed to have disappeared, along with Brenda and Alexandra's mother.

Gradually, the group's thoughts turned from rescue to ensuring that their community was safe from the tide of banditry and lawlessness that they were witnessing on an almost daily basis. Thomas suggested returning to the Lammermoors and to try and speak to the surrounding villages and towns about mutual support in times of need and a warning system when raiders were seen. Alexandra saw the sense of this, and though reluctant to admit that her mother was lost to her, agreed with Thomas that they had to prevent other women meeting the same fate as her mother and Brenda.

From Musselburgh, they didn't head straight back to Stainton, but headed first to Haddington, which they found all but deserted. The food distribution point in the super store had never been re-opened and people began to leave the town to seek food wherever they could. This turned into an exodus when heavy winter rains had flooded the centre of the town.

Without a functioning civil authority, the water had remained until the floods had subsided, causing havoc with sewerage systems. The floodwaters quickly became rancid causing outbreaks of water borne disease to those that remained in the town.

Next, they travelled to East Lowtown where they found that the community had learnt from Stainton and had organised defences. East Lowtown had focused on trading in all kinds of farming implements and renewable energy technologies. One family who had a background in engineering had inspired this; initially they had arranged barters for food in return for help with developing renewable energy sources. The villagers had then converted an old garage into a very busy workshop for producing wind turbines, watermills, and for repairing or adapting wood stoves, under the guidance of the two engineers.

Their suggestions for mutual aid and defence from raiders were received warmly. On the advice of the East Lowtown villagers, they avoided North Berwick, which was said to have recently been taken over by the crew of a Russian naval ship seeking supplies. At Dunbar, not even Alexandra and her red coat could get them a hearing with a very hostile group that manned the barricades set up around the village.

At Cockburn, a small and frightened group were found who explained that all they were able to do was hide when strangers approached, that they kept anything of value hidden and women were kept hidden during daylight hours. They were delighted to find that others were trying to respond to the threat from the raiders and were keen to offer and receive whatever help was possible. Cockburn had many connections with what was left of the farms in the area who could provide excellent eyes and ears for their developing defence system.

Alexandra promised to return with some method of communication between the different groups. In Garvally, a village close to Stainton, they found a very warm welcome and instant agreement that the villages should work together for mutual aid and defence.

As Alexandra approached the gates of Stainton, she knew she had failed to find her mother and Brenda, and the sadness of this was very strong, but against this was the success in beginning to develop alliances with the local towns and villages. Also she had found feelings in herself towards Thomas, which were powerful and hard to resist.

As they approached, she saw that the gates of the village were wide open, but no one was to be seen, no guards, no one rushing out to meet them or raising the alarm. Suddenly, Alexandra was alert, her mind full of a thousand explanations as to why the gate was deserted, none of them pleasant. She gunned the throttle of the quad bike to race for the open gate; the men momentarily taken by surprise, quickly followed on behind her.

Through the gate, she slewed the quad to a halt. For a few moments, all she could hear was the idling of the quad bike engine and then an explosion of welcome and shouts of surprise as people appeared from seemingly nowhere. The young men came running through the gate to find Alexandra being hugged by Prisca and the start of a party. Thomas sort out Natalie, who seeing him hesitated for a moment before throwing herself into his arms.

Across the street, Alexandra suddenly stiffened in Prisca's arms as she saw her heart's desire being stroked and caressed by one of her best friends who only weeks ago struggled to look a man in the eye. She forced away the feelings of anger at Thomas and the cruel thoughts about Natalie to return her focus to her joyful return to Stainton, but the feelings she crushed in that moment would haunt her for many, many years to come.

It was some time before Natalie became aware of Alexandra's feelings for Thomas. She had confided in Prisca that Alexandra was behaving differently towards her, that there was a sharpness in her words, and that she seemed to be excluding her from her company. Prisca had said, 'Oh, Natalie, you must be the last one in the village to realise that Alexandra has fallen in love with Thomas.'

This knowledge exploded in her head, instantly fitting all the facts and overwhelming her in its rightness. She let out a little moan followed by a flood of silent tears. The first since she was comforted in the back of a car by Prisca and Alexandra after her ordeal at the hands of the Haddington rioters. Prisca hugged her and mentally reprimanded herself for being quite so blunt.

'But Alexandra can have any boy she wants. Why does she want the one that loves me?' Prisca had no easy answer, and Natalie pressed her, 'Why, Prisca?'

'Natalie, you too can have any boy you want. It seems that poor Thomas has inspired love in you both.' Prisca held back the unvirtuous thought that Alexandra may just want what she could not have. She may be an inspiring personality and an aspiring community leader, but there was a part of Alexandra that was still the precocious child who wanted to be noticed first and foremost.

Natalie accepted that Alexandra was better than her in almost everything. She was prettier, stronger physically and mentally, faster and more intelligent. Natalie had never dreamed of trying to compete against her for anything. She loved Alexandra like almost everyone else that came into Alexandra's life, looked up to her as a role model in so many things. She would have followed her anywhere, but instantly, she understood that she would not give up Thomas to her, and she was confident in Thomas' feeling for her.

She sought out Thomas, who was helping Andy with checking and assembling a new wind turbine that they had bartered for with the people at East Lowtown.

'Why, Thomas? Why didn't you tell me she wanted you?' Natalie said with hurt and anger in her voice after she had managed to get him out of Andy's hearing.

'How could I tell you that another woman was in love with me, and not just any woman but Alexandra?'

'But Prisca says that everybody in the village knows and I am the last to find out,' she replied fighting back tears. The anger she felt towards Thomas for not telling her about Alexandra's feeling towards him rebounded on herself for being so stupid or at least so naive that it hadn't dawned on her.

Thomas smiled. 'Yes, it took you a while to catch on, didn't it?'

'Oh, Thomas, don't laugh at me. I can take the rest of village laughing at poor dim witted Natalie, but not you.'

Thomas drew her into his arms and she yielded readily. 'I think that I love you so much because you're the kind of person who would be the last to notice that your best friend was trying to steal your lover.'

'Are you my lover, Thomas?' Natalie asked.

'I want to be, if you will have me,' replied Thomas.

'And Alexandra, is she to be yours too?' Natalie said unable to keep the jealousy she now felt out of her voice.

'Alexandra is very beautiful and is going to be a truly amazing woman.' He paused feeling Natalie grip on his waist slacken. Pulling her even closer, he went on, 'But she will always be more in love with herself than any man. If I let myself fall for her, she would grow bored with me in a fairly short time and move onto somebody or something else. Besides from the first time I saw you, I somehow knew you were right for me.'

Natalie arms once again tightened around his waist and her hands began to explore the firm muscles of his back.

'If you are my lover,' she whispered, 'then you had better take me somewhere you can prove it to me.'

Soon after Natalie and Thomas announced to the village that they were to have a child together and wanted to celebrate by having a party for the village. Everyone seemed happy for them but Alexandra. She had grown colder and colder towards them as their romance had blossomed.

Chapter Fifteen

Housing and accommodation in the village was managed at one of the regular meetings of the women in the village hall. These meetings at first informal get togethers, increasingly became formalised and consciously excluded the men. The men in the village went along with this for fear of attracting the displeasure of the women or a woman in particular. If they didn't like decisions that came out of these meeting, they would approach Jim, who would then go to Prisca or Alexandra and relate the grievances of the men.

Although there was much grumbling the system seemed to work. Men that wanted some resource that belonged to the community like accommodation approached Jim, and if he agreed, he took the request to Prisca or Alexandra. Thomas followed this route when he wanted to take an empty house in the village for himself and Natalie so that they could prepare for the arrival of their baby.

James was happy to take this to the women and was sure that they would agree. When no decision was forthcoming after the meeting, he asked Prisca what the problem was.

'Problem, the problem is Alexandra,' spat out Prisca. 'She is being so petty, and it's all because she couldn't have Thomas. Of course she has half the women eating out of her hands, and supporting her no matter that they all know she is being spiteful and petty.'

Natalie had gone to Thomas straight after the meeting and explained that the women hadn't come to a decision. Alexandra was arguing that they should have a smaller house that would be vacated by the Andrews when they left the village to go and stay with their son in England. Alexandra argued that the larger house might be needed for others whose families were bigger. She ignored altogether Natalie and Prisca's argument that the house had been empty for months and nobody had asked for it, and might be empty for a lot longer yet.

In the end, the meeting was adjourned. They had never had this situation before, a consensus had always been reached. As news of the disagreement spread throughout the village, a debate began to spread about how the community should deal with disagreements. Men began to join the discussion saying that they should have more of a say in the decisions. For a week, the debate raged without any resolution. A special meeting of the women's group was convened.

As the women gathered in the village hall with a fuller attendance than was usual, the men of the village had gathered in Dave's house, which for all practical purposes had become the village pub. Dave did a thriving trade selling or bartering his home brewed beer and wine, and had great aspirations to one day produce his own whisky.

Thomas had almost universal support amongst the men for his request for the empty house, and there was a general agreement that Alexandra was acting out of spite and jealousy. However, the younger men in particular were acutely aware that the younger women were backing Alexandra and that if it came to a vote, it would be very close. A second round of drinks stoked up the fire of their resentment at being left out of the decision making.

'Why don't we just go and move Thomas into the house right now,' said Dave, 'and let them go on clucking about it.' Many were inspired by Dave's practical approach to solving the problem.

But Thomas vetoed it and said, 'Hold up, that would solve my problem, but if this community is to survive, we will have to find proper ways of dealing with situations like this. It will be chaos if we start solving arguments with action rather than words. Who would then be able to stop anybody taking what they wanted?'

'Thomas is right,' said Jim from the back of the room where he had sat quietly throughout the discussion.

'Well maybe,' replied Dave, 'but we can't just let Alexandra boss us about because the women can't or won't see that she is acting like a spoilt brat.' Again Dave was speaking the minds of the gathered men.

Thomas, ever reasonable, said, 'Don't fire people up against Alexandra, she has done a lot for this community already and I'm sure will do a lot more yet.'

'Bloody hell, Thomas, are you out for sainthood, lad? You should be spitting nails that she trying to stop you from getting what you have a right to and what you need just because you chose Natalie over her.'

'I'm no saint, Dave, and I know Alexandra is not either, but she is a fine leader. You didn't see her when we were searching for her mother. Stainton is going to need people like Alexandra.' He paused and turned to look at Jim. 'No offence, Jim, but you and Prisca are getting old and won't be here forever.'

'Well, we don't want anybody lording over us whether they are a good leader or not,' said old Bill, getting in just as Dave was opening his mouth.

'Aye, you're right, Bill,' replied Jim again from the back of the room. He got up and moved to where they could see him without swivelling their necks. 'Maybe it is time to think about how we want to pick those that are to lead. There has to be a way of controlling leaders or you end up with what that Captain Peters has got going in Stirling Castle. Alexandra is young and has a lot to learn about the world, but there is no doubt she is going to be a force in it. If for no other reason than that she leads a lot of you younger men by the balls.'

He paused to let the rumble of laughter acknowledge the truth of his statement. 'There is no doubt she is bright enough to know that being young and female in this new world gives her a power beyond her undoubted good looks. She has all the other young women looking up to her and ready to follow her because she is the one who is confident and ready to use it. Have you noticed how confident the young women are about their sexuality lately? Where only a few months ago, you hardly saw them out and certainly not dressed like Alexandra dresses.'

'I'm glad of it,' said Tim. 'It makes me think things might be normal again to see women dressing nice and not afraid to go about the streets.'

Tim's comment was met with a general assent, and the room filled with the thinking of the men as they pondered the implications of what Jim had been saying. Then Dave burst the bubble with, 'Aye, well that all very well, but what's it got to do with Alexandra saying no to Thomas taking his wife into an empty house.'

Jim replied, 'Because, my good friend, the world is never as simple as your brain makes it out to be. Don't you see that Alexandra, whether she knows she's doing it or not, is setting up for a fight. She is saying to the whole community that the women should decide who gets what and when. Thomas here has strayed into the middle of it by having the cheek to choose another women over Alexandra.

'I don't think Alexandra meant it to happen like this and she has let her jealousy get the better of her in the woman's council, but if she backs down now, she loses face in front of the women. There is no doubt that Alexandra thinks women should make the decisions, but it's not just Alexandra, most of the women agree because they fear that if men make the decisions, then there will be chaos because we would only be interested in fighting over women.'

Thomas picked up where Jim had finished. 'The truth is she is probably right. I think we have done so well here because we have let the women organise the community whilst the men have been focused on defending it. East Lowtown has followed our lead and is doing well, but lots of other places have been torn apart because too many men were pursuing too few women and used any lever to advantage themselves in this.

'You all know the tensions in Stainton over women, those with wives or partners are envied by those that don't have them. Those that do fear that they will lose them, and us young men will do practically anything to get noticed by the women. It wouldn't take much for that to get out of hand and ruin the chance for the decent life we have all worked so hard for.'

'Well, this is all fine philosophical chit chat, but what the fuck are yer gonnae do aboot yer hoose, man,' exploded an exasperated Dave, who was as ever focused on the immediate and practical. There was laughter in the room at Dave's outburst. He pleaded to Jim, 'For fuck sake, just tell us what we should do. We cannae let Alexandra get her way on this.'

'I think you're right, Dave, she is out of order,' said Jim. 'Perhaps we should call for the election of a leader, somebody to settle disputes. Like a town mayor.'

'Aye, that fine then,' said Dave. 'I nominate you, Jim, all those in favour raise your right hand.'

All the right hands in the room were raised except Jim's.

'Well, thanks very much. But that will never do. A straight vote is always going to disadvantage the women; if we are to have an election, it's got to give the women an equal voice.'

Dave was quick to react to Jim's suggestion. 'That's no problem, we're all one big family now here in Stainton. We'll have a women and a man as joint leaders, they can sort out the hassles just like a mother and father do. What do yer say to that then, Father Jim?' Dave laughed.

Jim was stuck for an answer. The good sense of what Dave had proposed hit him with the force of a solution that is obvious once seen, but the rightness of the proposal was at odds with the proposer. Dave could usually only be relied on to say the wrong thing at the wrong time, or occasionally the right thing at the wrong time. Jim looked to Thomas for support and Thomas smiled back at him, before saying, 'By God, I think Dave has hit the nail on the head this time.'

A big grin appeared on Dave's face and he received plaudits from all around. Then Thomas said, 'But…'

'Oh fuck, 'ere we go,' responded Dave swallowing the last of his drink.

Ignoring Dave's interruption, Thomas went on, 'But if we are going to elect a father and a mother, to use Dave's phrase, then I think it should be the women that elect the father and the men who elect the mother.' Pausing to assess the impact of his thoughts, he scanned the crowd to see mostly puzzled faces. 'Don't you see, this way the men can't complain about the women that's elected, and the women can't complain about the man.'

For the next half hour, they batted the ideas back and forth, until eventually paper and pen was called for and they wrote down their thoughts. Once completed, they left Dave's place and proceeded to the village hall where the women were still meeting. Jim was pushed forward as spokesperson and accompanied to the door. Dave was all for them all going in and making sure things were sorted out, but he was prevailed upon to be quiet and to let Jim get on with it.

The hubbub at the door brought Prisca out to see what they were up to, fearing that it might be men out to confront the women about Thomas and the empty house. She opened the door to find her husband standing there with a piece of paper in his hand.

'Jim, you know we don't allow men into our meetings. What are you lot doing here,' she said looking over his shoulder at the gang of men standing behind him.

'It's alright, love, we have been thinking and have come with a proposal we want to put to the women about how we can govern ourselves and deal with disputes like that of Thomas and the empty house.'

Prisca eyed her husband a little sceptically. 'You all came up with this together, did you?'

'That's right,' came Dave's voice from behind Jim. 'All of us together.' The others hushed him as he showed signs of preparing for a speech.

She saw Jim rolling his eyes as the others hushed Dave and said quietly for his hearing only, 'Of course you came to this understanding in Dave's house if my nose doesn't mistake me.'

'Prisca,' said Jim firmly, but also for her hearing only. 'This is important,' and with that, he brandished the paper.

So the others could hear and pointing to the paper in Jim's hand, she said, 'And is that the proposal you have then?'

'Aye, we want to…' began Dave as Prisca neatly plucked the paper from between Jim's fingers, and before he got to the end of the sentence, the door was closed in his face.

'Well, how'd yer like that then and from his own wife too,' came the irrepressible Dave.

The men hung around outside the hall for over an hour, but seeing that there was no sign of the women emerging, they began to get bored and some started drifting away back to their homes and beds. Thomas, Jim, and Dave and a few others stuck it out until the small hours of the morning. Thomas was becoming increasingly worried about how Natalie was faring inside and was just about to share his worries with Jim when the door to the hall was thrown open to reveal a resplendent Alexandra with the other women, including Prisca, bunched behind her.

Framed in the light of the door, Alexandra spoke to the dregs of the men who had persevered.

'We accept the proposal of the men. An election will be held in three weeks' time—the men voting for the women and the women voting for the man.'

'That's great,' said Jim. 'You have to thank Dave and Thomas for coming up with the idea.'

There was a titter of laughter from behind Alexandra and Dave's name was mentioned amongst the laughter. The laughter would have grown had they been able to see the redness swelling in Dave's face underneath the mass of unruly beard and hair.

Alexandra ignored both the laughter and Jim's suggestion of thanking Dave and Thomas. She cut off the laughter behind her with a loud 'But,' pausing for a moment and then in a rush, 'We want the women, the mother of the community, to be elected for life. The man to be re-elected at least every five years. The mother can only be replaced if a majority of the women vote for it.'

Thomas and Jim looked at each other but before they collected their thoughts to speak, Alexandra voice came again from the lighted doorway, 'Can you accept this on behalf of the men.'

Thomas and Jim were too slow, Dave got in first. 'Aye, aye, but what about Thomas' hoose.'

Alexandra spoke over the top of the start of protests from Jim and Thomas. 'We will take that as an acceptance then. As to Natalie and Thomas' request, that will be the first decision of the newly elected Community mother and father.'

She then moved to the side of the doorway effectively ending the debate as the men and women ceased to be two separated groups. The women streamed out of the hall and took up with their respective partners or groups and headed to their homes.

Along with the other men, Jim and Thomas let their relief that the argument seemed to be over submerge any doubts about letting Dave speak on their behalf. Looking back on it, neither Thomas nor Jim could say if they had agreed with the amendments to their proposal, were too tired to argue, or whether they had simply being trammelled by the force of Alexandra's personality.

When Natalie came from the hall, she hurried to Thomas' side. She swallowed her embarrassment as he bent to kiss her and yielded to him. Whether it was to remind Alexandra that she could not control everything or a result of the release of tension, their clasp was more passionate than their short separation merited, and occasioned a few hoots from the crowd.

An election campaign got underway the day after the meeting of the woman's council. It was hastily agreed that candidates had to be nominated by ten signatories of either sex. Alexandra, Prisca, Jim and Thomas were all nominated along with Natalie, much to her surprise and annoyance. Thomas spent the three weeks arguing that the women should vote for Jim. At first, Natalie refused to accept the nomination, but Prisca persuaded her that it was an honour to be nominated and that she should accept.

So she followed Thomas' lead and argued with the men that they should vote for Prisca. The campaign was very positive. Alexandra was very conciliatory towards Thomas and Natalie in the one public hustings of the campaign. On the issue of the house for Thomas and Natalie, she argued that it was important that the communities' resources be used wisely and to the benefit of all but that if she were elected mother, then she would be guided by the views of the community, hinting therefore that Thomas would get his house.

Three weeks later, the entire community of Stainton filed through the door of the village hall and one by one were ticked off a list of all entitled to vote, and then placed their x on to ballot papers one for the female community leader and one for the male community leader. The general consensus was that Jim would become the community father and that it would be very close between Alexandra and Prisca for the position of community mother.

The eldest of the young people not eligible to vote read out the result. It had been agreed that you had to be sixteen years or older to vote, but that the older teenagers would officiate at the election. The vote for the father was read out first and to Thomas' surprise and many of the community's, sixty-two women had voted for him, despite his best efforts. He lost by only six votes to Jim. The vote for the mother was also close, but the result came as a shock for the women of Stainton, as Natalie was declared the winner.

Of the one hundred and ten men of voting age in Stainton, thirty-nine had chosen to vote for Natalie, thirty-six for Alexandra and thirty-five for Prisca. The announcement was applauded, but as the applause faded out, it was followed by a murmur of discussion. It was clear that the women in particular had thought that the men would have chosen either Prisca or Alexandra being the strongest women in the community. Many thought that Natalie had only been nominated out of sympathy because it was believed that Alexandra had treated her badly over the empty house.

Truly, if the people of Stainton had chosen a proportional system rather than first past the post, then it is probable that Alexandra or Prisca would have come out on top. The loudest discussion in the community had been about whether it was better to have the youthful, energetic Alexandra or the proven strengths and capability of Prisca. In reality, many of the men saw Prisca and Alexandra as being very similar except in age. Both were strong, direct, even domineering.

Natalie's quieter virtues seemed to stand out in relief when compared to Prisca and Alexandra, and her modesty and lack of ambition in relation to the position simply magnified this in the minds of the men. Nor had it gone unnoticed that she had the strength to stand up to Alexandra in her feelings for Thomas, but also in the matter of the house. Most of the men that had voted for her did so in the belief that of the three she was the one that was most likely to take the views of men seriously.

Prisca and Alexandra were the acknowledged founders and leaders of the woman's council, which some of the men had come to resent.

So Natalie and Jim became the first ever community mother and father of Stainton, but also the first of a new political system that developed across the planet in response to the imbalance of the sexes.

Speeches were called for and Jim motioned to Natalie that she should be the first to speak.

On hearing the announcement, Natalie's mind had gone into overdrive. She really hadn't wanted to stand for the position, and had only allowed herself to be persuaded because she had felt sure that Prisca or Alexandra would be chosen. Her first instinct was to decline, but a voice inside her head was saying, *If the men of the community that saved your life trust you, then maybe you should trust yourself.*

When she became aware of Jim smiling and prompting her to be the first to speak, she made her mind up. She knew she wouldn't be doing this alone and she would find the strength from somewhere.

She stepped forward and everybody applauded politely. As the applause died away, she gave a big smile and said simply, 'Well, what a surprise!' Immediately, these four words broke her own tension and that of the gathered community, because it said what she and many others had been feeling. She went on, 'I know many of you have said you have been voting for a mother and father of our little community.'

Pausing she sought out Dave's face in the crowd before her, and said directly to him in as stern a voice as she could muster, 'I believe it was you that first used these terms for the positions, Dave.'

'Aye, that's right,' he shot back in a bristly tone, ready to defend himself.

'I suppose then, that we shall have to call you the midwife of Stainton,' she said with grave irony. The room broke into waves of laughter as an image of Dave, the midwife, filled their imaginations. The men around Dave slapped him on his back and generally congratulated him on his new title.

From that moment, Natalie assumed the authority she needed as leader of the community. She raised her hand to quieten the more boisterous in the crowd. 'As you all know, it won't be too long before I become a mother of a child. I can ensure you that I will try as hard to be a good mother for this community, as I will try to be a good mother of my own child. Finally, just as I know I need the support of my husband in being a mother, I know I can count on the man the women have chosen as father of the community.'

The crowd applauded as she stepped back to indicate that she had finished speaking, and this time, there were no murmurings of doubt as the applause died away.

Jim spoke briefly thanking everyone and expressed the hope that he would live up to the trust they had placed in him. Prisca said that she was confident that Jim and Natalie would make a great team and that Stainton would be secure under their leadership. Alexandra gave a rousing speech about the community of Stainton having taken a brave step that others would follow, and that these elections in the small community of Stainton would be taught in the classrooms of the future as a turning point after the devastation of the collapse of the old world.

As Natalie listened, she knew that Alexandra was unlikely to be happy playing second fiddle within the community of Stainton.

Chapter Sixteen

The very next day, Alexandra let it known that she was going to leave Stainton to travel to other emerging communities and talk to them about how Stainton had adopted a new political system. She argued with Jim, who was against her going, that it would help Stainton if it had strong allies that were able to cope with internal tensions as well as the many external threats. She did not consult with Stainton's community mother.

Jim's first instinct was to get Prisca to reason with Alexandra. But Prisca reminded him that she was only his wife and that he should go to Natalie to discuss this latest development in the life of Stainton. She added if Natalie agreed with him, she would try to reason with her, but didn't think she would have any more luck than he had.

Jim went to Natalie.

'The thing is she is bound to take some of the younger men with her and perhaps some of the younger women. Stainton is pretty boring for them and many are itching for excitement.'

'We can't make people stay. If they want to leave for excitement, or whatever other reason, we would be wrong and foolish to try and stop them.'

'But we need everybody that's here to make sure we can defend ourselves as well as feed ourselves,' protested Jim.

'Jim, you know as well as I do that we have to turn people away all the time. If we need more people to make the community work then that will be the least of our problems. Besides, Alexandra has a point. What we have done here is probably worth other people knowing about and copying. What's more, she is not going to be happy raising cabbages and teasing the local boys. She needs a bigger stage.

'If we try to force her to stay, and I'm not sure we can, then she would be miserable, and no doubt cause all kinds of trouble. Even if she had been elected mother, I doubt it would have kept her here for more than a couple of years. She would have left sooner or later, probably sooner. Stainton is just not big enough for someone like Alexandra.'

'Are you saying we should just let her go without saying a thing? It's a bit of a slap in the face coming straight after the elections.'

'Well, I don't think we can stop her, so we either give it our blessing and the support of the community, or we say that Alexandra is acting as an individual and does not have our, and therefore, the support of the community for her "mission". If we support her, then we can influence what she does, and who she takes to support her.'

'And what if she ignores us and does just what she wants,' he asked and then in frustration added, 'God! I so much want to take her over my knee and paddle her backside. She's behaving just like a little girl in a strop. All this just because she can't have what she wants.'

'Now that I would love to see,' laughed Natalie.

'Well, I can tell you that I am sorely tempted, only…'

'Only what?' Natalie prompted with a broad smile.

'Well, if I tried that, I think I might well come out of it for the worst,' Jim responded.

'Yeah, she is stronger than most men and fast. In the old world, she would have been an athlete or sportswoman of some kind.'

'All of you young people talk about the "old world". Do you really think that it's all over that we are not going to get back to what we had.'

'I don't think we can ever go back,' she said quietly. 'You know, Jim,' she continued, 'I was thirteen when my parents died, barely fifteen when you rescued me from underneath that car in Haddington, twenty when we had to fight for our lives against Nathaniel's band of thugs. Lots of other young people have similar stories to me. There no going back. No matter how much we all crave the comforts and security of the old world.'

Jim simply nodded.

Natalie continued, 'And part of Alexandra's beauty is that she is not looking back, in fact she is passionate about tomorrow and what she thinks the future can be. Let's work with her, Jim, not because she is pushing us, but because maybe she can help us all face up to what is ahead, rather than mourning what has passed.'

'Okay, okay,' said Jim warming to the energy that he felt in their conversation. 'But I don't want her taking half the young people with her. How about we ask for three volunteers to accompany her and give them enough provisions to last for a week or two. She is not taking that quad bike either, it is too useful around here for her to be prancing about on it. They can take a pony to carry their supplies. Of course, they will have to be armed.'

'That sounds good,' agreed Natalie, adding, 'They should also send back regular messages about their progress.' After a short pause, she asked, 'Should the volunteers all be men?'

'Well, no matter what Alexandra thinks about the power of the feminine in this new world, four women on their own is simply going to be a magnet for every marauding gang in Southern Scotland. I think she will want to choose her volunteers and I suspect they will all be men.'

A fortnight after the elections, the community of Stainton turned out to watch Alexandra and three young men lead a laden pony out of the gates of Stainton on the first steps of a journey that would seal the reputation of Alexandra in the stories of the new world.

Chapter Seventeen

Power had become a rare commodity, power stations had been well protected by the state, but had gradually failed or been closed because of lack of spare parts, or failure of fuel supplies or because essential elements of the national grid failed. Floods, landslides, vandalism, and the destructive aftermath of civil disorder, all took their toll on systems that became increasingly difficult to repair or rebuild. People desperate for power but unable to pay had illegally plugged themselves directly into power lines with frequent disastrous effect for themselves and the electricity infrastructure.

Attempts to stop this by the state simply led to more disorder and to acts of reprisal against electricity infrastructure.

A few months after Alexandra left the gates of Stainton on her mission to bring word of a new political ideology for the new world, the last functioning nuclear power station in the north east of England caught fire and began to burn uncontrollably, releasing a toxic plume which rose from the sight for over a month. For most of that time, the plume of smoke was blown across the sea to plague the people of Norway and Sweden, but shifting winds took it into Yorkshire, and across the Pennines into Cumbria.

It would cause miscarriages and deformed babies for many years to come, but the immediate impact was a flood of people desperate to get away from the epicentre of the fallout, as more and more people showed signs of radiation sickness. There was no effort from state authorities to try and manage or restrain the mass migration from the area or to help the desperate people, most of whom were simply running away but had no idea where to go or where to turn for help.

Alexandra's group learnt of the disaster from a family they found trying to push a caravan off a road and into a field after the car that had towed it away from Darlington had run out of fuel. They stopped to help the family of one woman, three male children, and three men, the woman's husband and two uncles. They had decided they were going to stay where they had stopped, having little hope of getting more fuel. They had tried to gain help at communities all along the A1 as they came north into Scotland, but the most they had received was a kind word and some water.

Nobody wanted them and they guessed, probably rightly, that they could have gone on to John O'Groats without finding a community that would welcome six males and one female with little to barter. They had no idea how long they would stay in the overgrown field into which the caravan had been manoeuvred, or if they had come far enough to be safe from the fallout. The women's name was Simmone and she insisted that Alexandra and her men stay for a cup of real tea as thanks for their help and kindness.

Real tea was something of a treasure and it would have been rude to turn it down. Over the carefully brewed tea, Alexandra and her companions described the communities in the area, careful not to raise their hope of access, but saying that many would provide pay for work with food. She said that they could use her name to vouch for them, but warned that no community would tolerate the approach of more than one or two unknown men at a time. She asked if they had any skills they could trade.

Simmone replied, 'Well, I was a midwife, well trainee midwife really, but I only had a few months of the training left. My husband was a civil servant but he's very good at growing things.' She added quickly, 'His brother, Arnie, was a sergeant in the army. He knows everything about weapons and how to survive in the wild. He's been teaching the boys, who just love that sort of thing. The other brother, Stuart, was a butcher. The boys, well only the two oldest, had any school at all, but I have taught them to read and write, and they have learnt a lot of practical stuff from my husband and his brothers.'

Alexandra had warmed to Simmone's easy manner and felt this was a woman she could trust. The men she had with her obviously saw her as the centre and the leader of the little family group. Trying to be encouraging, she said to the family gathered behind Simmone, 'A very practical group,' and added with a smile, 'it's just a pity you're men.'

Alexandra's joke met with silence for a moment before Simmone laughed and said, 'Well, I reckon Arnie would look alright in a dress.'

'Wouldn't be the first time he's wore one either,' added Simmone's husband.

'Ha bloody ha,' responded Arnie with a smile that revealed a line of perfect teeth. Arnie was in his early thirties, with Crewe cut hair in the military manner. He was the kind of man that would draw looks in a crowd. Apart from his perfect smile, he had a strongly masculine face, in fact he looked like he could have easily have been the model for "action man". Rugged yet handsomely symmetrical features and a body that looked, beneath his loose fitting clothes, to have the proportion that could have graced any of the old world's men's health magazines.

Altogether, he had the look of a man who lived very easily in his body. Even the most casual of movement revealed controlled power and a fluidity that lent grace to his good looks. Alexandra looked at him with a directness that was almost rude. Arnie returned her gaze comfortably as he was used to women looking at him, although Alexandra eyes seemed to be assessing rather than appraising him. He didn't know anything about this young woman but recognised the air of command that she wore so well.

He let her eyes appraise him, catching the smile of his brother and sister-in-law who had seen this situation many times before. Finally, Alexandra took her eyes from Arnie and looking at Simmone, said, 'Sorry, but I think he would look like a man in a dress.' As the laughter died and the sense of sexual tension was reaching a peak, she turned her attention back to Arnie and said, 'I guess a lot of men would fancy you in or out of a dress, Arnie.'

She felt as much as heard the intake of breath of the men in her group, but from the smile on Arnie's face, and the disappointed looks on the face of his family, she knew that she had got it right—Arnie was not in the slightest bit interested in women and never had been.

Simmone looked at Alexandra with a new respect as very few people picked up that Arnie was gay. 'How did you know?' Simmone asked.

The tension of the Stainton men disappeared with this confirmation that Alexandra was right and that Arnie and the family did not seem put out by Alexandra's manner.

'Like Arnie, I'm used to being ogled by the opposite sex.' This frank statement produced a shuffling of feet and eyes amongst the men of the group. 'In fact, Simmone, I notice it more when men don't look at me than when they do. Arnie didn't look or at least he didn't try and undress me with his eyes as most men do.

'I put that together with the way you were all ready to try and wind me up about Arnie and his good looks, and something told me that Arnie's obvious attractiveness to my sex, yet his unavailability, was a tension that been played out many times amongst you.'

'If you have quite finished talking about me, maybe we should start to make camp. There's only a few more hours of daylight,' said Arnie.

'If it's alright, we will camp here tonight as well,' said Alexandra.

That night, Alexandra spoke to Simmone on her own.

She came straight to the point. 'Simmone, I could use Arnie. It would be a relief to have a capable man who is not interested in me sexually. His military skills would also be very useful given what I am trying to do.'

'If you want him to go with you, Alexandra, you must speak to him yourself, he is his own man.'

'Yes, but things are hard enough for you without me taking him away. Besides, I don't think he would listen to me if you weren't behind it.'

'We do need him. My man and Stuart are great but Arnie knows how to fight. On the way here, he killed three men who tried sneaking up on us at night. We didn't even know we had been attacked until it was all over. He killed two with a knife and broke the neck of the third. To be honest, he frightens me a bit. I know he would never hurt us, but since I saw how he killed those men, it's a bit like carrying a loaded weapon; you're always aware of its power and potential for injury.'

'The way things are, you're much safer with a loaded weapon always to hand. Listen, Simmone, I think I could get you and your family into my community at Stainton. Your men appear happy to work and a midwife would be a big help.'

'And in return you want Arnie?'

'Well, I want to put the proposition to him and I don't think he would consider it unless he thought you and your family are going to be safe.'

'Alexandra, I don't really know whether to think of you as our fairy godmother or as the most manipulative bitch that I've come across in some time.'

Alexandra laughed. 'It works for me both ways, but what do you say. If I get you a place in the community of Stainton, then I get to ask Arnie if he will join me.'

'What if he says no?'

'Well, it's win-win for you. If he says yes, you're part of a community, if he say no, you're still part of the community.'

'But you must be confident he will go with you?'

'Yes, I'm pretty sure of it, once he knows you're safe. I think he's not the sort to settle down. Am I right?'

Simmone replied, 'Probably,' but she was pretty sure that Alexandra was right. She knew that Arnie was staying with them to protect them and when he judged them to be safe, he would leave.

'Look, Alexandra, I'll have to discuss this with my husband and his brother as well as Arnie, but I don't see how we can say no. Stainton seems like a good place and it's got to be better than setting up a permanent camp in this field which is our next best option.'

Alexandra frowned, and rising from her seat, she said, 'Simmone, the decision is yours. They would not get into the community without you no matter what I say. I won't debate the pros and cons of it with them—they either accept your decision or they don't. I'll be leaving in the morning, let me know what you have decided.'

The next morning, Simmone and Arnie came to Alexandra's tent, and after a short pause, were allowed in by the man who stood guard at the entrance.

Alexandra looked at Simmone waiting for her answer, but on this occasion was as aware of Arnie looking at her as she had been of him not looking at her at their first meeting.

'Well, I've told the men of your offer, or should I say deal, and they agree with me that we won't get a better offer any time soon. Arnie has a question to ask though.'

Alexandra turned her eyes to Arnie and waited.

'If you can get Simmone and her family through the gates of this community at Stainton, then I'll come with you, but what is it you want me to do for you?'

'Okay, first, I can't promise that I can get you all into Stainton, it's not my decision. I've told you how the community works.'

'My guess is you are pretty confident or you wouldn't have made the offer. You're a gambler but you only take risks you are confident about,' replied Arnie.

'Okay.' She smiled. 'I want you as my bodyguard. I can look after myself but I need somebody to watch my back.'

'I thought the four guys with you were already that. Why do you need a fifth?'

'They agreed to come with me to spread the word about a new world order, and I value them as volunteers, and as friends. No doubt they see themselves as bodyguards, certainly the community parents of Stainton saw them that way. But I think I would be protecting their bodies in a real fight rather than the other way round. You have probably already formed a judgement about their abilities. So what do you think?'

'They seem like good men, but you're right, I don't think they would fair very well in a fight and would be easy prey for trained fighters.'

'Then you already have the answer to your question. You would be my protection, answerable to me and only me, taking orders directly from me and only from me.'

'What do I get out of it apart from knowing that my family are in a relatively safe place?'

'You get to do what your good at, and for the meantime, that will have to be enough,' said Alexandra, in a tone that said that was the end of the conversation.

'I'll go to Stainton and speak to Jim and Natalie. My men will stay here and Simmone and Arnie will come with me.' Looking at Arnie, she said, 'If you are going to be my bodyguard, you might as well start now.' Without waiting for a reply, she said to Simmone, 'Can you ride a horse?'

Simmone replied, 'No, but I can learn.'

'No, you will have to ride behind Arnie,' said Alexandra and added for explanation, 'There is always the potential for trouble on the roads, and we can't have your horse charging off with you, can we?' Looking at Arnie, she said with a hint of challenge, 'I'm assuming you can ride, Arnie.'

'I'll manage,' he replied and addressing Simmone, he said, 'She's right; you don't want to be learning if there's a chance of trouble. But I would suggest you ride with Alexandra. If I am to be bodyguard, I need to be free to move.' He looked at Alexandra. 'Either that or we take one of your men for her to ride behind.'

An hour later, they set out with Arnie in the lead, followed by Alexandra and then Simmone clutching a man she barely knew and feeling that she would never feel less than precarious on the back of a horse.

Alexandra soon learnt that Arnie was a natural horseman whose skills had been learnt in the British army's household cavalry with whom he had served before joining the Special Air Service. He was in fact a lieutenant but had come through the ranks so his family still saw him as a sergeant. She also learnt that he was going to take his role as bodyguard very seriously, and that she would have to have some patience and allow him to do the job that she wanted of him.

The journey to Stainton was uneventful and Jim and Natalie, having met Arnie and Simmone, understood what Alexandra was asking for and were happy to agree. Stainton did not have a midwife, and Prisca's burdens as the only medically trained person in Stainton were considerable. For Natalie, in the final trimester of her own pregnancy, having a midwife in the community was particularly timely. It was agreed that Arnie and Alexandra would send on Simmone's family when she re-joined her men.

The news of the fire in the nuclear power plant and the exodus of people was met with fear but also a fatal acceptance within the community. It was just more evidence that the old world was beyond repair and that events were marching to a beat that the people of Stainton were quite powerless to influence. There was much discussion about whether they would be affected by the fallout from the burning power station.

Arnie dismissed the fear by telling them that they had come north because that seemed to be the safest way. He revealed that the family had in their possession a Geiger counter, which they had monitored on their journey and they had not noticed any changes in the background radiation level. In fact, as soon as they had got past the city of Durham, the thing had not registered any appreciable radiation.

The rest of the evening was spent with Alexandra relaying the story of her travels round the local communities over the last two months since leaving the gates of Stainton. Her men had brought letters handed to them from friends and family who lived in other communities, which were eagerly received. Although the internet, and more sporadically mobile phones, continued to function to an extent, the post had long since collapsed and letters were a rarity to be treasured.

Alexandra let it be known that she intended to continue with her mission of finding new and developing communities and talking to them of how Stainton was surviving the collapse of order. She carefully explained what each of the communities they had visited could offer Stainton and encouraged the people to think of how they could establish trade between the communities for every body's benefit.

In particular, she was keen to trade with a community in Peebles for bio-diesel. This community had set up a considerable production system for producing the fuel from vegetable oils and animal fats. They were able to convert tractors and other vehicles to take the fuel and had started trading with surrounding farmsteads and some towns and villages. The community had very little medicine and nobody with the expertise to diagnose illness. A young man had died whilst they were there from what Alexandra was pretty sure was a burst appendix, but nobody knew how to treat it or what to do.

They had agreed that if Alexandra could find somebody that was medically trained who would come and live in the community, then they would help Stainton to establish its own bio-diesel production process. Hearing Alexandra's story, Prisca volunteered to go with her to Peebles and do what she could, whether or not they helped with producing bio-diesel.

Jim and Natalie were quick to veto that, arguing that she was needed in Stainton and that it was one thing to help some of the neighbouring communities that she could travel to and from in the course of a day, but Peebles was too far; she would have to stay there overnight at the very least. Alexandra said that it was quite a big and fairly disorderly community without clear leadership. It would be hard, and probably dangerous, for an outsider to simply offer help and leave. She would find them a doctor and in return, one of their people would come to Stainton and stay as long as it took to get a system up and running.

Natalie asked of Alexandra, 'And your mother, have you heard anything?'

Without looking at Natalie, she simply replied, 'Nothing.'

Chapter Eighteen

The next day, as Jim and Prisca once again watched Alexandra leave the gates of Stainton, Jim turned to his wife and said, 'I wonder what the world and his brother is going to make of those two when they coming knocking on the door.' Getting no reply, he added, 'Do you think she fancies him?'

Prisca laughed and said, 'Alexandra will always want what she knows she can't have.'

Stopping only to pick up her men and direct Simmone's family to Stainton with the news that Simmone was preparing to welcome them at the gates, Alexandra took her band south. She was determined to find a doctor, preferably a female doctor, to complete her trade with Peebles. The bio-diesel for Stainton was important to her, but most of all, she wanted to influence the developing community there to adopt Stainton's model of organisation. Peebles was a community with much energy, but to her, it was unstable.

The tensions between men were already beginning to pull at what cohesion its leaders had achieved. The trade in bio-diesel had allowed the community to begin to organise itself, because it was a huge communal effort to get enough vegetable and animal fat processed to produce a tradable amount of fuel. The benefits of the trade were immediate and visible to the community and this had so far held them together.

However, in the short time Alexandra had stayed in this community, the disagreements were many and they settled them through a council of self-appointed men, who naturally used their influence to improve their own situation first and foremost. Alexandra felt the tensions in the community, which had focused around the lack of medical services, but ever present underneath was the boiling resentment and jealousies caused by the gender imbalance.

Since hearing about the exodus of people from the vicinity of the burnt out nuclear power station at Hartlepool, Alexandra had thought her best chance of finding a suitable person for Peebles would be amongst these displaced people.

She reasoned that by heading south, she would increase the chances of finding a doctor or medically trained person that would be amenable to trading her or his services for the chance of stability and protection within a settled community. Having Arnie as leader of her bodyguard also increased the chances of surviving confrontations with people made desperate by displacement.

Alexandra knew that her little group would not be the only people who would try to take advantage of the people displaced by the fire and radioactive fallout. Inevitably, there would be scavengers seeking to prey on such ill defended people. She knew that it would be such people who would threaten her little group, rather than the refugees themselves. She also knew that they would be met with suspicion and fear even though their intentions were not to steal but to help.

As they rode south, they stayed within earshot of the old A68' but avoided travelling on the actual roadway, as to easy an option for being ambushed. After only half a day's travel, they came across the occasional body and burnt out vehicles which they took as increasing evidence of the presence of refugees and the scavengers that were preying on them. More poignant than the scenes of obvious violence were the possessions carelessly scattered about where people had been robbed of anything valuable and the remaining often very personal items simply thrown into the dirt.

So far they had not seen a single living person. If the road was out of sight for any length of time, Arnie would halt the group and send scouts out with strict instructions to stay hidden, and find a place where the road could be seen. Alexandra was beginning to grow impatient with the slow progress caused by Arnie's caution, thinking to herself that the whole point of the trip was to find people, one of whom might be the doctor they were looking for.

They paused on a wooded hill top waiting for one of Arnie scouting expeditions to return. The wind suddenly shifted direction and brought with it a low humming noise, like the noise of thousands of bees shuffling about inside a hive. As the wind dropped, the noise fell away and as it blew a little stronger, it picked up in intensity if not volume. The horses picked up the tension of their riders and began to shuffle restlessly.

Nobody had spoken but they all knew that the noise was not a normal sound; it carried a tone that seemed dangerous and foreboding. The young man whose turn it was to scout ahead came rushing up the hill, breathless with running he stopped a little way from the group and shouted, 'There are thousands and thousands of people coming along the road.' As he spoke, the wind again carried the noise of thousands of people moving towards them, but it was not the noise of an angry mob and definitely not of a joyous crowd.

The noise it made was a monotonous and low moaning sound, with none of the fall and rises in pitch to be expected in for example a crowd of expectant of music fans or a rowdy crown of football supporters. Arnie rode over to the man and interrogated him until he got from him more clear information about what he had seen. Arnie spoke to Alexandra but for all to hear in a clipped and brief military manner.

'It seems to be a crowd of refugees coming up the road about ½ a mile away. Mostly on foot, some handcarts and a few horse drawn vehicles, maybe one or two motorised vehicles at the rear, but he couldn't see if they were travelling under their own power or were being pulled. They're too far away to say if they armed or not, but I think we have got to assume in such a big crowd, there will be some with firearms of some sort.'

All eyes turned to Alexandra as Arnie finished his report.

'I want to talk to them; let's move to a place where we can observe them and then we'll decide how best to approach them. There will be leaders in such a large group—we need to identify who they are and how they are controlling the crowd.'

'Alright,' said Arnie. 'I will accompany Alexandra to reconnoitre the crowd. The rest of you stay here; no fires, stay out of sight. If they have any kind of organisation, they will have scouts out ahead of the main group.'

Arnie turned and rode down the little hill in the direction their scout had come from the road. Alexandra followed.

It wasn't long before Arnie had found a vantage point on a low rise ahead of a bend in the road above a few cabin style holiday cottage that appeared abandoned. The crowd of humanity was just beginning to come around the bend in the road, only three or four hundred metres from their vantage point.

After a moment or two observation, Alexandra said to Arnie, 'Tell me what you see.'

'I see as sorry a looking group of refugees as you're ever likely to see, but no sign of armaments, no scouts and it looks like very little organisation. Just a crowd of very miserable people.'

Alexandra smiled. 'Nothing else?'

Arnie looked again and for a whole minute strained to see what it was that Alexandra was obviously seeing in the crowd. Then it came to him. 'Of course they're all men, it doesn't seem like that there is any women at all. Maybe a few small girls but otherwise no females.'

'Well done, Arnie,' said Alexandra with a mocking tone.

'But I think if you look even more closely, you will see that we are meant to think that there are no females, but in fact, there are quite a few. For instance, look behind that cart,' she said pointing. 'If those are not both young women, I will eat my hat.' She laughed.

Arnie looked at the two people behind the hand cart she had pointed to and kicked himself for not having noticed it sooner. He had no doubt that those two were women poorly disguised as men. Their hair was cut short and they were bundled in male clothing to disguise their shape, but when you looked at them singly rather than as part of a crowd, it was blindingly obvious that they were young women.

As Arnie again scanned the centre of the crowd, he could see that a number of other were also probably female even if they were better, or more easily disguised than the two behind the handcart.

'So there is some organisation then,' said Arnie. 'They're disguising the women and protecting them in the centre of the crowd.'

'I suspect that they are also arms in that crowd but hidden not on show. They want to look like a crowd of beaten fleeing men,' said Alexandra. 'But have they just clumped together out of instinct and a belief that there is safety in numbers or do they see themselves as a group, and if so, who are the leaders?' She asked as much of herself as of Arnie. The front rank of the crowd was now level with their position but the rear of the crowd had not yet cleared the bend in the road.

'Why no scouts then?' Arnie countered. 'That would be the most basic thing if they were an organised group, so they could be alerted to threats in advance.'

'Basic if you're an army and can defend yourself by hiding or attacking first. Maybe they have decided there is no point in knowing what is ahead. They can't hide, and they can't go back, so they simply have to face whatever comes and endure it.'

As Alexandra finished this thought, they heard a noise behind them. Arnie instantly crouched, and he motioned Alexandra to do the same. Then they heard frantic whispers and made out their names. Thinking it could only be one of their own men, Arnie gave a low whistle, and they heard movement towards them until one of their men came into sight.

Catching the look on Arnie's face that said "this better be good or you will be roasted alive", the man was quick to say, 'Sorry, but we thought you should know that there is a band of twenty or so men moving towards the road. They haven't seen us but we had to move to be sure.'

'You did right,' said Arnie, but shot out the question. 'Are they armed?' before the man could respond to the praise.

'Yes, from what we saw, it looked most of them had rifles or shotguns.'

Alexandra, asked, 'You're sure they didn't see you?'

'Yes, we had put out guards, and luckily, one of the lads spotted them well away from us and we were able to move before they could get into a position to see us. But I think they were intent on heading for the road and weren't taking much notice of anything else anyway.'

'So it looks like we will find out how well organised the crowd is very soon then,' Arnie said to Alexandra. 'But I hope you're not having thoughts of our little band taking on twenty armed thugs intent on murder and pillage.'

'We may be able to help and use it our advantage as well, as long as they don't know we are here.'

'Yes,' said Arnie. 'We could let them attack the crowd and then take them by surprise in the rear. That would probably be enough to at least frighten them off.'

'Good, but we watch first. I want to see just how organised that crowd is. If I'm right, then the thugs may get more than they bargained for.'

The group set off to follow in the tracks of the gang heading for the road. Arnie and Alexandra led the group, moving slowly and quietly, never getting to close. They were almost on the road themselves when they saw the band spread out on either side loosely hidden from the view of the road, but easily visible from their rear. Alexandra settled down to wait and watch, whilst Arnie gave instruction to the small group of Stainton men. He checked each man's weapon and made sure that they were carrying spare ammunition.

It wasn't long before the front rank of the crowd could be seen making its weary way along the road. The closer they got, the more dejected and pitiful and helpless they seemed. When the front of the crowd was about a hundred metres away from the hidden men, one of them arose from the verge and strode into the middle of the road. The crowd just kept coming as if it hadn't noticed the man loosely pointing an automatic weapon in their direction.

Almost as if he had to register his presence or be walked over, he fired a short salvo from the weapon above the heads of the crowd. At that, the rest of the gang rose from their hiding places and pointed their weapons at the crowd. Slowly and hesitantly, the crowd came to a halt no more than ten metres from the gang. As the crowd came to a halt, an expectant silence replaced the shuffling groan that had accompanied the crowd on its way along the road.

For a few moments, the small armed gang and the head of the crowd simply faced each other. The leader of the gang was the first to break the silence. Addressing the whole crowd, he said, 'We won't harm you if you give us what we want.'

'Leave us alone and we won't harm you,' came a feminine voice from the crowd. The gang leader could not locate the source of the voice and neither could those waiting on the hillside, but they had heard it.

Watching from his hiding place, Arnie whispered to the man next to him, 'Get ready.' He in turn passed on the warning with a feeling of excitement and expectation.

Alexandra was scanning the crowd with a pair of binoculars trying to find the owner of the quiet yet resolutely defiant voice.

Rattled, the leader shouted back at the crowd, 'Who said that? Come forward, so I can see you.'

'Go away! Leave us alone!' The voice came again. The gang started to get nervous despite the fact that they were the ones pointing the weapons. The leader pointed the weapon at the crowd and said, 'I will shoot unless you come forward now.'

The centre of the crowd shuffled apart to reveal a man slowly pushing a wheelchair forward. In the wheelchair sat a middle-aged woman who let slip the shawl that covered her hair as they came to a halt at the front edge of the crowd.

'Who are you?' The gang leader said.

'Go away!' The woman replied. 'We don't have any food to spare and I am the only woman here.'

'You're lying bitch, and we will take what we want,' he spat out, his confidence returning. 'My men are going to search for food. If anyone tries to stop them, you will be the first to die.'

He signalled to his men to move towards the crowd.

'Now!' A male voice came from the crowd.

Instantly, most of the crowd fell to the ground with those left standing unleashing a hail of fire from a wide range of weaponry. The leader of the gang never knew that he had died as his head exploded apart from the impact of a round from a hunting rifle at short range. Convulsively, his finger pulled on the trigger to send a spurt from the automatic into the body of the crowd. Thirty seconds of madness followed as fire was exchanged between the standing figures in the crowd and the few members of the gang that hadn't been caught in the initial salvo.

Alexandra's group was also caught by surprise, but it had been Arnie's shot that had killed the leader of the gang. His rifle sight had never left the man's head for an instant during the confrontation and he had fired the instant the crowd reacted to the shouted order. Arnie had never like bullies and that guy seemed to him to be a first class bully, so he had determined that if nothing else worked out, that man was not going to outlive the encounter.

One of the gang tried to run from the fight. Seeing this, Arnie sent three of his men to bring him back alive if they could. A prisoner might help in the negotiation that Alexandra seemed intent on having with the crowd's leader. When the firing stopped, it was replaced with the screams of wounded people in the crowd. Alexandra watched as the wounded men from the gang were dragged towards the woman in the wheel chair who had survived the encounter unhurt.

Of the four wounded gang members that were brought to her chair, each had to watch whilst their companion's throat was slit and their bodies thrown down to twitch in front of the wheelchair.

Alexandra and Arnie lay next to each other as they watched the grizzly execution ceremony from their vantage point. It was apparent that the people of the crowd had not been alerted to their presence. Arnie passed the binoculars to Alexandra saying, 'I think we have found a doctor, but I don't know what you intend to use to trade with them.'

'Hope, Arnie. Hope for a future is what I am going to trade.'

Arnie rolled onto his back and said in mock prayer, 'Dear God, please deliver me from true believers and hungry people.'

'When you have finished with your prayers, perhaps you would fetch the horses. I think it's time to have a chat with the lady in the wheelchair.'

'How do you know that they won't give us the same treatment they gave the last lost.'

'Come on, Arnie, they are not looking for trouble. I can't figure out exactly what they are looking for but it's not trouble. They're organised and for that you need to have a sense of purpose, so they are going somewhere. We need to find out where and what they intend to do when they get there.'

By the time that Alexandra and Arnie had organised themselves, the men had come back with the prisoner in tow. Alexandra said, 'Put a rope around his neck and bring him along behind the horses.'

Raising her voice to include the whole group, she said, 'I am going to meet the crowd. You will stay on the road visible, but well enough away not too spook the crowd. When I signal, you will bring him forward,' she finished pointing to the prisoner.

Ten minutes later, Alexandra pulled her horse onto the road a few hundred metres in front of the crowd which had only just started to move forward along the road once more. In her ear was a small receiver and she had on the lapel of her red coat a small microphone that Arnie had produced from his saddlebag. Slowly, she walked the horse towards the crowd, and as she had observed from the hillside, the crowd appeared not to react to her presence.

From the back of her horse, she scanned the crowd for the women in the wheelchair, or of the man who had pushed the chair, but failed to find them. She waited until they were a few metres from the horse, which was now becoming restless at the shuffling approach of so many people.

'My name is Alexandra. I am unarmed. I want to help you. Let me speak to the woman in the wheelchair,' she said addressing the crowd. Her words appeared to have no effect the crowd kept shuffling forward. Alexandra had to work to reassure the horse that wanted to turn away from the oncoming people. She let the horse back a few steps as she thought whether she wanted to risk being swallowed within the crowd.

Arnie was talking in her ear telling her to move away and that she shouldn't be caught up in the crowd. She snapped at him to be quiet, then whispered into her coat lapel, 'Arnie, I need to speak to this women. If they were going to shoot, they would have done it by now. Stay away from the crowd but keep me in sight.'

She halted the horse and steadily reassured it as the first people in the crowd shuffled around her. There were many furtive glances but no hostile acts as the crowd parted around her horse.

Arnie felt completely powerless as he watched Alexandra. A blot of brilliant red being swallowed into the amoebic crowd. If the crowd took her captive, there was nothing he and the little band of Stainton men could do about it. He started to think being a bodyguard was one thing but being on the coat tails of this woman was going to be quite a ride.

For many long minutes, Alexandra sat astride her horse and let the crowd pass her by. It was a strange feeling, like being ignored in a room full of people. Even the children steadfastly refused to make anything but the most fleeting of eye contact. Of the women in the wheelchair, she could see nothing. At the rear of the crowd was a small tractor pulling a flatbed trailer which carried those that could not walk. From the activity around it, it looked as though this included those that were wounded in the fight.

When the last of the crowd passed the spot she stood, she heard Arnie in her ear, 'Give it up, Alexandra, they don't want to talk. Just let them be.' But Alexandra was not for giving up. She had almost forgotten about her mission to find a doctor for Peebles and now was simply intrigued to know what motivated these people, and above all, she wanted to meet the women in the wheelchair.

'Any sign of the wheelchair woman, Arnie,' she said into the microphone on her lapel.

'Negative,' replied Arnie. 'Although I thought I saw the guy that pushed the wheelchair by the cart in the middle of the crowd, but couldn't be sure.'

'Ok, Arnie. Let's just tag along behind them for a while and see what happens, and you might as well come and join me now. I'm pretty sure they know I am not alone.'

The crowd kept moving along the road for the rest of the day covering another fifteen kms. It was dark before they stopped, and as they did, the crowd seemed to come to life breaking into a myriad of smaller groups. Small fires started to appear and spread on both sides of the road. A hub-hub of voices rose up replacing the silence in which they had spent most of the day.

Alexandra had her group make camp, hobbling the horses in a field so that they could graze but not wander too far. The night was very warm, although it was late in September and promised to be dry so they didn't bother with tents, or looking for shelter, intending to sleep on the ground around a campfire. They cooked a stew from rabbit meat and a few vegetables they carried with them. The talk of the men was all about how the crowd had reacted to the gang, with many theories about where they were heading to and what they wanted.

Outside the circle of sociable warmth spread by the campfire, lay the survivor of the gang who had fled but been captured by the Stainton men. He lay with his arms tied behind his back and his legs tied at the ankles, and a rough hood tied about his neck. He had come through the fight unwounded, although his capture had left him more than a little bruised. Throughout the meal, he lay completely still and noiseless as if he hoped he would be forgotten about if he remained as motionless and as inoffensive as possible.

In reality, he did not harbour any feelings of hope, in fact his stillness was a symptom of lack of hope. He had given up on his life. He understood that he was only alive because he was to be used in some kind of barter with the crowd, and although he was unaware of the fate of his wounded comrades, he expected little mercy from any source.

Once he had been a man who made a comfortable living as an information analyst. He had been married with two teenage daughters and a son. Then his wife and daughters died in the "death", and his son had been killed during a food riot in Aberdeen—he became a vagabond, wandering the country in search of food and solace. Eventually, he fell in with the gang that had decided there would be easy picking amongst the refugees from the nuclear power station fallout. His name was David.

After the meal finished, Alexandra said to Arnie that they should talk to the prisoner to see if the gang was part of a bigger group. Although there were lots of small bands of displaced men who were happy to use violence for their own ends there were a smaller number of more organised groups, like Nathaniel's band, who would later be known as raiders.

Arnie went to the man and removed the hood and untied his feet but left his arms tied, and then told him to get up and walk to the fire. With some effort, the man rose to his feet, walked slowly towards the fire and sat where he was told. He answered Alexandra's questions mechanically and made no effort to lie, nor to elaborate. The gang had been together for about a year originating from Aberdeen travelling south in search of food and women.

They had started out with over a hundred but had got into a fight with Colonel Peters men from Stirling Castle. Licking their wounds, they had fled from Stirling but only to the village of Kippen just outside of Stirling. Colonel Peters had been prepared to tolerate them in Kippen but insisted that they had to surrender anything other than shotguns to the castle. Their leader had refused and so Colonel Peters effectively made them prisoners in the village. Each day, their band dwindled from very accurate sniper fire.

Divisions grew in the dwindling band, and he found himself sneaking out of Kippen with about twenty others one night. They managed to get out undetected and moved west, eventually finding themselves in Glasgow, where they joined with a larger band of men living off the remnants of civilisation as he put it. They spent most of their time scavenging in abandoned homes and buildings. Moving from place to place, carrying with them only weapons and food. A few women had been part of the group under the protection of the group's most ruthless men.

The leaders of David's band tried to avoid fights with the other bands of rootless men and the few settled communities that had established defences, preferring to scavenge or take what they could from the undefended. Despite this policy, fights were frequent as the band came into contact with other groups. Such fights were usually very short, merely a sizing up of the strengths of the opposition before one side withdrew.

Sometimes they were forced to fight as opposing bands persisted in attacking. It was after just such a fight, in which they had lost a number of men, weapons and above the all the few women of the band that they had decided to look for easier pickings. They had travelled across the country having learnt of large numbers of refugees following the nuclear fire at Hartlepool.

Alexandra had just decided that she was finished with her prisoner when a warning whistle sounded. The men dived away from the light of the fire and brought weapons to the ready. Alexandra crouched low to the ground with Arnie kneeling to her left. She heard a male voice from the gloom shout, 'Hold your fire.'

She replied, 'Who's there? Come into the light. We won't harm you.' Arnie was signalling for men to move so that the direction from which the voice had come was covered.

Slowly from the dark of the night, they made out the form of a man pushing a wheelchair.

Alexandra moved so that she could be seen by the advancing pair, and raising her voice to be heard, said, 'Welcome, come to the fire so we can talk.'

She looked at David, the prisoner who had remained by the fire where he had been put by Arnie, and said to the nearest man, 'Take him away.'

It wasn't till they got close to the fire that the realised just how odd the couple approaching appeared. The man could only be described as huge. He was at least seven foot tall with huge shoulders and arms. He was not particularly muscular, just huge. In contrast, the women in the wheelchair was small, barely five foot tall, and very thin, with masses of black hair surrounding a pinched but beautiful face.

As they drew close, Alexandra caught Arnie and the giant behind the wheelchair silently sizing each other up like two boxers at the weigh in before a fight.

Alexandra who was anxious not to let any machismo get her conversation with the women off to a bad start, said, 'Arnie, I think we will want to talk in private, so take all of the men away from the fire.' She was addressing Arnie but looking at the woman in the wheelchair.

'Yes, private would be good. Bernard, see to it that we can't be heard,' replied the woman in the wheelchair in a distinctly upper class English accent, but with no hint of superiority and arrogance that so often goes with such an accent.

'My name is Ann,' said the woman in the wheelchair. 'And you must be Alexandra. Thank you for your help earlier today, but as you saw, we are not defenceless.'

Alexandra spoke diplomatically but warmly. 'I am glad to meet you, Ann, and congratulate you in being able to lead and defend such a group.' She added by way of hospitality, 'Can I get you a drink or something to eat. We don't have much but I can offer you tea.'

Ann laughed. 'Tea would be very nice.'

Arnie and Bernard had not moved from their respective positions during these introductions. Again without looking at him, Alexandra said, 'Arnie, if you are going to loiter, you might as well make the tea.' Bernard let loose a guffaw on hearing Arnie ordered to make tea.

'Oh, Bernard, you are still there too, then be a dear and bring me a rug, it's getting cold,' said Ann.

Bernard lumbered off grumbling under his breath at which both women laughed.

Whilst they waited for the tea and the rug as well as for Bernard and Arnie to relax enough to leave them alone, Alexandra asked, 'Is it very bad in the north east of England?'

'Yes, it is bad. The first effects of the fallout were already starting to show as we left, people vomiting and starting to lose hair, bleeding gums. But the worst of it is that people went crazy, like it was the final straw that detached tens of thousands from their sanity.'

Ann paused for a moment before adding, 'I mean totally crazy. At first, people contented themselves with attacking the army and police that had been sent to try and put the fire out, which was madness in itself. Then they started ransacking any and all public buildings. Finally, they started attacking each other. Those that are still alive and have stayed, are barricaded into little tribal groups whose main occupation is attacking the people in the next street or town or village. We are lucky to be alive, and have had to fight to survive.'

'Is there anything we can help with,' said Alexandra.

'Who are you to offer over two thousand five hundred people help?' Ann asked, in a curious but friendly way.

Rather pompously, she replied 'I am Alexandra from the community of Stainton, and will help anyway I can. Friends and allies will make your journey easier.'

'You are the Alexandra who writes the weblog. I have heard of you and people tell me often I should read it.'

'Yes, that's me. If you know of my blog, you know that I want to see something new come out of the chaos of the old world. That I think we can do better for people than the old world achieved despite its power and technology.'

'The "old world". You don't believe that what you call the "old world" will come back. That it's gone forever.' Ann paused, then said, 'Sadly, I think I have to agree with you. I suppose it has gone now, hasn't it?'

'No,' said Alexandra. 'It's not coming back, but neither has it gone yet and the danger is that it drags us all down with it as it dies.'

'Well, what do you see replacing it?' Ann asked.

'That's a big question, but before I answer it, I have one to ask of you,' said Alexandra, whilst refilling Ann's mug from the teapot at her side.

'Let me guess. You want to know what our plans are. Where are we going as we shuffle along this road?'

'Yes, I don't believe you're just running away from the disaster of Hartlepool, though that would be understandable.'

'You're right of course, and I don't think it will do any harm to tell you that we are heading for Jedburgh.'

'Why Jedburgh?' Alexandra asked.

'Bernard is from Jedburgh and he says that the town has been all but abandoned; the people that the plague didn't kill have fled from raiders into the countryside. He says we could take over the town and make it habitable and defendable. Most of us are from Blythswood, just north of Newcastle and had managed to avoid the worst of the chaos, before the fire at the power station. It took quite a bit to convince people that we had to leave what we had spent so much time organising and defending.

'When we left, we had a convoy of thirty trucks and about five hundred people crammed into buses and an assortment of vehicles. We thought we would do the journey in a day—that was two weeks ago. The roads were crammed with people and with broken down or burnt out vehicles. It turned out that our vehicles or at least the fuel we had were like a huge magnet for people, some just desperate and looking for help, others looking for whatever they could take.

'It got very ugly, very ugly. We had to abandon the vehicles and everything we so carefully packed into them. As soon as we did, the number of attacks and raids fell away, but by then, our original number had swollen to what you saw today. Most of them don't know where we are going, they are just glad to be able to tag along.'

Alexandra nodded in acknowledgement of this story. She said, 'The way you handled the raiders that was worked out in advance, wasn't it? You deliberately make yourselves look weak and defenceless.'

'Yes, it's a big risk for the men at the front and rear of the convoy, but it lulls the bullies and cowards that try to prey on us into a false sense of security. They see us as weak so they don't sneak up on us or fire at us from a distance as they did at the convoy of vehicles. Instead, they march right up and make their demands just as they did today. But moving so many people by foot is very slow, very slow especially when we are attacked every other day.'

She paused and staring into the flames of the campfire, said, 'We have been lucky—all the bands that we met since we abandoned the vehicles have been quite small and led by stupid bullies.'

'And tomorrow you will probably make it to Jedburgh or at the worst, the day after,' said Alexandra.

'Thank God, I seriously need a bath. I'm definitely not an outdoors girl. I would love to be in a real bed under a real roof preferably with central heating and a home entertainment system, but I'll settle for the bed and the roof,' laughed Ann. 'But what about you, Alexandra? I sense your ambition is greater than a soft, warm bed, to sleep in.'

'Oh, I am taking what we have learnt in Stainton and sharing it with others, so that something new can grow out of the chaos of the old world,' said Alexandra without any sense of embarrassment or doubt.

'Ah yes, Stainton. The community parents, the genderisation of politics.'

'You're very well informed, Ann,' said Alexandra.

'I do try my best, Alexandra. You know, Bernard wanted to just ignore you, but you made a big impression today. Astride your horse, healthy and beautiful, in your red coat, calmly letting our crowd pass you by. That took courage and the people in the crowd respect you for it. Then our gossips got to work and the information about you and your weblog flowed forth.

'In my camp, the talk is all about you and what you want and whether you can help us. As I said, only the original group from Blythswood know where we are going and they have been told to keep it secret until we arrive. Though I'm not sure how that is working out. Most of our people are desperate for hope and now you have arrived offering help, unspecified help, they are ready to follow you.'

'I don't want and don't need followers, Ann.'

'Then what do you want, Alexandra?'

'As I said, I want to build communities where people can live decent lives, where women can be safe.'

'Hmm, very noble. And what do you want of us? Why did you risk your life today? A beautiful young women in a crowd consisting mostly of men. There would have been many that were tempted to take what they know they might never be able to have any other way.'

'It was a risk, but I knew from the way you dealt with the raiders that you were no undisciplined mob, and I wanted your trust, Ann. I knew that there was a leader and that the leader was more than likely a woman. You asked what I want. Actually, I came hoping to find a doctor amongst the refugees from Hartlepool for a community in Peebles, but most of all, I want to influence women like you that are leaders. I think it is people—no not people—women like you who are the key to a new world.

'Everywhere I go, it is women that are the organisers for creation and safety. Where men lead, it is more likely to be of raiders or a destructive inward looking community to protect their hegemony over a few pitiful and frightened women.'

'I'm not much of a candidate for a new world led by female Amazons,' laughed Ann.

'And yet thousands of people follow you along a road they know not where and a man the size of a bear gently does your bidding.'

Very quietly to avoid listening ears, Ann said, 'Bernard's a real sweetie. I knew his parents, both dead now, and I think he sees me as family.'

'Is he…' whispered Alexandra.

'My lover, no. I don't think he even has aspirations in that direction. He treats me like I'm his mother. Very affectionate and protective, but not in a sexual way. And what about, what's his name, the muscle that accompanies you.'

'Arnie, no, he is my bodyguard, and probably more interested in Bernard than me sexually.'

A moment of silence followed this personal interchange, which Ann broke by saying in a normal voice; 'So, Alexandra, we are hogging your campfire, and no doubt causing some resentment amongst your men. As I can feel Bernard fretting even though I can't see him, it's time to return to our camp. Accompany us to Jedburgh tomorrow and let us talk so more there.'

'We will, happily, though I think Arnie would advise that our small group go ahead and see if they're any further surprises awaiting you.'

'We have found that scouts only succeed in alerting the enemy to our defences, and knowing that an enemy is just around the corner we must travel is of no help to us. With such numbers, we cannot avoid what is ahead of us, we can only endure it. But it is probably better not to add your men to my host, their proud bearing and fondness for their weapons would stick out like a sore thumb. Perhaps you could take some of my men on ahead and make preparations for our arrival; there are sick and wounded amongst us. Fires for cooking and hot water for washing would be a joyous welcome.'

'You're sure that the town is deserted?' Alexandra said. 'It's not a place we have not been to, but many apparently deserted towns have people hiding in their ruins.'

'Yes, we sent a man ahead. He came back to us before I came to speak with you. There may be a few people hiding but it has been abandoned.'

'Good, then we shall leave at first light. Have your men meet us on the road. We will circle your camp so as not to cause alarm.'

'It has been good talking to you, Alexandra, and I look forward to continuing the conversation in Jedburgh.' Then without raising her voice, she said, 'I think I am ready to return to our camp now, Bernard.' A moment later, Bernard's great form emerged from the shadow beyond the fire, and with a nod to Alexandra, pushed the wheelchair in the direction they had come from.

When Bernard's back had disappeared into the gloom, Alexandra spoke as if to the fire, 'Well, Arnie, what did you make of that?' For though she had not caught sight of him during her conversation with Ann, she was confident that he had not been out of earshot.

Emerging from the dark, Arnie said, 'A remarkable woman, but as to what you want with a horde of refugees in a world full of refugees, I haven't a bloody clue.'

Chapter Nineteen

Alexandra and her group stayed with Ann and the refugees for over three months as they settled themselves into Jedburgh. Arnie split his time between helping with making the town defendable from raiders and scavenging for food. Feeding two thousand five hundred people was horrendously difficult task for the self-appointed leaders of this new community, and no small source of friction and dissent. They had arrived with little and Jedburgh itself had been picked clean of anything edible.

Small parties were organised to hunt in the surrounding countryside—a popular chore for the young men in the group. Community kitchens were established providing everybody with one meal a day.

Alexandra, impatient of all the detailed arrangement and internal bickering involved in establishing a new community, urged Ann to venture out and meet the friendly communities in the area. She knew that Ann's new community would receive little in the way of charity, because there was little enough too spare, but she knew that communities were eager to trade. Alexandra persuaded Ann that the other communities could help with food if they had something to trade with.

All of the communities Alexandra had visited lacked or craved something that they could not get from their own resources or from scavenging. She knew some had surpluses from agricultural enterprises and suspected that some had successfully stockpiled preserved foods scavenged from far and wide. The problem was that the new community of Jedburgh had very little to trade with. It was Ann that came up with an answer after a conversation with Alexandra about education in the new communities.

Stainton was one of the few communities that had been able to support a school. Many of the new world's young people were growing up without an education, or had to make to do with what they had received before the schools and universities collapsed after the "death".

Ann's first step was to organise a census of the community's skills so that she would at least have the potential to trade. The first fruit of this activity was that two doctors, a paramedic, and several nurses were found amongst their number. Ann brought this little medical group together and explained that she intended to trade their skills for food with a community Alexandra had identified as in particular need of medical skills.

She was careful not to name the community or its whereabouts, afraid that they would simply set off and strike their own bargain. After some discussion and a degree of competition for the post that Ann had not suspected, a male doctor and a female nurse were chosen for the journey to nearby Peebles. It was no surprise to Alexandra that the nurse, who was a young and attractive female, proved to be a strong bargaining point with the community.

Alexandra and Ann returned from Peebles with a truckload of grain and potatoes and a promise of more at the next harvest. They also had a set of plans for producing bio-diesel, which is of course what powered the truck that brought the food to Jedburgh.

The arrival of such a quantity of food, though limited enough to feed such a large number of people, brought hope and sense of mastery over their future. A little hope which succeeded in spreading a much needed psychological warmth through the new community that winter. Spurred on by this initial success, other trades of "people" and their skills were made, a male electrician was taken to the community of East Lowtown who needed somebody that could help with repairing generators for wind turbines.

From this journey, Ann and Alexandra returned with a cow and a basket of eggs, which they were assured were fertile and would hatch out if they could keep them warm.

Gradually, this new community began to form and, six months after they arrived, elected Ann as its community mother and Bernard as community father. In the next few years, Jedburgh prospered under Ann and Bernard's leadership, becoming a centre of knowledge skills and learning, and a place where Alexandra would return again and again.

Alexandra was not there for the result of the election or the party that followed, she was roaming across Scotland and the North of England looking for surviving communities to cajole and argue with. As the months and years since her decision to leave Stainton went by, she found fewer and fewer communities that were not willing to listen to her. Her influence and stature amongst the communities grew and grew.

No doubt helped by the fact that those who were willing to listen to her argument of mutual support and the importance of gender balance in political governance of the communities were the ones that tended to prevail against the onslaught of barbarity that still prevailed across Scotland and the world. She became a symbol of feminine power in the new communities. A woman who was not afraid to travel between communities.

A women whom men followed and respected. She was never known to have a male partner and this added to her stature with stories circulating about the virgin in the red coat who brought order to communities and kept the raiders from the cities at bay.

In 2045, Alexandra was with a small community on the outskirts of what had been the town of Motherwell in North Lanarkshire. She had been there for two weeks helping the leaders of the community assemble a wind turbine and a small facility for producing bio-diesel from the effluent of pigs kept by the community. Alexandra had found that raiders from Glasgow had destroyed most efforts at building stable communities in the areas within easy reach of the city.

This community had been particularly effective at defending itself, partly because the core of the community was an army platoon that had decided they had enough and deserted not long after the chaos following the "death". Many of them had family connections in Motherwell and decided to stick together as a unit. Unusually, it was led by a male, a man in his late fifties who had been the platoon sergeant. He had teamed up with a younger woman called Beth, also from a military background.

They had fortified a small area of the town and defended it from all comers so successfully that most of the raider gangs gave it a wide berth. However, they found it hard to produce enough food for their community as land out with their fortified town was difficult to defend and constantly exposed to theft from raiders or the more pathetic gangs of community less men. They kept large number of pigs that were herded out of the town in the morning to forage in woodlands and herded back at night time—a time consuming and difficult occupation aided by many dogs.

From these people, Alexandra learnt about the raider gangs based in the city the worst and most organised of which was led by Nathaniel. Alexandra knew that it could only be the same Nathaniel that had raided Stainton all those years ago and taken her mother and friend. She had often heard the name Nathaniel connected to some depredation of the communities that she visited, but these people seemed to know where his gang was based.

Arnie had heard the story of the raid on Stainton and how it had been desperately fought off, but had resulted in the loss of two of the communities women, one of them Alexandra's mother. He had also heard the story of Natalie's rape at the hands of a gang apparently led by this Nathaniel. Watching Alexandra's reaction to the news that Nathaniel had a base in the buildings around George Square in the heart of Glasgow, he saw for almost the first time doubt and fear in her face.

Alexandra fought hard not to show it but having knowledge of Nathaniel's whereabouts had hit her hard. It was dragging up all the emotions of her mother's loss, and Jim almost dying from a gunshot wound, and the near loss of the community that had given meaning to her life. She had always refused to let herself believe that her mother and her friend, Brenda, could still be alive. It had been her way of coping, somehow dealing with the grief of believing them to be dead was easier than the feelings that arose in her at the thought of their fate should they be still alive.

Finishing her business with the community leaders, she made excuses and left earlier from the discussion than was diplomatic. Arnie let her go and, over a dubious fluid that was described as beer by their hosts, sought to get more information about Nathaniel and his band of raiders. In particular, he hoped for information about Alexandra's mother. Pretending that a female relative of his had disappeared after a raid by Nathaniel's gang, he asked what happened to woman taken by the gang.

'Is she important to you, Sir?' Mikey asked, the ex-sergeant who led the group. Mikey and Arnie had briefly known each other and Mikey found the habit of deferment to an officer a hard habit to break.

'Yeah, she's family, that's important don't you think, and drop the sir. There ain't no army any more, Mikey,' replied Arnie with a note of irritation in his voice.

'Yes, Sir,' was the swift and military reply, 'and if you don't mind my saying, there might be no army but it is the army way that stopped us going under.'

Knowing when he was beat, Arnie replied, 'Okay, Sergeant, you did good, and no doubt about that. Alexandra is backing your community and she only backs winners.' Pausing to make sure that Mikey had climbed down from defending his military honour, he then brought the discussion back to female captured by the raiders.

'What do you know about the woman held by this Nathaniel?'

Mikey sighed. 'Most he puts in a brothel, access to which is bought in food or weapons or as a direct reward from Nathaniel. The best looking can avoid the brothel, if they agree to serve his captains. His captains are a small circle of men around him that he allows to have women of their own. Most of the men have to use the brothel. The brothel is run by a woman, by all accounts the most vicious person you would ever want not to meet.'

'Do you know the location of this brothel?'

'They move it about from time to time. No shortage of space you see, it's usually in one of the hotel in the city centre.'

'Have you lost women to the gang?'

'Yeah, the bastards got in with the pigs one evening and dam near overrun us. They took two women and three girls. One of them only eight. Bastards!' Mikey spat with venom remembering the loss.

'Did you try to get them back?'

'We didn't, and we got our ass kicked good and proper when we tried. I shouldn't have allowed it, but the blood was up, and we went charging in. No problem until we got into the city centre, then it was ambush after ambush. Street fighting, dirty and deadly. We lost a dozen men, including a couple of my best, before we were forced to retreat. The truth is we were lucky to get out of there.

'Don't be in any doubt that bastard's a clever one, Sir. He sucked us in, bled us and then when we weakened, he turned on us. Pursued us right out of the city and back here. Laid siege to us for a week, but once we were back here, we could handle them on our terms. Do you know the bastard even brought a challenger tank. Luckily, they didn't have the skill to use the thing properly and we had a couple of Javelin anti-tanks missiles from our original kit. So they got more than they bargained for.

'After that little escapade, I spoke to Colonel Peters in Stirling Castle, and between us, we scoured every army, navy and air force base we knew of in Scotland and disabled anything we could get access too, stripped out tank control system, trashed helicopters, spiked field guns. We also brought home tank mines we found stashed in a hard shelter in Cupar. We have buried the mines on the most likely approaches from the city—so if he tries that again, he'll get a shock.

We've got their position mapped but they're safe enough, you would have to jump on them pretty hard to set them off.'

Arnie listened with half his mind whilst Mikey rattled on about his adventures roaming around Scotland with Colonel Peters vandalising military equipment that had cost millions and millions of pounds of tax payers' money. The other half of his mind was busily engaged thinking about how to deal with the problem of Alexandra's mother. He knew the knowledge that her mother could still be alive would eat away at Alexandra and deflect her away from her self-imposed mission that he had come to believe in as much as her.

To Arnie, family was sacrosanct; he would do anything to protect what remained of his own, and these emotions coloured his thinking about Alexandra and her mother. The plan that was hatching in his head, as he listened to Mikey, was as much an emotional response to Alexandra's plight as a rational way to protect the woman who he had given his allegiance to. He reasoned that if he didn't act, then Alexandra was likely to act, and that might have disastrous consequences for her and everything she stood for and was in the process of building.

Realising that Mikey had stopped regaling him with stories of his exploits and was now directing a question to him, Arnie had to pull his attention back to the sergeant.

'Don't tell me you're thinking about going to get this woman, Sir.'

'Well, she is family, Sergeant. And besides, that Nathaniel sounds like he's got it coming to him, if you know what I mean.'

'She will have been ill-used. If you want to know how bad it is for women in there, go and speak to Rosie,' said the sergeant.

'Rosie?'

'You have met her. The red head with the knife scar on her face,' he said demonstrating the scars position with his finger on his own face.

'What does she know?' Arnie asked.

'By a series of miracles, she managed to escape from the brothel about three years ago. Our dogs found her, half frozen to death, hiding beneath some upturned tree roots. She is how we know so much about how women are treated in the brothel, that and talking to men that have run away from Nathaniel's gang. We never let them stay. Too much of a risk, but Rosie has lived with us since we found her. She got the scar on her face and many others you won't see whilst she was in that brothel.'

'I'd like to speak to Rosie, maybe she would recognise my relatives name or description,' said Arnie.

Mikey replied, 'She won't thank you for bringing up the memories. What are you thinking? You have heard how we fared when we went after our women.'

'Well, Sergeant, sometimes one man can achieve more than a whole army.'

The next day, Arnie sought out Rosie and from what he learnt from her, he was pretty sure that Alexandra's mother had not only been an inmate of Nathaniel's brothel, but also had been used by Nathaniel himself. However, Rosie's information was three years old. There was no way of knowing whether she was still there, or indeed whether she was still alive.

He also learnt a great deal about how the brothel was operated and the plan that had formed in his mind talking to Mikey the night before began to on a more solid form. He had to get Rosie to promise not to say anything to Alexandra under the pretence that she would be annoyed that he was planning something without her permission.

After speaking to Rosie, he went to speak to Alexandra who was working on the plans for the bio-fuel plant with Beth and a couple of men. As he went into the room being used for the meeting, Beth was mid-flow, berating a couple teenage boys for indolence in her broad Glaswegian accent.

'Yer a right pair of wankers, so ye are. If yers could keep yer 'ands off yer cocks a wee bit longer, yer might be a bit brighter, so yer would.'

Arnie's arrival in the room interrupted the flow of abuse she had lined up for the young men so she dismissed them with.

'Oh, piss off, why don't yer.' The lads turned to leave quickly, obviously relieved to be getting off with a verbal roasting for whatever their misdemeanour had been. Beth shouted to their backs, 'And yer can go tell Mikey that yer on shit duty for the rest of the week.'

They groaned and the bolder of the two turned to argue. 'But…'

'No fucking buts, tell him I said yer a pair of wankers and I dinnae want to set eyes on yer ever again.'

His mate dragged the complainer with him through the doorway before he could get another word out.

'Trouble?' Arnie said.

'Not really,' replied Alexandra. 'That pair of jokers were meant to be stripping copper pipe from abandoned houses to use in the bio-diesel plant.' She pointed and Arnie's eyes noted a mangled heap of pretty useless looking copper pipe in the corner of the room.

'Beth wasn't impressed with the result of their labours,' Alexandra added in her matter of fact way, which she never intended to be humorous but so often was.

'Pair of dickless wonders; a week shovelling pig shit will be good for them,' spat Beth.

'I'm right, sorry, Alexandra, I reckoned we'd be ready to start putting this together, but I guess we cannae get on wi oot the piping eh.'

'No, we need between thirty and fifty feet of copper pipe and some plastic piping to connect everything up.'

'Aye, right well, I'll get a squad on it right away,' she said and marched off.

Arnie and Alexandra were left alone, and he told her what he had learned from Rosie.

Alexandra stared quietly at the components of what would be a small bio-diesel plant enough to produce a couple of thousand a litres a year. Mostly from pig fat but the community was going to experiment with rape seed; there was little point in the raider stealing or destroying such a crop. So far the raiders had followed a strictly parasitical lifestyle and produced little of their own.

They lived off the leavings of the old world, producing nothing for themselves. What they could not scavenge, they sought to steal or extort from organised communities.

Arnie broke the gloomy silence that had fallen in the room as soon as Beth had left.

Speaking to her back, he said, 'You are thinking about your mother.'

Alexandra did not turn to speak to him, and Arnie felt rather than saw tears in her eyes.

'Yes, Arnie. I am thinking about my mother and my friend, Brenda. She was only seventeen when she was taken and now she will be thirty-two, the same age as me.

'If she is still alive,' said Arnie.

Alexandra ignored Arnie's reality testing statement and continued still with her back to him.

'I have been racking my brains to try and think what age my mother would be—the best I can come up with is late fifties / early sixties. I was her only child but I think she had me in her late twenties or early thirties. During the "death" plague, she was really, really ill for a while. I was not allowed to see her of course, but I think she very nearly died.'

Half turning to face him, she said, 'I've tried to imagine what she might look like, but the more I try, the vaguer her features become so that it's even hard to remember her as I last saw her.'

Arnie listened quietly. This was the most personal and emotional Alexandra had ever allowed herself to be. Somehow before his eyes, Alexandra the commander, the visionary, the prophet of the new world who stood so proudly and was so certain in everything, seemed to melt away, leaving a small frightened girl.

Taking a large gulp of breath that was almost but not quite a sob, Alexandra continued almost as if Arnie wasn't there.

'If I saw her or Brenda, would I recognise them? What has all those years in Nathaniel's brothels done to them? Those religious nutters we met are completely fucked up. How could a God allow a plague that kills good and bad indiscriminately. How could He allow so many good people to die horrible deaths but allow a creature like Nathaniel to live and to prosper on the misery of others?'

Arnie hated what the realisation that her mother may be alive but beyond her reach was doing to the Alexandra he had known. He was desperate to support her but above all, to break her out of this inward looking self-pity that he so little recognised as Alexandra.

'You don't know that they are still alive. You know there is every chance they are dead and gone,' he insisted.

'No, Arnie.' She still had not turned fully to look at him. 'I think I've always known that they are still alive somewhere. Possessing women gives him power, he would use them but not kill them.'

Finally, she turned towards Arnie. He had to force himself to look her in the face, afraid of how would deal with it if she showed signs of the distress she was so obviously feeling.

'He would protect what gives him power, he would not allow them to die, not whilst he had a use for them.'

Arnie stayed silent allowing Alexandra the time to win the battle to regain her composure.

'They say that all power corrupts and that absolute power corrupts absolutely, but that's only half the story, don't you think. A lack of power can be just as corrosive as too much. Don't you think so, Arnie?'

Arnie was no philosopher, and was happy to admit that he didn't understand what she was getting at.

'The really dangerous people are those who lack the power to believe in themselves and so seek power over others to protect their own weakness.'

Arnie faced must have betrayed the struggle he was having trying to figure out where Alexandra was going with her argument.

'Give me that gun you are carrying, Arnie,' she said with something of the usual self-possession returning to her voice. He gave her the gun without question, guessing that a lesson was to follow.

'The gun gives me power over you, does it not,' she said holding it to his head.

Sweeping the weapon and her hand away from his forehead, he said, 'Not whilst the safety is on.'

He brought her hand still with the weapon back until it pointed directly at his chest and with his free hand, snicked off the safety catch. Letting go of the weapon, he said, 'Now it gives you the power to kill me.'

'Or to make you do my will,' said Alexandra.

'Only whilst it is pointing at me, and I don't believe I can take it from you.'

Lowering the weapon, replacing the safety and giving it back, she said, 'You see. You believe in your own power, you don't need a weapon to feel powerful. You need it only to counter the power that a weapon can give to another person. That power strengthens you, makes you a decent person, it doesn't corrupt you. Men like Nathaniel do not believe they are powerful unless they possess power as an external thing like a gun, or absolute control over other people.

'In the end, with all the power he exerts over his raiders, the thing that corrupted Nathaniel was his lack of power, his lack of belief in himself. He's obviously clever or devious enough to hold together his raiders, but ultimately, he is as pathetic as the man who beats his wife or child so that he can feel powerful and in control.'

'Well, he may be a pathetic shit but he does wield power and more than we can directly counter.'

'I know it and I can think of only one way to indirectly counter that power,' she said with some reluctance.

'Oh,' said Arnie warily.

'I've been racking my brains but I can't think of any other way than of letting myself be captured by his goons, and...'

'NO, absolutely not...I won't...can't allow it.'

'Won't...cant, who do you think you are?' She snapped the sad tension in her face replaced with irritation and the beginnings of anger.

'You've lost your marbles,' and seeing the anger rising in her face, he raised his voice countering with his own anger. 'How dare you say that you're going to throw your life away when you've made so many people see you as hope for the future?'

'I can't see another way, and I can't just leave knowing that they are there.'

'Maybe there,' he insisted. 'But there is another way, a better way.'

Alexandra looked him in the eye, and said, 'How? What are you thinking?'

'I will go. I will join them, and find out if they are living, and if they are, figure out some way of getting them out.'

'You, someone would recognise you. They wouldn't trust you, they would kill you rather than capture you. No, that won't work.'

Calmly, Arnie replied, 'It will, it's what I was trained for—counter insurgency. I won't be recognised, or at least it's a risk I will take. Mikey tells me Nathaniel rarely lets new men into his group, preferring to cherry pick from other bands that owe allegiance to his. That's how I'll do it. I'll join up with one of the other raider bands and get myself noticed. The only thing is that it will take time. It's not something that can be rushed. I mean months even a year or more.'

'You would do that for me, put yourself in amongst those barbarians?'

'To stop from you killing yourself on a hopeless cause. And so that you can get on with your work. Yes, I will do it.'

Then Alexandra did something she had never done. She kissed him.

'Thank you, Arnie. You don't know how much this means to me.'

Arnie covered his feelings with a return to practical planning. 'You will have to make up a story to cover for my absence—perhaps, that I was killed in an attack by Nathaniel's raiders, everything gets blamed on them anyway. I will ask Mikey to assign one of his guys to you. There's some good soldiers in his group and I trust them.'

'No, I'd planned to spend some time in Jedburgh with Ann anyway. So I'll go there as soon as we're finished here and then to Stainton if you're not back by the time I've done there. I'll be safe enough in the communities.' After a short pause, she looked directly at him and said, 'When will you go?'

'Soon,' said Arnie. 'I need to make some arrangement with Mikey. Assuming I get in, and that your mother and friend are still alive, he will be able to help with the extraction. Also, it's only fair that he knows, because with what I'm planning, it is likely to cause trouble. It may also cause trouble for Stainton if Nathaniel figures out what has happened and who has caused it.

'So it might serve well to make sure they haven't grown complacent in defence. It wouldn't do any harm to get Beth to return the favour you are doing for her by getting her to go and review defences in some of the other communities.'

'That's a good idea. I don't know why I didn't think of that. Their military skills are as tradable as any others. Yes, I'll talk to Beth about that.'

And with that, the Alexandra that Arnie knew and had grown to love had fully returned, the self-doubt gone as quickly as it had come. Alexandra was again focused on the task ahead as she trusted Arnie to do what he said he would do. She put the fate of her mother and friend in his hands, knowing that for the moment she could do no better and so she would worry about it no more.

Chapter Twenty

In late March, Arnie and Alexandra left North Lanarkshire alone, having given instruction to the Stainton men with them to make their own way back to Stainton. They explained that they were going to Jedburgh for the summer and would join them again by Christmas.

Arnie accompanied Alexandra to a short ride of Jedburgh's gates and then left after letting loose enough rounds from an automatic pistol to get the people of Jedburgh worried and excited. Alexandra, playing her part, made her horse gallop as if both their lives depended on it. Arnie watched through binoculars with a degree of concern as she approached the gates at full tilt.

This was the part of their plan that could go wrong; some over eager guard might shoot first and ask questions later. She reined the horse to a halt a hundred yards short of the gate, and although he couldn't hear her, he knew she was shouting for them to open the gate and they were to fetch Ann and Bernard at once.

The gate opened and a mob gathered around Alexandra. Twenty minutes later, riders appeared from the gates heading along the road with Alexandra at their head. This was his cue they were coming to rescue him, for in the story she would have told them, he had remained behind to hold off a band of raiders whilst she rode for help. He let off a few more rounds. He had already shot the pack horse they had brought with them, having first stripped it of everything he would need, throwing the rest about to make it look as if it had been stripped bare by raiders.

News of Arnie's death or capture at the hand of raiders would spread fast— of course there would be no body, but they had decided this would simply add spice to the story of Arnie's demise and spread it further and quicker. It would be hard for his family in Stainton but he had insisted that nobody other than Alexandra and Mikey should know the real story. He knew that the story had lots of holes in it if anybody cared to look carefully. He gambled on Alexandra being believed without question and hoped the confusion and excitement of the search would erase any doubts that occurred to the brighter of his would be rescuers.

The rouse worked, although Alexandra hated lying to his family and the many people who loved him. It would be the following spring before Alexandra would hear from him again. She spent the summer working with Ann on the college she was developing for the young people of the communities. Alexandra had spent many hours discussing with Ann the lack of educational opportunities in the new communities. She saw that many of the people of her own age had not had formal education beyond primary or early secondary school level.

Almost all of the communities made it a priority to teach their children to read, write, and use basic arithmetic, but few could resource anything more than this. Any other education was informal and focused on achieving practical day-to-day tasks within the communities. For many of the young people who had known nothing but the new communities, that were now in their late teens, the communities became restrictive.

This caused tension and strife as in the time honoured way, young people explored the boundaries of who they are and what they can expect and want out of adult life. Ann saw the college as way of developing the trading in skills that Jedburgh had grounded itself in with Alexandra's help. Alexandra had a bolder vision of a college where people learnt not only practical skills needed by their communities but a college that was a training ground for the young people of the new communities. She wanted Ann to equip young people to be leaders of a new world, to learn from the mistakes of the past.

She also wanted an outlet for the brightest from the restrictive atmosphere of communities focused on the practical task of survival. She wanted a place where the boundaries and differences between communities could be blurred enough for their common agendas to be seen clearly and explored by willing minds.

All through that spring and early summer, they debated the form the college would take. They interviewed people for the post of teachers, argued and cajoled community leaders about the importance of education. They spent long hours arguing over how it could be paid for and sustained. Ann sent out anybody that could be spared from the community's defence and food production effort to scavenge for books and equipment.

Through nothing more than the sheer force of their personalities, they opened the college to its first fifty students after the summer harvest. Alexandra had picked the external students, and Ann had chosen from the Jedburgh youth. They both would have preferred to have chosen more young women but families and communities were still very loath to allow females out of their gates. Alexandra chose the young people because she knew they were straining against the confines of their communities, but also because in her judgement, they possessed the self-discipline and aspiration to learn.

She spent the winter with these young people and the educators she and Ann had chosen working out how they wanted to learn as well as what. She insisted that they must use a part of each week talking about how and why the old world had collapsed, and how humans were responding to that collapse. Working for the community of Jedburgh was part of how the college was to be paid for by the students. The other part of their fees was to come from their communities in the form of an agreed sum to be paid at the start each term.

Ann was taking a risk with this development, some of her already large community saw it simply as bringing in more mouths to feed and were not shy at saying so. A lot of work and time had gone into setting it up, and both Alexandra and Ann knew it was likely to take time for Jedburgh to benefit from its investment. They had countered the argument of extra mouths to feed by getting each of the student's communities to send them with enough supplies to see them through their stay in Jedburgh.

The fee payable from the communities was a source of much frustration, debate, and aggravation. So far barter had been the only means of exchange between the communities but how do you value education in terms of potatoes, bags of grain, or machine parts. Even the communities who agreed to send some of their young people were often at best lukewarm to the idea, so when it came to parting with real and immediately useful items, the negotiations became difficult.

The community of East Lowtown was the exception; they had got behind the idea of the college and five of the young people had come from East Lowtown. They were all young women and they brought with them a dozen water heating solar panels and a water pump adapted to work from bio-diesel. Ann and Alexandra drummed up a reception committee to make a fuss over the arrival of the East Lowtown group, mostly because they knew the site of a lorry load of equipment and a large group escorting the five young women would create quite a bit of excitement in the community.

The effect was electric; the community buzzed for days with the interaction between the East Lowtown people and the Jedburgh people. Ann and Alexandra used to travelling between the communities had not really appreciated how isolated most people felt in their communities, nor how much people craved for the different, the out of the ordinary, the not every day. The arrival of the group from East Lowtown had made the people of Jedburgh feel at the centre of something important rather than people lost in a place they didn't come from.

Suddenly, the voices of the critics of the college project were no longer heard or were reduced to mutterings in corners.

So it came as shock to the people of Jedburgh when, just before the student were to leave at the end of the colleges first term, the news reached them that East Lowtown had been attacked by raiders probably out of Edinburgh or one of the Fife towns. They learnt of the attack from Stainton on the short wave radio. The people of East Lowtown had managed to hold off the raiders until help had arrived from Stainton and other communities.

However, much damage had been done and a number of people had lost their lives with more injured. Alexandra, and the East Lowtown girls, camped out by the radio waiting for news of their families. They were reassured that their families had survived, though the brother of one had been wounded in the attack. The young women from East Lowtown were desperate to return to their families. Ann and Bernard were against it, saying that the area would be dangerous for travelling.

They argued that the girls should wait until they had word from East Lowtown that it was safe to travel, and that they wouldn't help by getting themselves captured by retreating raiders. Despite Bernard and Ann's attempt to stamp their authority on the decision to stop the girls from immediately returning, the whole community of Jedburgh became engaged in the discussion, everybody had an opinion on what should be done.

The next day, it was discovered that the girls had taken matters into their own hands and had left Jedburgh under cover of darkness, accompanied by of some of their fellow male students. Ann was furious, blaming herself for not acting to prevent such an eventuality. Alexandra said the girls were not children and should not be thought of as such. They had made their own decision and should be allowed to do so. It was the first time that Alexandra and Ann had publicly argued over anything since they had met.

Ann sent a company of men headed by Bernard to try and catch up with the girls and make sure that they got to East Lothian safely. Alexandra decided to accompany them.

The evening after Alexandra had left with Bernard and the other Jedburgh men in pursuit of the East Lowtown group, another message came over the shortwave radio from Jim of Stainton. Arnie had come back from the dead bringing with him Alexandra's mother and her childhood friend, Brenda. Ann was tempted to send someone racing after Alexandra with the good news, but Jim had passed on another message from Arnie, which was not quite as positive.

It seemed that in rescuing Alexandra's mother and friend, Arnie had also infuriated Nathaniel, who had taken his revenge on some small communities on the outskirts of Glasgow. Jim said that Stainton was warning all the communities to take precautions until they could be sure that he wouldn't travel east. Ann decided she had to focus on preparing Jedburgh, and besides, by the time any riders she sent caught up with Bernard and Alexandra, they would most probably be at Stainton already or as near as to make little difference.

Chapter Twenty-One

Whilst waiting for Alexandra to get to Stainton, Arnie had begun to have serious doubts about what he had done. He had rationalised that he was rescuing them, but couldn't ignore the reality that he had added kidnapping to his professional CV. Marina was distraught about being parted from her children and expressed her grief in furious, physical and verbal onslaughts at Arnie in particular, but was happy to include anybody that came within her orbit.

People she had known in Stainton before her capture came to try and talk to her, but she simply demanded to be allowed to return to Glasgow, She refused to speak about anything else unless it was to pour venom on her rescuer / kidnapper—Arnie.

Natalie came to Arnie to tell him that she had word that Alexandra was on her way back from Jedburgh in pursuit of some missing women students from East Lowtown, but had set off before she could be told of her mother's return.

'Good, that's good,' said Arnie unconvincingly.

'What's the matter, Arnie?' Natalie replied, sensing his discomfort.

Arnie looked at Natalie, Stainton's community mother, and decided that he had to confide his worries with her. Arnie was surprised how easily he and everyone else accepted the authority of Natalie and the other community mothers. He supposed that people needed leaders, figures of authority. Voicing his line of thought, he said, 'Why do you suppose people need leaders, Natalie?'

'Oh, that's simple,' laughed Natalie.

'Oh yeah, tell me then,' challenged Arnie.

'Well,' said Natalie changing her manner to suit Arnie serious mood. 'Humans are social animals. We can't get by without other humans, but at the same time, we are all individuals constantly rubbing up against other individuals.' As she spoke, Natalie watched Arnie's face trying to get behind his uncharacteristically oblique and philosophical question to what it was that was worrying him; a man that she had never seem perturbed by anything.

'Do you understand, Arnie? We are both social and individual.'

'You're saying we need other people to get by, but we don't always like the people we have to get by with.'

'That's it. That conflict between the social necessity and the individual aspiration is why we need leaders. Basically, leaders are the people we entrust to try to balance the conflict between the social and the individual.'

Although Arnie was interested in what Natalie was saying, he knew it was a diversion that he was putting off what he had decided he was going to do, confide in this woman.

'I'm scared, Natalie.'

'We all get scared, but I admit it's not something I expected to hear you say, Arnie.'

'Oh, I've been scared plenty in my life, believe me.'

'What's scaring you now, Arnie?' She prodded.

'I'm afraid for Alexandra. I'm afraid of how she will react when she sees those creatures that used to be her mother and friend.'

'You're afraid that you have done the wrong thing bringing them to her.'

Arnie thought for a moment. 'Is that what's bothering me? Am I afraid that I've made a mistake; am I just dressing it up as concern for how Alexandra's reaction is going to effect the communities?' Out loud, he said to Natalie, 'Marina said that I should have told Alexandra that she and Brenda were dead. I think that maybe I should have done that. I can't see any good from bringing them back here.'

'Everybody here thinks you did the right thing, Marina and Beth were part of this community and we all wanted them back, even though few believed that we would ever see them alive again.' Natalie paused and then added, 'If you're afraid of reprisals, then we have confronted Nathaniel before and will do it again if we have to.'

'It's not Nathaniel and his thugs I'm worrying about,' said Arnie. 'I think it was a mistake to bring them here, but not because of Nathaniel. Dealing with raiders is going to be a reality for all the communities, no matter what happens to Alexandra and her mother.'

'I don't understand, Arnie,' said Natalie. 'What is it that your afraid is going to happen?'

'I'm afraid Alexandra will turn her back on the communities when she sees what has happened to her mother and Beth and when she learns that she has a step-sister and step-brother, and that they are Nathaniel's children.'

'Why on earth would she turn her back on us? You're not making sense, Arnie.'

'Blood runs deep. I know Alexandra, she will side with her mother and won't rest until her step-brother and sister are free or dead,' sighed Arnie.

Natalie thought for a moment. 'You're afraid that she will go back to Glasgow with her mother and be captured or killed.'

'She's not stupid, Natalie, she knows she can't take on Nathaniel on her own, but she does carry a lot of credibility in the communities.'

Natalie began to share Arnie's concern. She could easily imagine a hot-headed Alexandra trying to rouse the communities into an attack on Nathaniel.

'You don't think…' she began

'I don't know, but if it was my sister's kids, I would go back for them, and like me, she would do whatever it took to make the mission more likely to succeed. I've racked my brains, Natalie, but I can't think of any way of getting those kids out of there other than a full scale onslaught. Marina says he is devoted to the children, and now that she is gone, he is bound to be suspicious and keep them close to him in the centre of his power.'

Natalie spoke her thoughts out loud, more than directing them at Arnie, 'Attacking Nathaniel in his lair would risk everything we have built up and have little chance of getting those kids out alive.' Looking directly at him, she said, 'But as you said, Alexandra is not stupid, she would see that, and so would the people in the communities. I don't think they would follow her.'

Even as she said it, Natalie knew this wasn't true. Many of the younger men especially would join her. 'I won't let her take people from this community on a hopeless rescue mission for Marina's children. You know we cannot afford to seek out confrontation with Nathaniel.'

'I know, Natalie, I can only hope Alexandra is as rational about this as you are.'

Chapter Twenty-Two

Bernard's group had so far seen no sign of the young women they were pursuing as they came north. They decided the girls would probably have taken the old A68 as it was the route that they knew and so they did the same. It was late winter turning into early spring as they travelled. Although very mild the rain was continuous, only slowing rather than stopping, and the sky cycled between grey, leaden grey, and occasionally black, but never blue.

Where the road drains had become blocked through neglect, the road turned into a river and they often had to leave it to find a drier route. Alexandra plodded along in the midst of the group trying to ignore the wet that was migrating from her waterproofs into the seams of her clothes, and thence to her skin. Her mind travelled back to the time that she and Brenda had been taken in by Prisca and Jim.

The decay of the road they travelled, and the fact that she was cold and uncomfortable on horseback, rather than warm and dry in a car for some reason made her think of lessons that Prisca had given her and Brenda when they had all lived together in Prisca's home.

Prisca had found books and DVDs about lost civilisations. The Inca people of Peru, the Khmer people of Vietnam, the Egyptians in the time of the Pharaohs, the Romans and so on. Prisca had impressed upon them that they were all great civilisations that had risen and fallen, leaving behind great monuments like the Sphinx and Pyramids, lost cities with beautiful stone carvings now covered by jungles or buried under sand. She had said that had they been young women living in the land of the Pharaohs, they would have thought themselves in the most powerful and advanced civilisation that had ever existed.

Had they been Roman's at the time of Julius Caesar, they may well have believed that the Roman Empire would conquer all of the known world and last for ever. Even then, she knew that Prisca was trying to help them come to terms with what was happening to the world around them. They had spent evenings talking about how the Egyptians must have felt when their crops failed and the Roman invaders came, or how the great cities of the Khmer people came to be abandoned and absorbed again into the jungle.

Prisca had challenged them to think like an Egyptian, or a Khmer, or Roman who saw their civilisation failing and asked them what it was that they would want to save to pass on to whatever came after them. At the time, Alexandra and Brenda had competed to come up with silly ideas, or thought of things they really missed like chocolate chip ice cream. The question had stayed with Alexandra long after their lessons had moved on. Her mind came back to it again as she rode on trying to ignore her discomfort.

What was it that was most valuable about the old world that should be protected and handed on to future generations? As she had thought about Prisca's question through her teenage years, she had always settled on knowledge, learning, understanding about the way the natural world was and how it worked. In large part, this is what motivated her support of Ann's aspiration for the community of Jedburgh, a community that traded in knowledge and learning. Such a community would be able to protect and shelter some of what was valuable about the old world whilst making it useful for the new world.

Maybe it was the physical discomfort of the journey that soured her mood, but as she thought on Prisca's question once more, her usual answer seemed unsatisfactory. The old world had accumulated a great wealth of knowledge, but she asked herself, had it been used with wisdom and creativity? In the old world, information or knowledge was power. Initially, people had seen the internet as subversive because it made information more widely available as long as you had access to it.

The old world wasn't a place where wisdom was seen as powerful, or a time in which people had sought the power of creativity unless it was to come up with an imaginative advertising slogan.

Suddenly, she was aware of Bernard to her left. Moving aside the hood of her cloak so she could catch his eye and speak clearly, she said, 'Bernard, what is the difference between knowledge and wisdom?'

Bernard showed little apparent surprise at the question as he looked at her, rain dripping from his beard. She could see the effort of thought chasing the ever present smile from his face for a moment. The smile came back as he said, 'Well, knowledge is knowing that rain is wet and cold, wisdom is having the sense to get under cover when it's raining.' Pleased with his answer, he guffawed, and slapped his leg, and then rode off to share the joke with the men in front, never bothering to ask the reason for the question.

Alexandra adjusted her rain coat and her seat in the saddle before resuming her thinking about what was most important to save from the old world. The sky took on a darker shade and the rain came in sheets of fat rain drops that bounced from the already sodden ground. She had backed Ann in her attempt to establish a community in Jedburgh because Ann seemed to have the determination to succeed and the qualities of leadership needed in a successful community mother.

Supporting Ann to develop a community that used knowledge as a trading commodity was a practical solution to helping a community that had nothing but its people's old world skills to establish itself. However, the idea had excited Alexandra because it fitted with her belief that old world knowledge was something that had to be protected and husbanded into the new world. She had been very aware that the little circle of new communities in south east Scotland, under the pressure of self-protection, were in danger of closing themselves off to each other and to new ideas.

Partly because of her efforts, the communities had established communications between themselves and trade followed. However, psychologically, most of the communities saw interaction with other communities as a necessary evil, a risk that had to be taken, rather a blessing and the start of a new opportunity. East Lowtown, Stainton, and Jedburgh were different, actively pursuing contacts and communication in order to trade for the things they needed to live and prosper rather than simply survive.

Alexandra had felt the difference when she visited these communities. There was an excitement, a hopefulness and a creativity that the less outward focused communities lacked. The attack on a well defended community like East Lowtown by raiders would only serve to make the other communities even more focused on survival and self-protection.

Squirming in the saddle as a rivulet of water found its way from the hood of her raincoat under her scarf and onto the skin of her neck, she felt her mood lift despite the pounding rain and her awareness of the length of road still to travel. Alexandra suddenly felt certain that what Ann had started in Jedburgh was the best hope that the communities had to escape from the cycle of narrow survival and to learn to live in a new world.

The communities had organised themselves in a way that dealt with the internal tensions caused by the gender imbalance following the "death", and had, at least so far, defended themselves from the external chaos and disorder caused by the collapse of the old world. Yet if they were to prosper, she knew that they had to overcome their fear of the raiders. That fear was real but it fuelled a degenerate parochialism and insularity.

Firstly, she reasoned they must build on and protect what Ann had achieved so far. Ann was like all the other community mothers elected so far. She was a vigorous, competent woman, dedicated to protecting and nurturing the communities that had elected them. However, Alexandra recognised that to one degree or another all the community mothers had become focused on their own particular communities.

Few of them travelled between the communities like she did, even Ann resented the disruption to her management of community issues that was caused by the trips, no matter how necessary to the development of the college. It had only been Alexandra's insistence that had built an ethical and philosophical dimension to the college. Left to her own devices, she was sure that Ann would have stuck to technical knowledge that was the immediate needs and demands of the communities.

Producing young people who could become leaders with access to the knowledge and wisdom of hundreds generations of human beings, was not yet part of Ann's vision.

Alexandra's mind began to turn to how she could move the communities beyond the trading of goods and technical skills to the development of "wisdom". She thought about what Bernard had said and knew that many would share his view of wisdom as the practical use of knowledge. For Alexandra, that was too narrow; she felt that wisdom had to have an ethical dimension. She thought, *For me, wisdom is the practical use of knowledge for the betterment of people we live with and the planet we live on.*

To her surprise, she heard Bernard saying, 'Aye, that's altogether better, so wisdom is knowing that rain is cold and wet and having the good sense to get you and your pals under shelter.'

She had not realised she had spoken aloud or that Bernard was again riding close enough to hear what she had said.

She replied, 'Well, Bernard, I guess we are lacking in the wisdom department then.'

Bernard laughed and shook his head so that water span from hair and beard like a dog shaking itself dry. 'Oh, aye, not very wise at all to be oot on a day like today.'

As her horse plodded on amidst the small knot of men she was travelling with, her mind joyfully grabbed at the conundrum of how to develop wisdom in the communities that balanced both practical and ethical knowledge. She drifted into the warmth of her mind, away from the physical discomforts of the journey relying totally on the men in Bernard's group for direction and safety.

It was in this mood of reflection and aspiration for the future that she spent the rest of the fruitless search for the girls of East Lowtown. A few miles out from Stainton, the village community she regarded as home, in countryside that was very familiar to her, she was almost sorry that the journey was coming to an end. The men's mood was lifting at the thought of warmth and shelter from the incessant rain, which had never let up for the whole of their two day journey.

Bernard, however, seemed wary and chastised the men to keep their wits about them. She urged her horse up to his side. 'Is there something of matter, Bernard?'

'Oh. You've come back to us, have you?' Bernard smiled.

'I've been thinking.'

'Aye, well,' he replied, with a complete lack of curiosity as to the content of the thinking.

'You seem tense. What is it?' Alexandra persisted.

'Aye, well, it's probably nothing, but it seems very quiet if you know what I mean. We haven't seen a soul. I should have thought to see somebody out and about by now.'

Alexandra smiled at him as she said, 'Maybe the people of Stainton are wise enough to know to stay in indoors when it's raining.'

'What, ah well that could be it,' laughed Bernard, remembering one of the few laughs he had on this journey. 'But all the same, I've got a bad feeling, you know just a feeling that things aren't quite right. Can't put me finger on why, but the feelings there all the same.'

Alexandra replied, 'Okay, well, you're right to trust your intuition, Bernard. Let's just hope it's wrong this time. We will be at Stainton in less than an hour I should think. Hopefully, they will have good news for us.'

Arriving at Stainton, they found the gates locked and barred and a warning siren sounded as they approached. A rifle shot sounded and a spray of stones leapt up from the road only metres in front of them. The group drew to a halt. They were too far to make themselves heard by the guard over the wind and rain. Alexandra pushed her horse to the front of the group and lowered her hood so that she might be recognised by the people at the gate.

'Looks like your intuition was right,' said Alexandra to Bernard, something has got them spooked.

The gates opened slightly to allow one man bundled against the rain to emerge from the fortified village. He immediately broke into a gentle lope towards the group. He had not taken twenty steps before Alexandra recognised the figure by its physique and lithe movement. Spurring her horse, she shouted to Bernard stay here until they see it's safe, and cantered to meet the jogging figure she knew to be Arnie.

A matter of seconds later, she pulled hard at the horse's reins and dived from its back to stand in front of the man that was her bodyguard and best hope of seeing her mother and friend again.

'Are they here with you?' She asked quietly, but with eyes that screamed at him for an answer.

'Yes,' he said simply.

He watched as relief filled her face, with more emotion than he had ever seen in her eyes before. She looked past him to the town gates, which were now opening in recognition of them as friends. She began to move past him, but he caught her arm, preventing her from going.

A moment of anger sprang into her face, to be replaced by concern for the man she knew had risked his life not as a bodyguard but as a friend. Arnie let go of her arm.

'What is it, Arnie? Just tell me.'

Arnie sighed. 'You should know that they have both gone through hell and that it shows. You need to prepare yourself for a shock, Alexandra,' he said this firmly but with a sadness in his eyes.

A matter of minutes later, Alexandra was confronted with a sight that shocked her despite Arnie's warning. Her mother and Brenda were being kept in a locked room that had only one door and no windows. The meagre contents of the room had been smashed beyond recognition. Two very dirty and dishevelled bodies lay on the floor. Alexandra went to move towards them but felt Arnie's strong hand on her shoulder, and before she could react, he whispered an urgent, 'Be careful, Alexandra.'

Anger flared in Alexandra. Arnie had always respected her physical space and now within minutes, he had twice laid restraining hands on her, but more than this, he was telling her to be careful of her own mother and best friend.

She stamped her foot and screamed at him, visibly regressing from the cool, calm leader of people to the girl who had lost her mother.

'Leave me alone, you bastard, how could you have left them like this.'

Her protest wakened the sleeping women and Alexandra found her mother in her arms but not in a loving embrace but a grip of fear and anger.

Alexandra had to hold her mother arms to stop her gauging at her with her fingernails, and endured a torrent of spittle and abuse as her mother poured forth a venomous and disgusting tirade of words. Brenda huddled in the corner and began to slowly rock backward and forward as she hugged her knees. Marina's rage eventually subsided enough for Alexandra to try and communicate with her.

'Mother, it's me. It's Alexandra, your daughter,' Alexandra repeated this over and over again. 'It's Alexandra, it's Alexandra.'

Suddenly, Marina slumped to the floor, all of the energy and fight leaving her.

Alexandra let go of her mother's arms which flopped lifelessly to her side. She stooped to gather her mother into her arms. It didn't take a huge effort for Alexandra to raise her and carry her over to where Brenda continued to rock, her eyes fixed nowhere in particular. Where moments ago Alexandra had to fight to stop her mother gauging out her eyes, she now carried her un-protesting and flaccid body easily in her arms. Alexandra squatted next to Brenda, arranging her mother so that she could hold her, and stroke her hair with one hand, whilst with the other she could stroke Brenda's back.

Arnie had stayed in the doorway throughout Alexandra's re-union with her mother and friend. Although he didn't feel completely comfortable with leaving them, his instinct told him that they needed to be alone. He dismissed the gaggle of Stainton people that had appeared in the house and sent the boy who had been guarding the door to fetch a lantern. When the boy returned with the lantern, he set it inside the door, and then settled himself in the corridor to wait and see how things developed.

In Stainton, a rage of gossip flowed through the streets and homes. Alexandra had returned to find her mother and childhood friend in a terrible state and Marina had responded by trying to murder her daughter. A debate started as to whether Arnie had been right to bring them back. People asked was it not better to spare the daughter the agony of knowing how her mother had suffered and changed.

Natalie and Thomas had not been in the community when Alexandra had returned. They had been visiting East Lowtown to see what help was needed, and to bring back the Stainton men who had gone to East Lowtown's aid. They saw that the community quickly returned to its normal rhythm, the dead were buried and the wounded cared for and repairs too damage started. Much grief, pain and fear were there also, but these were emotions that were very much a part of human life since the "death".

They also found the young students from Jedburgh, safe and sound but determined to remain. The young men that had travelled with the East Lowtown group also elected to stay for as long as they were needed to help rebuild. Natalie was reassured that the community was again able to defend itself and that the men from Stainton and other local communities could return to their homes. She and Thomas were keen to return to Stainton, particularly given Arnie's warning that Nathaniel might come east.

On their return, Natalie and Thomas went straight to the house that Marina and Brenda had been locked up in when they heard that Alexandra had returned.

'How is it?' Natalie asked of Arnie who she found lounging against the door frame at the entrance to the house.

'Alexandra's with them—its deadly quiet in there now, but at least Marina's stopped trying to gauge out people's eyes.'

'How's Alexandra taking it?' Thomas asked.

'Hard to say, she was angry about the state they are in, but she has seen what her mother has become so I guess she'll understand why they were locked up like that.' He added, 'Maybe she can reach them, bring them back, but it will be a long road.'

'Do they need anything?' Natalie asked.

'Well, I reckon Alexandra will want them somewhere else as soon as they can be moved, but it will have to be somewhere that they can be watched. Give her chance and I reckon Marina will go back to Glasgow, and we just can't allow that to happen.'

Quietly, he said, 'Between you and me, I'm not sure how Alexandra would cope with losing her mother again, even this creature that was her mother. I think she buried her feelings about their loss pretty deeply and now they're all dredged up.'

'What a fucked up world we live in,' sighed Thomas.

'Amen to that,' said Arnie.

'Does Alexandra know about the half sister and brother?' Natalie asked.

'No. There was no way to let her know, it was all I could to stop her rushing straight in there.'

'Are you stopping here or do you want someone to take over?' Thomas asked.

'I'll stay until she comes out. I don't want her to learn about her brother and sister from anyone but me.'

'I'll have some hot food sent over. Is there anything else you want?' Natalie asked.

'No, some food would be great. I do really need to speak to Beth. The last I heard, she was somewhere in Fife, but if you could get on the shortwave and ask the other communities to get her to call in, I would be grateful.'

'No problem. You're expecting trouble soon?' Thomas asked.

Arnie nodded and said, 'I think trouble is overdue.'

It was late in the evening when Alexandra emerged from the room. She looked more exhausted than he had ever seen her; it was as if the colour had drained out of her skin, her hair was flat and greasy against her skull, her eyes dull and unfocused.

Arnie waited for the control in their relationship had always been with Alexandra, and more than anything right now, he wanted Alexandra to re-assert that control.

'They're asleep,' she said avoiding his eye.

'Yes,' said Arnie.

'Sorry about what I said, what I called you.'

'That's okay, I'd forgotten already,' he lied.

'I need to know what happened to her, to them, Arnie.'

'I'll tell you, but first you need food and sleep. A few more hours before knowing will make no difference after all these years.'

She nodded accepting the sense of that but said, 'I can't leave them.'

'There's a camp bed in that room and some cold food but I'll ask Thomas to get some hot food over and some water for washing. I won't move from here and I promise, I'll call you the moment they're awake,' he finished.

'Good. Cold food will do. Get someone to bring my change of clothes from the saddlebag, would you. I feel like these are glued to my body.'

'All your stuff is already in there along with some fresh night stuff Natalie sent for you.'

'Ahh Natalie, the mother of Stainton. I hear she's expecting yet another brat.'

'Yes, but eat and sleep now, Alexandra,' said Arnie hearing and ignoring the childish spite in her tone.

'You sound like an old granny yourself nagging me to eat and sleep.'

'All part of the job,' he said with a smile.

'Hah,' said Alexandra and turned to go into the room Arnie had indicated. She turned back to look at him and said, 'I hope you know how much I owe you for finding them.'

He nodded and she turned back towards the room. Whether to herself or to him he wasn't sure but as she disappeared into the room, she said, 'I'll just have a quick nap then.'

Six hours later, and with great reluctance, Arnie woke her in order to keep his promise that he would let her know when her mother stirred.

'Alexandra, they're waking,' he said as he gently shook her shoulders.

She snapped awake.

'Bring food and water for them,' she said rising naked from the camp bed. She had never felt the need to hide her body from Arnie, in fact he was probably the only man that had seen her naked. Despite his sexuality, Alexandra was aware that Arnie wasn't completely immune from her sexuality, and on better days, it amused her to be aware of his interest. This day, nothing was further from her thoughts as she pulled on the clothes he had laid across an old chair in the corner of the room.

As Alexandra finished dressing, Marina began battering the door of the room she and Brenda were contained within. Arnie appeared at her side. 'Alexandra, there is something I must tell you before you see her again.'

'Not now, Arnie,' snapped Alexandra. 'Please just get some food and water for them.'

'It's coming but you should know…'

'Not now, Arnie,' said Alexandra, pushing past him towards the door that her mother was trying to batter down. On the other side of the door, obscenity was flowing from her mother's mouth as she thumped and kicked, hard enough that the thin door was in danger of breaking. The obscenity was mostly directed at what she was going to do to Arnie should she have the slightest chance.

Alexandra took a deep breath as she opened the door.

Marina was about to throw herself out of the suddenly open door, but a moment of recognition began to filter into her brain, just enough to make her pause.

'Mother, it's me, Alexandra, your daughter,' said Alexandra. Into those few words, she managed to imbue a sense of "enough is enough, this bad behaviour had been tolerated for long enough and has to stop".

'Is it really Alexandra,' said Marina quietly.

'Yes, it's me, and I have missed you,' she said letting softness and hurt come back into her voice.

Suddenly, Marina became the parent once again, hugging Alexandra, and saying, 'I have missed you too, darling.'

She broke the hug to look at her daughter with tears in her eyes, and said, 'I have missed you growing into a woman, Alexandra. Sometimes I would look at Brenda and think, "my Alexandra is growing older and changing into a woman just like her", and it made me so sad.'

Pulling Alexandra into her arms again, she said, 'Oh, Alexandra, I tried to protect her. I did try, just as if she was you that I was protecting.'

Alexandra looked at Brenda who had resumed her rocking in the corner of the room.

'Oh, Mother, I hate the bastards that took you away from me so so much. I want them to hurt, really, really hurt!'

Suddenly, fear came back to Marina's face, 'Promise me you won't go anywhere near him, Alexandra, he is evil, you don't know how evil.'

Concerned that her mother might lose her grip on reality again, Alexandra tried to soothe her.

'You're safe here, Mother, Brenda too. Nobody can harm you here in Stainton.'

'It's too late for me, Alexandra,' said her mother, letting herself slide down the doorframe to sit on the floor.

'Maybe Brenda could stay with you, Alexandra. She needs looking after, but maybe in time, she might…' Marina paused to think of the right words. 'Well, she might learn to live again, if you helped her, Alexandra.'

'You will both stay and both put everything that has happened since you were taken behind you.'

'I can't do that, Alexandra,' said Marina tears jumping into her eyes.

Alexandra stroked her hand, and said, 'Yes, yes, you can, Mother. It will be alright now.'

'No, it won't, Alexandra, you don't understand,' said Marina shaking her head.

At that point, Alexandra heard Arnie calling her name. Her mother became suddenly alert; fear springing readily back into a face that had got used to it.

'It's alright, its only Arnie. He has probably got food for you to eat and water to wash with.'

'Who the hell is he, Alexandra? He drugged me, the animal. How he got us out of the bro…' She couldn't finish the word and look at her daughter, so she said, 'Out of that place God alone knows.'

Looking Alexandra in the face, she said, 'Why does he want us, Alexandra?'

Before Alexandra could reply, her mother was shouting obscenities over her shoulder in the direction Arnie's voice had come from.

'Stop it, Mother! Arnie is my bodyguard, and a brave and decent man. He would not have done anything to cause you harm. Don't you understand that he rescued you.'

'The stupid bastard, what's going to happen to Nathan and Paula?' Marina exclaimed.

Arnie came round the corner with food and water before Alexandra could frame a question about Jake and Paula.

Alexandra felt her mother tense in her arms and held on to her tightly.

'Just leave it, Arnie,' pleaded Alexandra as she applied more pressure to the grip on her mother, who was either preparing to fly from or towards Arnie. She wasn't sure which would happen should she let her loose.

Putting the food down and ignoring the globule of spit that flew towards him from Marina, he said firmly, 'I need to talk to you, it's urgent.'

'Hell, Arnie, it's a bit difficult.'

Standing his ground, he said, 'It will only take a minute.'

'Well, talk then,' she spat at him with irritation in her eyes.

'I need to talk to you alone.'

'Go away, Arnie,' she said exasperated.

Arnie didn't move, which caused her mother to struggle even more in her grip as well as let loose another stream of obscenity.

'Be still, Mother, it's alright, he's not going to harm you.'

'Make him go away then.'

'Arnie, for God's sake, leave, I'll be right out.'

'Please, Alexandra, I need to talk to you,' Arnie pleaded.

'Yes, yes, I'll be right there,' she replied both irritated at his insistence and concerned at his unusual behaviour. She had never heard him plead for anything in the time she had known him.

It took five minutes of coaxing to get her mother into the room with the food and water. She succeeded in doing so only by appealing to her mother's instinct to look after Brenda, who had slowly rocked in the corner, apparently oblivious to everything.

Leaving the room, she found Arnie waiting around a corner in the corridor. She was aware that she was harassed, that her clothes were dishevelled and her hair uncombed, and she felt more out of control than she had ever done in her life.

She pressed her back against the corridor wall and took a deep breath.

Staring at the rain pouring down the kitchen's window, she said, 'Oh God, Arnie, what the fuck happened to my mother?' Before he could answer, she said, 'She was in his brothel house, wasn't she?'

'Yes,' replied Arnie calmly. 'But there is something else you need to know.'

'Tell me,' she sighed, mentally preparing for what she expected to hear about the brothel.

She was taken totally by surprise to hear Arnie say, 'You have a sister.'

Alexandra was already staring open mouthed at Arnie when he said, 'And a brother.'

This news was beyond Alexandra's imagination. She had known that any woman taken by raiders could not escape being raped and abused, and had not kidded herself that her mother would have escaped this fate if she lived. When she had learnt of Nathaniel's brothel houses, she had even prepared herself for the knowledge that her mother may have been an inmate of such a facility for all those years, but she had never entertained the thought that she would become pregnant.

The possibility was obvious to her now, her mother was in her early thirties when she had been taken. She laughed out loud at the absurd naivety of such girlish thinking that at no time had the thought of her mother becoming pregnant entered her head. Her laughter turned to silent tears.

She gave herself to the kind of tears that come when the emotional pain is overwhelming. Tears that come in uncontrolled waves and trigger your nasal ducts to join in the flow that drips from your face.

Arnie let her cry. He did not try to and comfort her with word or touch. He simply stayed with her and waited for it to pass. He had seen soldiers cry like for this for their dead comrades, and knew it was a pain that had to be gone through. Had Alexandra been a soldier, he would have waited for it to pass and then get him as drunk as possible, but losing control was not what Alexandra needed. She had to get back into the saddle. He had to get her focused on the mission that gave meaning to her life, but he had no idea how to achieve this.

The tears had stopped and Alexandra was coming back from the place her pain had taken her, when with a knock and a "hello", Natalie pushed open the door and stepped into the corridor.

Instantly, Natalie recognised that this was a bad time and regretted having pushed open the door. She knew instinctively Alexandra would hate that she had seen her in a vulnerable state. Arnie stepped between Natalie and Alexandra and whispered to Natalie that it was not a good time. However, she decided not to leave immediately, a decision she would later regret, but one she believed she made out of a desire to help the woman that had once been her best friend.

Her mind told her it was a bad idea but her heart wanted to help. So as she said over Arnie's shoulder, 'Alexandra, what's the matter, can I help,' she was following her heart.

'What can you do, Natalie?' Alexandra said with a sarcastic spite.

'I don't know, but I will do what I can, Alexandra,' said Natalie softly, all the time telling herself mentally that she was only making things worse and that she should leave her to Arnie who she seemed to trust.

'Well, I can see that you're good at one thing,' said Alexandra pointing to Natalie's belly, which was swelling slightly in that unmistakable way of pregnancy.

'Thomas and I are very happy,' responded Natalie defensively but again regretting her words. Mentioning Thomas was not likely to soften Alexandra's mood, as she had been distant with both her and Thomas ever since they had made their relationship public.

Alexandra found that making Natalie feel bad was making her feel better. Although she knew it was terrible and petty behaviour to snipe at this woman who was once her friend, it distracted her from her own feelings and brought back a sense of power in herself that she had not felt since her mother came back into her life.

Leaning closer to Natalie, Alexandra responded with a bitter sarcasm. 'Ooh, I'm so glad somebody is happy in this fucked up world. Even if it's a couple of hopeless cases like you and Thomas.' Without drawing breath, she rushed on, 'But maybe you need to spend less time on your back keeping Thomas happy and more time making this community safe.'

Natalie sighed and said, 'I don't know why you want to hurt me, Alexandra, but I will always love you for what you did for me.' She then turned and left.

'Stupid,' snarled Alexandra. She was referring to herself for she knew that Natalie had once again seen a side of her that Alexandra herself did not like.

Hearing condemnation in Arnie's silence, she realised he thought she had been referring to Natalie. She tried to both cover up her embarrassment at her behaviour and to fend off the complaints of her own conscience as she said, 'Well, I'm right. Have you not seen what the defences of this place has come to, it's pathetic!'

'Aye well, it could be improved upon and no doubt you will take that up with Jim as soon as you can manage,' said Arnie with only a hint of sarcasm. Alexandra knew full well that Jim, the community father, was primarily responsible for the defences of the community, and Arnie was reminding her that he had been unfair to Natalie.

Alexandra changed the subject. 'Before I go back to her, tell me how you got them away from that bastard Nathaniel, and about the children.'

'I had a choice to make: the children or your mother and Brenda,' said Arnie a little defensively.

'I believe you, Arnie, you don't know how much it means to me that you even tried to get them back, never mind succeeded. Tell me how you did it?'

Arnie continued with his story. 'The younger women are kept in different quarters from the children. The men don't want kids running around when they get the opportunity to visit the women's quarters. The kids are kept in a parody of a school come nursery, looked after by some older woman and a male, who styles himself as the headmaster. He's a particular nasty creature that I would dearly love to kill.

'The female quarters are run in the same way as many a brothel has operated down the ages in which a madam controls entry. The women have more freedom to come and go than you would think, but attempting to escape is severely punished.'

Alexandra asked, 'Do many try? I know Beth escaped.'

Arnie said, 'Beth is pretty exceptional. In truth, very few try to escape, most have given up hope. Quite a few are dependent on drugs, supplied by the madam of course, or controlled in some other way. In your mother's case, it was access to her children that they used as the hold over her. You see, when your mother was first captured, Nathaniel kept her to himself. He refused to allow the other men access to her.

'He kept her confined in his personal apartments which are guarded constantly. After a few years, he grew tired of her and replaced her with another woman sending her into the brothel, but your brother and sister had been born by then.'

'Oh God, they are Nathaniel's children,' sighed Alexandra.

'It would seem that way, but only your mother could tell you for sure. Everything I know about her early years with Nathaniel is gossip I learnt in the men's barracks. So you have to take it with a pinch of salt, Alexandra.'

'But you believe they are Nathaniel's children,' she said tiredly.

'They are your mother's children, and they are the reason I had to drug her to get her out of that place. There is no way she would have left without them. I thought once she was out of Glasgow, she would see reason and I could let the drugs wear off. Big mistake; she dammed near killed me with a little stiletto knife she had hidden in a boot. Had she succeeded, she would have marched straight back to Glasgow.'

Arnie paused his story to make sure Alexandra was taking it all in before continuing. 'I kept her drugged or bound for the rest of the journey. Brenda was a different problem; she is practically catatonic. She does exactly what she is told but nothing more. I could have left her standing in one place all day and she would still be there the next day. You have to tell her to eat, even to go the toilet, otherwise she just does it when her bladder or bowels are full. Like a baby.'

'How did you get them out of this brothel of his?' She asked.

'Getting in and out of the brothel was the easy part. As I said, a madam controls the women. If you want a woman, you give the madam one of Nathaniel's coins, or if you are trusted by the madam, she will trade for other things.'

'Coins?' Alexandra inquired.

Arnie fished in his pocket and passed Alexandra a coin of indeterminate metal with the form of a naked woman on one side and a date stamped on the other.

'That is Nathaniel's currency. It is distributed only by him and his henchmen, or captains as he calls them. His power is built on the brothels, only a few selected groups amongst his men are allowed to have their own women. There are five brothels, each with around fifty women. They give out these coins for work or in return for other favours. One coin gets you access to the brothel, but you will expect to pay more if you want to choose a woman.

'A one coin woman is a very sad creature indeed. Brenda was a one coin woman because her mind was so far gone, other's were one coin woman because they were old or disfigured or had venereal disease of one sort or another.'

Chapter Twenty-Three

Arnie had found joining up with Nathaniel's band was very easy; he simply posed as a refugee from the North East, looking for food and work and showed up at one of the areas of Glasgow controlled by Nathaniel's gangs. After a week or two of working in fields, he heard that Nathaniel had killed one of his captains in a rage about a failed raid.

The captain in control of the area Arnie was in had been tasked with mounting an attack to revenge the defeat of the raid led by the executed captain. Arnie let drop in a couple of drinking dens that he used to be in the SAS, and a few days later, he was summoned to see his captain. Arnie quickly made himself indispensable to the captain and was inducted into an elite band of men in the city, who wore Nathaniel's uniform of black.

It was this uniform that allowed Arnie to achieve his goal of finding out whether Marina and Brenda were still alive. The uniform was a passport between areas of the city controlled by different captains. Nathaniel's empire was based around the brothels, each brothel area had a captain, who maintained a bunch of thugs dressed in black to keep order amongst the population in the area. Movement of men between brothel areas was not prevented, but could easily lead to fights.

So men tended to stick to the brothel for their own area. As a mere labourer, Arnie would have stuck out like a sore thumb moving around the districts asking questions about two women called Marina and Brenda.

It is doubtful that Nathaniel had ever read a manual on the maintenance of power and order, but he was a natural leader and had quickly learnt the age old art of divide and rule. Only men attached to a captain's fighting force could move between brothels without drawing too much attention. Arnie set about visiting each of the district brothels which was almost expected of a new man wearing the black uniform.

However, he quickly learnt to spend most of his time hanging about in the local drinking dens as a regular topic of conversation for the men was the woman they had used in the brothel. He quickly established a reputation as a generous man happy to buy drinks and share stories about visits to the brothel. It took a few weeks but eventually, he had got what he wanted—a man that mentioned the name of Marina. He was keen to impress upon Arnie that this woman had been kept by Nathaniel himself for a number of years before being shared with all in the brothel.

Marina was not a common name in Glasgow and the description he had teased out of the man fit with the picture that Alexandra had given her of her mother. Arnie went that night to the brothel the man had talked of and asked for Marina. The madam bellowed the name and Marina appeared listlessly from an ante room. She followed Arnie to the room the madam had given him the number of. He had thought about how he would deal with this meeting should he find her alive, but had never really come up with a satisfactory plan.

He could not know how she would react to the knowledge that he was there at the request of her daughter, and he had come to get her out of the place.

She plonked herself onto the narrow bed as soon as she was in the room. She looked down at the floor or up at the ceiling and waited for him to speak.

'Your name is Marina,' said Arnie.

'Yeah, what of it?' She said listlessly.

'Marina Asquith?' Arnie asked, impulsively deciding that he needed to take a risk.

Her surname impacted upon her like a slap in the face. Suddenly, her face was bright and alert, fear and anxiety mixed with interest and excitement, as her eyes looked to search his face.

'Nobody knows my surname, not even my own children. Who the fuck are you? Do I know you from somewhere?'

'One of your children knows all of your name,' replied Arnie.

Her face betrayed the frustration at his response, before it dawned on her that he was referring to the child she had given up for dead.

She jumped to her feet and shouted at him, 'You're talking about Alexandra!'

'Quiet,' he urged. 'We don't want to attract attention now, do we?'

'Who are you? What do you want? I've never set eyes on you. How can you know my daughter?' She gasped stumbling for breath and the space to think.

'It doesn't matter who I am. All you need to know is that your daughter loves you and wants you with her, and her friend, Brenda, if she is still alive.'

'But...' stumbled a confused Marina.

'Is Brenda alive, Marina?' Arnie asked firmly.

'Yes...Yes...well, if you can call it living. Her mind is gone. I do my best for her but...'

'Where is she?' Arnie persisted.

'Here. Here. I look after her when she's not working. The bastards are awful to her. She's a one coiner...but worse...she gets all the perverted shites who get off on the way she is. Why am I telling you this? What do you want?' She had lowered her voice but Arnie could hear the hysteria rising in her again. Her dressing gown had fallen open, revealing her nakedness beneath.

She was completely unaware of this but caught Arnie averting his eyes from her body, which had the immediate effect of bringing a calmness to her, as she pulled the cordless nightgown around her more tightly.

She sat on the bed again, breathed out, and in a calm resolute voice, said, 'Tell me what you want. You paid for an hour, and by the end of it, I need to know why you are here and what you want of me or else, I am going straight to madam. You understand.'

He did; the Madam was the only woman in the place that could offer any kind of protection for her. Threatening to tell the madam was her only defence.

'It's simple, Marina,' he said quietly. 'I have come here to take you back to Alexandra, and Brenda to if I can.'

'Oh God, why now, why not seven years ago?' She moaned.

'She didn't know where you were then, and maybe that was for the best, because I think she would have come looking for you and more than likely ended up next to you rather than rescuing you.'

'No, she mustn't come here, don't let her for God's sake.'

'I am here to take you to her, partly to stop her coming for you.'

Marina looked at him with a renewed interest, as a link to a long lost daughter.

'Are you her...'

'No,' he answered anticipating the question.

'Then why take the risk of coming here? What are you to my daughter?'

'Her bodyguard,' he said simply.

'Bodyguard,' she said with surprise and with a volume that urged Arnie to shush her again.

'Yes, I work with her to bring on communities that are trying to cope in a more civilised way than this hell hole.'

'My Alexandra. She must be, oh, twenty-eight by now.' She patted the side of the bed, feeling only excitement at the prospect of hearing something about her daughter, and losing all the fear that had been with her only moments ago. 'Come, come, tell me about her. What does she look like? Has she married? Am I a grandmother?'

Then her face darkened. 'Oh, this better not be some kind of perverted shit. Get me all excited by selling me some crap about my daughter.'

'No,' said Arnie firmly. 'Everything I have said is true. Here is a picture your daughter gave me to recognise you by.'

Marina rose and snatched the picture from his hand.

'She gave me a letter as well but I had to leave it behind. It was too much of a risk to carry it on me. I could have been searched. You will get it when we get out of here.'

'A letter,' she said staring at the picture. She shook the picture and said, 'You could have got this from anywhere. How can I really know you are telling the truth?'

He replied in a quiet voice, 'You will have to trust me. After all, what have I really got to gain if I wasn't telling the truth.'

'Tell me about her then,' she said again sitting on the bed.

'Your daughter has become a leader of what she calls the new world. She is a truly remarkable woman. She is finding ways to put this fucked up world back together again, and who knows, perhaps it will be better next time.'

'A leader, my little Alexandra, but she was always was the one the other girls followed.' She smiled. 'Do you have a picture of her?'

He shook his head but started trying to describe her for Marina. 'She is about six foot one, and slim but not in a skinny way. She is well muscled for a women and doesn't carry a lot of fat. Not flat chested but not busty either, if you know what I mean.'

Marina had her eyes closed as if she was trying to build a picture of her daughter in her head using Arnie words and her own memories.

He continued, 'She doesn't exercise but seems to stay fit by being on the go most of the time. Of course you know her hair is fair, almost blond, and her eyes are blue. She has a strong face, but you know, she is intelligent just to look at her. Something about the eyes and maybe the way she holds herself just lets you know that she is somebody to be reckoned with. People see that in her straight away, men and women.'

'You like her,' said Marina.

'Yes, next to my family, she is the most important person in my life,' he said simply and without emotion.

'She's pretty,' Marina probed.

'Pretty is not a word I would associate with Alexandra. Too girly. There's no doubt she is attractive to men, though, I'm not sure whether she would be described as beautiful. She makes an impression on people as soon as they see her. She wears a red coat, a cloak really. It's become a kind of trademark, makes her instantly recognisable.'

'Does she have a man?' Marina asked.

'No, she has never chosen a man in the time that I have known her.'

'Never!'

'No, as far as I can tell, she is completely celibate.'

'Why? Did something happen to her?' She said aware that a lot of time had passed and many things could have happened to the daughter she had been taken from.

'Not that I know of. She seems to have made a choice. She doesn't talk about it with me, but I get the impression that she feels relationships with men would interfere with her work, her ability to influence and lead.'

'But…is she happy?' Marina asked.

Arnie, thought for a moment before saying, 'She has set herself a mission to protect and nurture the communities she has helped to create, and so she is happy in so far as she is pursuing the goal she has set for herself. For instance, she rarely takes part in the community celebrations or festivals except to make speeches, but this one time, she did. She seemed to enjoy it greatly, it brought out a different side to her, younger more carefree.

'However, she broke her wrist when a partner in a strip the willow let go. In truth, she was to blame as she was whirling like a dervish.' He laughed at the memory.

'The next day, she was in such a foul mood that everybody kept out of her way. The people in the community put it down to anger at the male who had let go her hand in the dance. But I think it was anger at herself for allowing her own feelings to get in the way of what she has to do. You see, we travel mostly on horseback, its quicker now for most journeys and doesn't draw attention like a vehicle, and the wrist prevented her from travelling.'

Arnie finished by saying, 'You should be very proud of her, she is a fighter.'

'Does she know about me? I mean about where I am, what I have become,' she sighed.

'Yes. We have never talked about it, but she knows how it is here, and she not stupid.'

Marina stood up from the bed and turned her back to him before saying, 'Tell her I am dead and that Brenda is dead also.'

'I can't do that,' said Arnie firmly.

She whirled around, and for a moment, Arnie saw Alexandra in her eyes. 'That is exactly what you will do,' she spat. 'Otherwise, Nathaniel will know there is a spy in his camp and you'll be dead. Painfully dead.'

'Then she would come,' he countered.

'To find you, she wouldn't do that if she is as clever as you say.'

'No, to find you. Your daughter is a remarkable person, but sometimes she is given to reacting to what's in her heart not what's in her head. If she thinks there still a chance that you're alive here, then she will find some way to get to you.'

'Then for God's sake, tell her we are dead, that we were here, but were killed. God alone knows that should be easy enough to believe. It could even be the truth by the time you get back to her. It only takes some crazy drunken bastard to get it into his head he's been cheated, or made a fool of. It could happen anytime.'

'She would know I was lying,' he said with conviction. 'I told you, she is far from stupid. She would find out, maybe not straight away but somehow it would come out, and I would hate myself for lying to her.'

'I can't leave,' Marina sighed.

'The whole world's gone through shit,' said Arnie. 'What you have gone through has got to have been hell, but she won't judge you for that.'

Marina slumped back onto the bed. 'You don't understand. I can't leave because of my children.'

'Children,' said Arnie, stupidly looking round the room as if they would magically appear in the empty space of the room.

'They don't use condoms here, love.' She laughed.

'How many?' He stuttered, trying to accommodate space in his head for the adjustment to his planning this revelation entailed.

'Two, and don't think you can go rescuing them as well as me and Brenda. They are Nathaniel's kids, you won't get anywhere near them. I think it won't be long before he won't let me see them anymore. I've become too dirty since he threw me out of his personal harem and into this cesspit. You can't say somebody like him can be a good father, but he is very attentive, and gentle with his children.

'He actually spoils them. The kids are the only reason he lets me see them, because they still ask and get upset if he says no.'

Tears came to her eyes as she said, 'But he will poison their minds. He'll manipulate it so that they stop asking, and then I won't ever be allowed out of this or some other rat hole until I am dead.'

Arnie sighed as he said, 'Shit'!

Marina laughed. 'Yeah, you've got that right—shit just about covers it.'

Arnie left the room after his allotted time, so deflated that the madam stopped him and asked him if he had any trouble. He made his excuses and left the building, his head buzzing.

He had not come up with an answer, when he went back to the brothel the next evening and asked for Brenda. The madam eyed him suspiciously but said nothing. He knew that Brenda was usually a choice for those that had no choice. As his uniform said he had coin to spare, he hoped the madam would be satisfied with the conclusion that his motive in choosing Brenda was to satisfy some sort of perversion.

Brenda was brought from the same room that Marina had emerged from the night before and left to stand in front of him. He turned to go to the room that he had been given, but was halted by the madam's voice. He turned and saw that Brenda had not moved from the spot she had stood on.

'You will need to tell her to follow you, she won't do anything unless you tell her to. I thought you knew what she is. What a fine fella like you want with her anyway?'

'That's my business,' said Arnie and seeing the suspicion rising in the madam's face, spoke roughly to Brenda, 'Follow me, bitch.' Brenda obeyed.

He heard the madam muttering about cheapskates as he turned his back to ascend the stairs.

Arnie soon learnt that Brenda was completely disconnected from reality. He told her to stand on one leg and she did so until her leg collapsed beneath her, and then simply lay where she fell. After that, he spent the time trying to think how he was going to solve what seemed the impossible task of getting an unwilling Marina and a catatonic Brenda out of the district without being followed. Then there was Marina's children.

A week later, he had found out where Marina's children were kept and where they went to a sort of school for part of the day. The children had their own black uniformed guard as well as an older woman that seemed to act as a nanny to them. He had reluctantly come to the conclusion that there was no way that he could take the children and Marina and Brenda, and get them all out of Nathaniel's grasp before the children were missed. His dilemma was simple but seemed intractable.

Taking the children alone would bring Nathaniel's rage down on Marina's head, he would undoubtedly suspect her involvement. What's more, he may be able to discover a connection with Stainton through Marina. Not taking the children meant Marina would not leave willingly, and kidnapping her would be a lot more challenging than rescuing her, particularly with a catatonic Brenda in tow. The campaign against Motherwell was developing and he now had only a few more weeks before his captain and Nathaniel would decide that all the preparations were made and commence the attack.

He knew that without his information, the community of Motherwell would have a hard time of it. He was being pressed into a decision, into making choices that had more cons than pros.

Arnie had persuaded his captain that they should set up a forward supply base for the assault on Motherwell. It would have been a good strategy except that Arnie had already given away the location of this supply base and plans were already in place for its capture. Stocking the base with ammunition, fuel and food gave Arnie the chance to leave the city without incurring suspicion. He had the use of a small battery powered van for the purpose of transporting heavy items, and it was in this that he intended to smuggle Brenda and Marina out of the city.

He had arranged for three night journeys to take the ammunition needed to the forward base. He had argued that moving at night was necessary to keep the base's location a secret. The first two nights he had established a routine of taking the van to the brothel in which Marina and Brenda were housed, and leaving the van with a guard whilst he visited the brothel. On the third night, he said to his companion that he was tired and would rather sleep. He generously gave his companion some coin so that he might visit the brothel whilst he slept in the van.

The man readily accepted and disappeared into the brothel. As soon as his companion disappeared from view, Arnie left the van and made his way to the back of the building, where he had previously hidden the tools he would need to effect the escape. Quickly checking everything was still present, he climbed up a drain pipe for three storeys and pulled himself over the gutter onto the roof of the building. Securing himself, he pulled up the equipment from a rope line he had trailed behind him.

He dropped through a roof light into what was the women's dormitory area. He was fairly sure that at this time of the night, all the women would be in the working areas of the brothel. There was always the chance that one or more of the women would be allowed to remain behind because of illness, but he was in luck and the room was completely empty.

He then set the room alight, making sure it would burn hard and fast by dousing the bedding in paraffin. As soon as he was satisfied that the room was well ablaze, he quickly started down the stairs carrying a small knapsack on his back. Arnie was confident that he could get down the stairs unobserved as the corridors and stairwells were used only to get to and from the rooms and nobody lingered in them. On the first floor, he listened in at the doors of the rooms to find a vacant one.

Having found a room he was pretty sure was empty, he slipped an old credit card between the door frame and the lock and in seconds, the door clicked open. He didn't have to wait for long before shouts of fire—fire could be heard all over the building. Hearing footsteps in the corridor outside him, he emerged from the room with his clothing looking suitably disarranged. Joining the growing crowd of people moving toward the stairs, he heard crashing noises above his head and there was a very strong smell of burning in the corridors though no smoke as yet.

He began to worry that his fire raising had been a little too effective, when reaching the ground floor where the madam usually sat, he saw pieces of burning building falling to the road outside of the building.

A few anxious moments later, he saw what he had gambled on, Marina leading a half-naked Brenda down the stairs. Arnie had felt sure that Marina would not leave the building without knowing that Brenda was safe. As the alarm had been raised, Marina had been in the back room and unoccupied, but Brenda had been engaged by a man over half an hour previously. Marina had found her rocking on the bed of one of the rooms abandoned by the man that had been using her.

Not able to find Brenda's dressing gown, which had been taken by the man she was with, she told Brenda to put on an old shirt she found lying on the floor, and hurried her out of the room. They were on the second floor and amongst the last to come down the stairs that were now starting to fill with smoke as the fire spread.

Arnie watched Marina leading Brenda down the stairs, making sure that he was not seen. As the pair got to the bottom of the stairs, there was a loud crash followed by a rush of smoke billowing out of the first floor corridor, which then slowed sinisterly as it clung to the ceiling of the ground floor. The noise and the smoke registered on Brenda who began to show signs of alarm. Marina tried to calm her and hurry her at the same time. Arnie thought this was going to be his best chance.

He emerged from hiding and quickly walked towards Marina and Brenda. Marina's attention was focused solely on getting Brenda and thus herself out of the building. As Arnie moved, he also fished a plastic bag from his knapsack, ripping it open as he stepped behind Marina he took a white pad from the bag. In one movement, he brought the pad up to Marina's face and clamped her body to his. There was a brief struggle before Marina collapsed in Arnie's arms, overcome by the anaesthetic he had soaked the pad with.

Throwing her over his shoulder, he took Brenda's hand and said with authority but quietly, 'Come, Brenda, you must follow me and Marina.' He did not know whether she recognised him from his several visits with her, or whether she was just instinctively responding to a male command, but she came without question.

He moved as quickly as he could out of the building which was now so well ablaze that even a trained fire service would have struggled to save it. No such thing existed in Glasgow and in fact, nobody was lifting a finger to try and put the fire out. As they emerged from the building, he heard cheers from the onlookers who saw a man rescuing two women, rather than a man kidnapping two women. Once onto the road, people rushed forward to help—he brushed them off and called out for them to clear the road.

A minute later, he was a few yards from the van. Arnie mentally commended himself for not parking immediately in front of the brothel as the road was now littered with burning debris from the building. Arnie's companion, Pete, saw him coming towards the van and rushed over to him.

'Where the fuck have you been? You were meant to be with the van. What if somebody had nicked it?' Pete spluttered.

'Shut up and help me get these two into the van,' snapped Arnie.

'Just leave them, the madam will look after them.'

'No, I'm not leaving them,' he said lowering Marina to the ground by the back of the van whilst he fished for the vehicle's keys.

'Oh Christ, have it your way then,' said the man who recognised that there was no changing Arnie's mind and he was very keen to get away from the crowd gathering round the fire.

They bundled Marina and Brenda into the back of the van and Arnie told Pete to drive.

'Where? We can't take those two with us to forward base,' he said leaning over the driver's seat.

'Just go, Pete, get us away from here to a quieter spot where I can think,' shouted Arnie, putting in a very good performance as a man who was losing it. Pete complied.

Five minutes later, Arnie could see they were in a largely abandoned area of the city and told Pete to stop.

He got out of the van, taking his little knapsack with him, from which he produced a pistol with the long barrel of a silencer on it.

Coming level with the driver's door, he pulled it open and pointed the weapon at his companion.

'What the fuck are you playing at,' gasped an amazed, exasperated but not yet frightened Pete.

'Out of the van,' said Arnie.

Pete tried to grab the driver's door as he said "get stuffed", but it was the last thing he did. Arnie fired once and Pete slumped out of the car, leaving behind a significant amount of blood, bone and brain.

In the back of the van, Marina remained unconscious and Brenda rocked as if nothing had happened. Arnie hid Pete's body in a long disused wheelie bin.

Returning to the van, he checked on Marina's condition, and then gently drugged Brenda in the same was as he had Marina. Carefully, he re-arranged the ammunition boxes so that they left a space for their inert bodies and then covered them so that the van would have to be searched properly for them to be seen.

The last two nights, he and Pete had left the city unchallenged and he guessed that this night would be just the same. Nathaniel had all the entrances and exits to the part of the city he was using guarded, but Arnie in his black uniform had never been seriously challenged. Coming to the checkpoint, he stopped at the barricade across the road and wound down the window. As the men on guard lazily got themselves in order to move the barricade, their leader sauntered over to Arnie.

As he came close, Arnie said, 'You heard about the fire?'

'We saw a fire,' he replied. 'What went up then?'

'The brothel in Renton's sector.'

'Madam Burkes' place,' queried the guard.

'That's right, but I think everybody got out safe. So I'm sure it will be business as usual tomorrow night in some other building.'

'Hah, that's alright then,' laughed the man.

'See yer later.' Arnie smiled as he put the van in gear and rolled towards the opening barricade. *Some guard*, thought Arnie, *he hasn't even noticed that I am on my own.*

An hour later, Arnie had stopped in sight of another more permanent looking barricade.

He got out of the van and flashed the word "friend" in morse code towards the barricade. No response came. *The bastards can't be sleeping,* thought Arnie and he flashed the message again. Five minutes later, he was starting to get concerned, he decided to try once more. But before he could, a light flashed from the barricade in morse code. It said simply "wait".

Ten minutes later, he was getting irritated.

Twenty minutes later, he was starting to fume, when he heard a voice cursing and swearing at people. A shape appeared on top of the barricade and a light flashed, "Identify friend" in morse. Arnie flashed back, "Santa Claus".

A voice he recognised boomed, 'Come in, laddie,' and Arnie returned to the van to drive it the short distance to the barricade.

Two days later, Arnie was in Stainton and a week after, he was telling the story of the rescue / kidnapping to Alexandra. He had suffered a constant stream of abuse from Marina once she had recovered from being drugged, and he had to keep her bound for the whole journey. He had been accompanied by an older woman from Motherwell who was to guard the women, and was glad that he had, for there was no way that Marina could have been untied without constant supervision.

Alexandra had listened to Arnie tell the story without interrupting. When he finished, she stepped close and hugged him tightly. She whispered to him, 'Thank you, Arnie.' She stepped away and said quietly, 'We will talk later, but now I must spend time with my mother. Can you ask Natalie and Jim if we can meet this evening?'

'Of course, but what shall I say the meeting is about?' Arnie asked a little anxiously.

'The children, Arnie, the children.'

Chapter Twenty-Four

Alexandra spent the whole day with her mother. Arnie hovered close to the room they were in, nervous about what was happening inside, but not wanting to seem like he was eavesdropping. He could hear that Marina and Alexandra were talking but not what they were saying. He was, however, relieved that whatever was being said was being done in calm voices.

Alexandra eventually emerged from the room and said to Arnie, 'One day, I will find a way to thank you properly for bringing my mother back to me.'

'Is she okay? Does she need anything?' Arnie replied unable to keep a pensiveness from his voice.

Alexandra smiled at him and said, 'Don't worry, Arnie, I think I have probably convinced her not to tear your throat out.'

'Probably, well, I suppose that's an improvement then.'

Alexandra actually laughed which instantly eased Arnie's tension. 'She is going to clean herself up and see to Brenda. Then I would like us both to meet with Natalie and Jim. Did you speak to them?'

'Yes, they will be at Jim and Prisca's place this evening. They like to have their meetings whilst cooking a meal together. Amazing, isn't it? I think the old world politicians had something called a "kitchen cabinet" but this really is running a community from a kitchen. Natalie says their biggest arguments are over what to cook. I think they are planning to eat at about 7pm. Shall I say to set two more spaces.'

'I need you to be there as well, Arnie. If I remember right, we will all squeeze round Prisca's table,' said Alexandra.

'Is that a good idea? Not sure me, Marina and steel cutlery is a good combination,' said Arnie not entirely jokingly.

'Arnie, I think you are scared of my mother. Imagine that, my hero bodyguard afraid of a five foot five inch, 8 stone female,' laughed Alexandra. 'Don't worry, this evening I shall be your bodyguard.'

'I might well need it if you are going to be talking about her children. I can't believe she has forgiven me for taking her out of Nathaniel's grasp and away from the children.'

When Natalie and Jim heard about Alexandra and Marina joining them for their evening meal from Arnie, they said in unison, 'What?'

'Yeah, I thought you would say something like that,' laughed Arnie.

'Seriously,' said Jim, 'what the fuck is she up to now?'

Just at that moment, Prisca came into the kitchen. 'Language, Jim. Who's up to what, or is it a state secret?'

Natalie responded, 'Alexandra of course, she's invited herself to dinner along with her mother.'

'Fuck,' said Prisca.

Alexandra and her mother arrived at Jim and Prisca's home. She immediately cut through the social awkwardness by assembling them all at the table and getting down to business.

'So the situation is that my mother is determined to return to Glasgow to be with the children that she bore to that bastard rapist, Nathaniel.'

'I can't just leave them, they didn't choose their father,' interjected Marina calmly but with an appeal to the friends she had known so well.

'Let me finish, Mother,' appealed Alexandra but with the firmness of someone who was used to being in charge. 'As well as what happened to mother, as you all know my best friend is catatonic and may never come back from the hell she was put through since being taken from here.'

Everyone gathered at the table shared the pain and anger Alexandra felt but knew there was a proposal coming. After a short pause, Alexandra continued satisfied that she had their attention.

'At the moment, we believe Nathaniel to be pushing forward with his attack on Motherwell. From all accounts, he is attempting to exert control on survivors and communities out with Glasgow city. It's my belief that bandits like Nathaniel can no longer survive by taking from the old world's resources which are becoming scarcer. Food and power are not easily scavenged anymore. So he and others like him are trying to control those like us that have found ways to feed ourselves and can keep the lights on. Like an ancient robber Baron, he hopes to keep his lifestyle, and above all his power, by turning people into slaves.'

Again, she briefly paused and looked round the table. Nobody was taking issue with her analysis, so she continued, 'That's the big picture; small communities like ours struggling to live a civilised life, harried and at constant risk from would be barons like Nathaniel. I do not underestimate Nathaniel. It would be easy to see him as a simple thug and bully, but it takes skill and leadership as well as ruthlessness to take and to maintain power. From everything mother, Arnie and people like Mikey in Motherwell have said to me, it's clear that Nathaniel has secured his place as top dog amongst all the "scavenger bands" in a large part of Scotland.

'Distance has probably insulated us a little from his influence but as we know, he does send small bands this way and he definitely holds influence over the bands in Edinburgh. Nathaniel is trying to be more than a raider living from day to day. All that organisation, the brothels, his own currency, organising his territory into departments. That's not a raider or scavenger, it's an empire builder. Nathaniel has ambitions; he wants to be great, to found a dynasty.

'Finally, it is unlikely that Nathaniel will believe that my mother was killed in the fire Arnie started and will probably connect Arnie's disappearance with Marina's; not to mention the loss of weapons and ammunition when the Motherwell people "discovered" the forward operating base Arnie was supposed to be establishing.' She paused and looking pointedly at Arnie and said, 'Correct?'

'Yes,' said Arnie. 'I tried to make it look like I was ambushed but we have to assume he will join the dots to make an arrow which points here.'

Jim decided it was time to speak up. 'So you're saying that he may come here to try and retake Marina, take revenge, and assert his authority as emperor of Glasgow.'

Arnie said, 'No, Jim, I don't think he cares about one woman, not even the mother of his children whom he was already trying to get rid of from Marina's account.'

Marina nodded and said, 'That's right. He has probably already told the children I am dead. He may send his thugs to try and make sure of it in fact, but certainly won't want me back. What he will do is make sure that I can't get near my children, and that no one else can get close enough to take them from him either.'

Natalie, sitting next to Marina, said, 'I think as a mother, I know something of what you must feel, Marina, but wouldn't going back to Glasgow simply give Nathaniel the opportunity to do away with you before you even set eyes on your children?'

Marina sighed. 'Yes, I have to accept that, thanks to Arnie, I am now separated from my children unless they can escape or be taken from him. I do need to be near them, to know they are well. Maybe if I agree to stay away, he may still let me live.'

Seeing that both Arnie and Jim were about to speak, Alexandra raised her hand a little and quickly said, 'On our own, there's now no way we can get the children back to Marina other than a full scale attack on Nathaniel in Glasgow and I am convinced that would be a bloodbath and probably fail. I think Arnie would agree with that assessment.'

'Certainly, apart from being heavily outnumbered, we would have to fight through city streets with prepared defence points. Absolutely the worst kind of fighting for an attacking force. Adding to that, we would be at least sixty miles from our base and much of that distance exposed to other hostile forces. It would be suicide.'

'Agreed,' interjected Alexandra.

Arnie almost sighed aloud in relief as he realised she wasn't planning to charge off to Glasgow with her mother.

'I sense a "but" coming,' said Jim.

'Yes, Jim, there's a "but",' said Alexandra. 'I suspect you and Arnie were worried I was about to propose a hare brained rescue mission and potentially threaten everything we have achieved here.'

She paused knowing that both Jim and Arnie looked awkward because that had been in their minds.

'Frankly, I'm disappointed that you men think I can't control my emotions. So old world masculine, don't you think?'

Prisca guffawed. 'Ha, she has got a point, Jim. You are such an old world man.'

Jim laughed. 'Well, if I knew what you were talking about, I might even agree.'

Natalie looked at Arnie's quizzical expression and saw he had no idea what Alexandra was planning for them all and it was worrying him. She said, 'You haven't got to the "but" yet, Alexandra.'

'Thank you, Natalie. I said we can't do it on our own but I fully intend that that bastard will fall. He has to be stopped. Not for revenge for what he has done, but to stop what he is capable of doing if we don't stop him.' Alexandra paused and everyone waited expectantly.

'To beat him, we need allies and we need to be clever, use our strengths and his weakness. I hope I am going to be able to count on your support as leaders of this community as I need to count on my mother's patience.'

Natalie spoke into the silence. 'If you are right about Nathaniel, then we are going to have to deal with him at some point. It makes sense to do it on our terms and as you say, use our strengths, allied with others that want to live peaceful and civilised lives. You wouldn't have come to us unless you already had a plan, so maybe you should just tell us and then we can eat.'

'I'm going to pay our respects to Colonel Peters in Stirling,' said Alexandra.

'What!' Arnie exploded, nearly falling off his chair.

Marina giggled and Alexandra smiled as Arnie got himself seated steadily again.

'It's not funny,' said Arnie. 'Stirling is an armed camp, and unlike a lot of the others, these guys actually know how to use their arms.'

Jim said, 'So you think you can make an ally of this Colonel Peters. I recognise the name. Isn't he the one who hanged looters in Haddington when Natalie was found.'

'He is,' said Natalie. 'It's strange but Nathaniel was also there that day. He was the ring leader of the looters.'

'I had forgotten that, Natalie,' said Alexandra. 'Another reason to bring the bastard down and perhaps, a man like Colonel Peters might see it as unfinished business.'

Prisca said thoughtfully, 'What do we know about this Peters other than he once hanged looters. I don't know much about the community at Stirling, but I don't think women are free there. How do we know he's really any better than Nathaniel's and his gangsters?'

'It's a risk, Prisca, but I learnt a bit about him and the community he leads in Stirling from Mikey. All I can say is that they might not be a lost cause, and they do have the military skill needed to deal with the would be emperor of Glasgow. I think Arnie can tell you more about him, but let's do eat please, I'm famished and the food smells delicious.'

'Amen to that,' said Jim, jumping up to organise the food he and Natalie had prepared earlier.

Waiting for the food to appear, Alexandra whispered to Arnie, 'What are you smirking about? Perhaps happy that we will be going to see your soldier pals.'

'Just delighted that you have surprised me yet again, and sorry if I disappointed you with my old world masculine thinking.' He laughed.

'So what do you think, will Peters see things our way?' She asked.

'Colonel Peters is an honourable man, he is just responding to the situation he finds himself in. His moral compass came from the chain of command and army traditions. Not having a chain of command all this time probably means he's a bit lost. You may be just what he needs if you can get past the gate.'

'That's what I'm gambling your, mine, and my mother's freedom on, that's he ready to accept a new chain of command. To be honest, my real fear is getting to the gate and finding that Nathaniel has already been calling, and persuaded Peters that strength rules in this new era and that they can carve up Scotland between them.'

'Hadn't thought of that, but I'm pretty sure Nathaniel is smart enough to see advantages to negotiating. Peters may not be concerned with Glasgow and its surrounds but Nathaniel is vulnerable if that changed.' He added, 'Why take Marina, you can't keep an eye on her all the time. She will distract you from the mission.'

'As you said, Peters is an honourable man, or at least honour is important to him. I heard from women in Motherwell that he punishes any man who abuses a woman in his community. My mother will open his eyes to what is really going on in Glasgow. I suspect he knows but chooses to ignore. Our mission is to make Glasgow an affront to Colonel Peters at the same time as drawing Nathaniel out of his lair and to a place he can be destroyed.'

Chapter Twenty-Five

Three weeks later, Alexandra once again sallied forth from the gates of Stainton. She had with her Arnie, her mother, Marina, and a small group of men handpicked by Arnie. Marina was almost unrecognisable, transformed by her freedom from the brothels of Glasgow. Her desire to be with her children by Nathaniel had not lessened, but she had promised her daughter she would not return to Glasgow until they had time to test her plan. In reality, she knew she had little alternative as returning to Glasgow would probably be the end of her and for no advantage.

They travelled in two cars and a small truck rather than horseback which had been their usual mode of travel. Arnie had decided the risk of vehicles attracting attention was outweighed by the ability to move quickly using the wide and still mostly usable motorway network. They were armed well enough to deter all but the most desperate or brazen raiders.

A few days before their deputation was due to leave, Arnie led a small group on horseback to scout for any traps or hazards on the roads they were to travel. He was being cautious as he knew the road would provide very thin pickings for raiders, as for some years now, few people travelled out of their own communities and when they did, they tended to avoid main routes.

Alexandra had been able to establish a radio communication with Colonel Peters, when a local short wave radio enthusiast had come across some coded radio traffic between Colonel Peters and a group of his men who for some reason had ventured to Kincardine. The man had brought the information to Jim as it was now unusual to have any kind of radio transmission other than that between the new communities. Taking the risk that the message could be overheard, Alexandra had messages broadcast on the frequency Colonel Peter's men had been using.

After a week of rebuffed and ignored messages, Colonel Peters himself spoke with Alexandra and a meeting was set up at an old motorway station on the outskirts of Stirling. It was now a fortified outpost permanently garrisoned.

Although Natalie and Jim shared some concern that the mission to Stirling was foolhardy, though both understood that the worst thing their little community could do was to pull up the drawbridge and try to survive in isolation. Arnie had reassured them that Nathaniel at least was probably fully occupied trying to break the community of Motherwell. However, many in the community they looked after grumbled and it was left to them to persuade and reassure as Alexandra left the community once more.

Alexandra, however, felt confident that at the very least, they would return safely and with a better understanding between Colonel Peters and the new communities. The radio communication had convinced her that she could work with Peters, even if they weren't going to share a vision of the future. The very fact that they had made contact by radio and were able to fuel vehicles to make the journey to Stirling had clearly impressed Peters.

Alexandra thought about Arnie's insight that Peters would not be comfortable without an external authority to report to. Arnie knew men like Peters, had worked with and for them. Having come from the ranks to the status of an officer, Alexandra understood why he both respected, but also mistrusted such men. Arnie had said that men like Peters outside of the institution of the army could be slightly comic figures with their mannerism and devotion to tradition and duty.

However, he said they were unusually dangerous men and should never be underestimated. They could be as ruthless in enforcing tradition and discipline as they could be efficient in the business of killing. He had said a man like Peters would be unfailingly polite, would not condone barbarity of any sort, but at the same time, would slit your throat without a second thought if it was in the line of duty. He said that Alexandra would find Peters to be a precise man, always well-groomed no matter the circumstances.

To an officer like Peters, cleanliness and order in all things was essential and applied with an almost obsessional quality. He would be completely confident about his right to command and to act independently within the authority proscribed to him by his superiors. He would tolerate no challenge or disruption to his chain of command. His soldiers would always be aware of his presence, but rarely hear more than stock phrases such as "good show", "well done that man".

He would listen to his junior officers but only on the rarest occasion discuss or debate. He would live with the decisions he made, justifying if called upon to senior officers but never to juniors. He would be used to being alone, responsible in charge. She thought about this; the man had been alone without superiors for over three decades. What had that done to him? What ways had he found to cope? What kept him going knowing that what had given him meaning was gone and wasn't coming back?

The journey to Stirling was uneventful and completed in half a day, so Alexandra arrived earlier than expected. Arnie had met her a mile away from the old service station. Thanks to the radio communication they had maintained with Colonel Peter's men, Arnie was confident that they would get past the barricades at least. As they approached the road barricade at the old service station and brought the cars to a halt, nerves began to grow taught.

After a few moments, a tall man in an officer's uniform and peaked cap walked casually up to the barrier, nodded to an unseen person and the barrier lifted. He walked casually forward with his hands clasped behind his back, then stopped and rocked gently on the balls of his feet.

Still sitting in the back of one of Stainton's vehicles, Alexandra smiled at Arnie. 'Time to go, let's not keep the gentleman waiting.' Arnie got out of the vehicle and held the door for Alexandra.

She strode forward confidently in her bright red coat, stopped in front of Colonel Peters and thrust out her hand.

'Welcome to Stirling, Alexandra. I am very eager to hear more about your travels around Scotland. I have to admit to having become quite insular.'

'Thank you, it's wonderful to have this opportunity to learn about the community of Stirling and to explore any mutual aid we may be able to help each other with.'

'Wonderful, will you let me escort you to the castle which is much more comfortable than this outpost. I assure you will be completely safe as will be your people.'

'Thank you, I would like my mother to accompany us. I think you will want to hear her story.'

'Be delighted to meet the lady, of course, and perhaps the tense looking chap by the car will want to join us. He has a military bearing about him so I am guessing he is your bodyguard I have heard about.'

'I believe you might have come across Arnie in the past. He is, as you say, my bodyguard, but more than that, a very trusted adviser.'

It took a few moments to organise the trip to the castle in the centre of Stirling. Alexandra and Colonel Peters, content that arrangements were in hand, went ahead in an open top jeep driven by one of Peter's soldiers.

As she had hoped, Colonel Peters was intrigued by news of the world outside of his "zone of control" as he saw it. During their conversation, he admitted to Alexandra that he and his people were largely unaware of how the rest of the world was coping. The radio contact from Alexandra and the "New Communities" had been the first outside communication they had received for many years.

After the failure of central power, he had seen his task as maintaining order in his force as best he could until the proper authorities were restored. When it had become apparent to him that this wasn't ever going to happen, he had simply given up trying to communicate with the rest of the world.

He said to Alexandra, 'I would be happy to take you on a tour of inspection later. Tomorrow perhaps if the weather is fine. We haven't done too bad you know. Life's not as comfortable as it is used to be but we are safe and won't starve in the immediate future. Power is our main problem. We have fuel and generators but it's a diminishing resource.'

Over a fine meal served in a banqueting hall in the ancient castle, Alexandra spoke of the new communities emerging all along Scotland's east coast and even extending into Northumbria. She spoke of how they defended themselves from the depredations of raiders and their support for the community at Motherwell against the forces of Nathaniel in Glasgow. Colonel Peters had some intelligence on Nathaniel as he had some problems with Glasgow based raiders looting remote farmsteads and stealing livestock.

He had laughed when she told him that Nathaniel had been in a group of looters in Haddington during the period of the transitional authority and narrowly escaped being hanged by Peters himself.

After the meal, they moved to a smaller room with a log fire and were served whisky by an immaculate soldier in a formal white uniform. Colonel Peters introduced the soldier. 'Matlock here has the most important duty in the whole garrison. Isn't that correct, Matlock?'

Matlock replied, 'Sir, yes, Sir.'

'Good man, Matlock, I think on this occasion, you could leave the bottle.'

'As you say, Sir. Will that be all?'

'Thank you, Matlock, that will be all, but please do make sure arrangement for accommodating our guests comfortably are in hand.'

Matlock left closing the door behind him.

'Perhaps you can guess what Matlock's most important duty is,' asked Colonel Peters smiling, and obviously enjoying this rare chance to socialise. 'Oh come, I admit to have been very impressed with you "new community" people, but you will go down in my estimation if you have not divined Matlock's function.' In response to the blank looks, he said, 'What, not even the SAS intelligence officer?'

Arnie laughed. 'I wondered if you remembered, lot of water under the bridge since those days, Sir.'

'Perhaps you have grown rusty, Lieutenant,' said Peters taking a sip of his whisky.

'Probably, but if your referring to Matlock's function, I would suggest that you have given the reformed alcoholic the critical security role of guarding the drinks cabinet. No more dangerous task in an army barrack than protecting the booze.'

'Well done, Lieutenant, but not just the cabinet but every drop available in this castle, and the whole community. My men are only allowed to drink when off duty and drunken behaviour is punished severely. Hard to maintain discipline when they have seen order collapse around them.'

Marina asked, 'Why on earth did you put an alcoholic in charge of alcohol. It seems, cruel?'

'Ah well, all of us survived, therefore we all know how cruel the world can be. However, being cruel to Matlock was not my objective. I'm sure the lieutenant can explain, Marina.'

Arnie understood that he was being tested and mildly ribbed at the same time but he played along. 'Well, let's see. I would suggest that Matlock is the kind of alcoholic who can resist until he takes that first sip. Once that sip hits his throat, his brain switches off and he won't stop until he falls over. Therefore, you don't have to worry about marking the bottles, the evidence of theft would be an inebriated Matlock.'

As Arnie finished, they all looked to Colonel Peters with expectation. Peters raised his glass to Arnie and smiled. 'Spot on, the years have not blunted your wits, Lieutenant. Matlock is a good soldier, but his younger days were blighted by drink. He often ended periods of leave in civilian or military jails. Just couldn't cope when he had the freedom to decide for himself. Never drank in uniform, could always be relied on and was even promoted a couple of times.

'Only to be punished with demotion after periods of leave. He would probably be dead by now if old world order hadn't collapsed. He would have finally been kicked out of the army and then, whether through violence or liver failure, he would have ended his days a miserable and pathetic figure. My solution has been that like me, he is never out of uniform and always faced with the temptation that he knows will be the end of him if he gives into it.'

Alexandra, who had listened as much to the interplay between Arnie and Peters as the story about Matlock, said to Peters. 'So if Matlock is like you in never being out of uniform, are you like him and always faced by a temptation?'

'Very perceptive, Alexandra,' said Colonel Peters. 'I can see that you and the lieutenant make a good team. Though I never have more than one measure, well maybe two for special occasions.'

'Power,' said Alexandra. 'That's the temptation you are always faced with.'

'Indeed, and like Matlock, I have to protect it, measure it, and serve it out every day.'

Marina spoke up. 'I know men who use their power badly, and you don't seem to be one of them. We haven't seen a lot of this community but it doesn't feel like a place where power is abused.'

'I am glad that Stirling is to your liking so far, Marina, but believe me, the temptation of power is with me always. For instance, if I was to lift that little bell and ring it once, Matlock or a guard would appear. I could if I so wished then order you all to be shackled and thrown into this castle's darker spaces. My soldiers would do it and would not question the order.'

Marina responded, 'That would be a poor end to a lovely evening, Colonel.'

'Agreed, my dear, but you take my point about temptation.' He continued with a smile. 'Perhaps if guests aren't so convivial, the temptation would be greater.'

'Now I think it's time for me to retire. I look forward to showing you more of our community tomorrow, as well as hearing more about the world beyond our walls. Please do use this room for as long as you wish. Do use the bell if there is anything you need.'

The following day, Peters continued to be a generous and amiable host as they spent the day touring the area controlled by his men. They met many people and began to discuss the ways they could help each other. It was obvious that power generation was their greatest problem as they were relying on a fast dwindling supply of stockpiled fuel.

Great windmills dotted the hillsides but were useless without the systems to take the power they could generate to where it was needed. Colonel Peters said he really needed an engineering regiment instead of his rifle and artillery men.

Marina and Peters were of a similar age and she became quite relaxed in his company and said as much to Alexandra.

'He doesn't seem to have a wife or a female companion,' said Marina in conversation to Alexandra and Arnie. 'Do you think he is gay?'

'No,' said Arnie. 'Matlock told me he was happily married. She survived the "death", but never recovered fully mentally or physically. He cared for her but she just seemed to fade away and nobody was surprised when she died about five years ago. Apparently, he has never looked at another women since. There was a daughter but she was lost in the "death".'

'I think he likes your company, Mother. Have you spoken to him about Nathaniel and the situation in Glasgow yet?' Alexandra asked.

Arnie added, 'We can't be too relaxed here. I'm worried about Mikey's situation in Motherwell. Nathaniel is pressing hard and they need help. They can fend him off but the attacks are strangling the community. They will have a tough winter if Nathaniel's not pushed back into Glasgow.'

'I will talk to him this evening, but I have a feeling he will not be easily persuaded even if he is sympathetic to my plight and to our cause,' said Marina.

Chapter Twenty-Six

Marina did speak to Colonel Peters of her personal situation and her need to rescue her children from Nathaniel. He had been generally aware of the plight of women in Glasgow, but she could sense his personal disgust as he learnt about how organised the abuse of woman was and how Nathaniel used woman to maintain his power. However, when she asked directly for his help in getting her children back, he simply said it was not possible.

Although he completely understood her asking, it was not in his power to help, and she would have to accept that for the time being they were lost to her.

At other levels, their mission to Stirling was going well. Alexandra was working with one of Colonel Peters' junior officer on plans to establish a bio-fuel facility. She was also arranging for people with appropriate skills to travel to Stirling to look at options for restoring some electrical power from existing turbines or establishing smaller scale new turbines.

In return for their help, Arnie persuaded Colonel Peters and a small group of his men to travel to Motherwell with him to establish a relationship with Mikey and his community. However, Colonel Peters was very clear that this would be recon only. If he thought there situation was not sustainable, he might be willing to bring Mikey and his community to Stirling, but they would have to accept his command.

A force of almost two hundred men set out from Stirling in a motorised column fuelled by bio-diesel brought from East Lowtown, which had been partly traded for surplus grain and cattle from farmsteads close to Stirling. A large part of the force were men from the Lammermoor communities. Arnie, although now used to working with untrained "irregulars", was well contented to have twenty of Colonel Peter's trained and well-armed men at the core of the force.

Peters and Arnie had agreed that the Lammermoor men should be formed in small groups of eight men under one of his soldiers who would give them some basic training and assess capabilities as they travelled. The force would be spearheaded by Colonel Peter's men commanded by one of his officers with Arnie in support.

Amongst the men from the Lammermoor communities was Thomas, the husband of Natalie Stainton's community mother.

'Thomas, what are you doing here?' Arnie asked by way of greeting.

'Nice to see you too, Arnie. I'm here to do my bit like the rest of our men,' said Thomas.

Arnie steered Thomas away from the group he was with and said, 'I didn't think Natalie or Jim, for that matter, were very keen on "Alexandra's latest adventure" and yet they have sent the largest contingent, including you.'

'Ah well, maybe I was after some excitement like a lot of our guys are. It seems my luck was in. Life can be a bit dull in our communities, endless work, endless squabbles and not much in the way of entertainment these days.'

Arnie knew Thomas, though brave enough, wasn't the sort to seek out adventure. He said, 'But aren't you about to become a father again. There are plenty of childless, partner-less men in the communities, why not send them?'

Thomas frowned at him. 'I have to take my chances the same as the rest of them. You know that, and besides, as I said, my luck was in. Haven't been to Stirling since the old world collapsed. Hope to have a look around before we move on. See you later, Arnie.'

Arnie later learnt that Jim and Natalie had decided who should go from Stainton's men by organising a lottery of all the able bodied adult men in the community. That explained Thomas insistence that his presence in the force was down to luck. To Arnie, it was the worst way possible to select men for a fighting force. However, he could see why Natalie and Jim would have taken the decision to do it this way.

It meant the whole community had a stake in the campaign, and thus helping to prevent splits between those in favour and those against. Hard for men chosen by lady luck to back out once the decision to go with a lottery had been made. In fact, there had been a general enthusiasm for the adventure by men in the communities, so the lottery chose from a group that would mostly have volunteered anyway. As Thomas had said, life in the communities offered limited chances for adventure.

Arnie reflected that things had changed for people in the communities in the last five years or so. The constant struggle for survival was now more mundane and peaceful enough that young men in particular were looking for excitement and adventure.

The journey to Motherwell was uneventful and with the men all in vehicles, it was relatively quick in spite of the constant stopping and starting whilst the roads were scouted out. They could have made it in one day but decided that they wanted to arrive with plenty of daylight left, so set up camp in an abandoned village with about ten miles still to travel. A festival mood grew in the men as they bonded in their new groups and had the opportunity to meet new people.

When they arrived, they found that Motherwell had been enjoying a reprieve from the constant low level fighting that had been taking place over the last three months. In fact, there had been no contact with Nathaniel's forces for over twenty-four hours. Arnie was instantly suspicious. Mikey was delighted and a little overwhelmed that this two hundred strong force with Arnie, Alexandra, and Colonel Peters had come to the aid of his community.

After introductions and welcomes, Arnie was keen to share his suspicions. 'Nathaniel's not stupid, why would he back off when he knows he has you pinned down?' He asked Mikey. There had been no counter attack or blow that would make him lick his wounds.

'We are not sure, maybe he got wind of your group arriving,' said Mikey. 'After all, no one around here has seen two APC's (armoured personnel carriers), two heavy trucks and a couple of bikes with side cars for quite some time. It would make me think again.'

Colonel Peters said, 'Not impossible, Sergeant, but this trip hasn't been long in the planning. Two weeks at the very most and information doesn't travel as quickly as it used to. Even if we have loose talk in the camp or even a traitor, it would take time to learn about us setting out from Stirling only thirty-six hours ago. It's more likely that somethings afoot, and that he has been planning it for a while.

'Our arrival might well give him pause for thought in whatever he was planning though. If he is as smart as you both think he is, then he will have had people watching your gates. However, that we arrived completely without resistance suggests he had no conception of you receiving aid from outside. Otherwise, one presumes he would have made some effort to stop said aid arriving. You have had scouting parties out I assume.'

'Yes, we do, and as far as we can tell, his forces haven't moved. We still have a couple of working drones and have had them out for a look. They are where we expect them to be. They are just not attacking.'

'Hmm, more intelligence needed, gentlemen. What's the enemy up to? Is he having a rest, short of ammunition or plotting dastardly deeds. Perhaps some real human intelligence might do the trick, Lieutenant. What do you think?'

'Prisoners you mean,' said Arnie. 'He keeps a tight ship; the only ones that would really know what's going on would be his captains.'

'Captains have to give orders to get things done so we might learn something from a prisoner from the ranks, but maybe the two of you could come up with a ploy to tempt one of these captains into a place where he could be bagged alive.'

Alexandra could sense that Colonel Peters was enjoying the company and the sense of a shared mission. She smiled as she said, 'You will need something very tempting to bait your trap with if you want to catch one of the big rats.'

Mikey said, 'Have you got something in mind then, Alexandra?'

'What is the greatest prize for those men?' Alexandra asked.

'Women of course,' said Mikey.

'Oh no, that is not happening,' said Arnie.

'Not your decision, but I'm sure you will able to protect me, Arnie. After all, it is us that will be setting the trap.'

'I'm afraid I agree with the lieutenant. You would be too great a loss, and these things have a habit of not going to plan.' Colonel Peters held up his hand as he saw she was about to protest. 'However, the idea of baiting a trap with women is a sound one, but perhaps a little play acting would suffice.'

Arnie eager to divert Alexandra, said, 'Yes, yes, that would work. We dress up some men. We make them believe the famous Alexandra is amongst them. Not so difficult with that red coat.'

Colonel Peters said, 'Well, that settles the bait. How shall we set the trap?'

Mikey said, 'I have an idea that might just work. That red coat is probably famous enough that it might just do the trick. We know where they are and where we can be seen from. So if we let them see the red coat in what seems a vulnerable spot then word will get back of an opportunity to capture women and Alexandra in particular.

'The bio-diesel facility you helped us establish is in fact a vulnerable spot for us and we know they keep an eye on it. Hopefully, someone who knows the significance of the red coat is watching and that somebody might just want to impress the boss enough to risk a close encounter.'

Arnie scowled and said, 'Maybe, or maybe a sniper will be sent to put a hole in the coat.'

Over the rest of the day, a plan was worked out to try and lure some of Nathaniel's force to a position where they could be captured. Under cover of night, they moved men into the most likely approach positions with instructions to remain invisible until a signal was given. Their task was to cut off and capture retreating men if the bait was taken and the trap sprung. This task was given to Mikey's men as they knew the ground well.

Thomas volunteered with some good humour to be dressed up as Alexandra. Arnie stressed that he was to make sure the coat was seen coming and going to the bio-diesel plant but not too make to obvious a target. This was both for his own safety and so that his disguise was not put under too much scrutiny. Beth often looked after the plant anyway and so may have already been observed coming and going would make sure he didn't take too many risks.

Everything was in position Thomas and Beth settled down to wait and see if the bait would be taken. They worked on the bio-diesel plant just running checks on the process and adding more feed stock as much to pass the time as to take their mind off what might happen.

But nothing happened. Twenty-four hours later, there was no sign of any activity by Nathaniel's men. They couldn't leave Mikey's men in their hiding places much longer so they decided to call off the operation. It was then that an attack did develop but at the community's main gate. The gate came under fire from a mortar and after a half dozen mortar rounds, a pick-up truck with a heavy gun on the back bumped over a field and started to lay down fire on the gate.

The community was well drilled in how to respond to attacks on its perimeter and were soon responding. The pick-up was quickly disabled and its weapon was silenced. At least one of the occupants was wounded or killed and the others took to ground.

Arnie, Mikey, and Colonel Peters had been debriefing the men who had been hiding in anticipation of an attack on the bio-diesel plant when the attack happened.

'Got to be diversionary,' said Arnie as they heard about the pick-up being disabled and the mortar attack seeming to have stopped.

'Agreed,' said Peters, 'but what are they up to it doesn't seem to be the bio-diesel facility or Alexandra.'

Mikey joined in the discussion. 'This is the first attack even attempting to get into the town through a direct assault. The others have all been sneak attacks or opportunistic on farmsteads or on groups out with the walls. Maybe they are just probing.'

Colonel Peters replied, 'Possibly, but strange that they had let up on attacks and now attempt a siege on your main gate, and we haven't seen any evidence of their forces since we got here.'

Arnie said, 'We still need more information, and maybe that's their goal, especially since they must know of our arrival in force.' Mikey suddenly interrupted the discussion, 'Shit, what's that now.' Arnie and Peters looked at each other and then they both heard what Mikey must have heard first, a noise of tearing metal getting louder.

One of Mikey's men burst in. 'Trouble, Mikey, they seem to have found a way to get to our scrap wall without us seeing and they are using some kind of winch to pull it down.'

Mikey said, 'Right, get a perimeter behind the wall and be prepared for an assault.'

Arnie and Peters left the room, Peters to assemble the men under his control as it had been agreed that their best use in the event of an assault was to fill gaps and repel any breeches of the defences. Arnie went to find Alexandra, her protection being his role.

As he left to find Alexandra, he heard small arms fire and then the plopping sound of the mortar fire starting again.

Alexandra was with Thomas and Beth and hurriedly exchanging clothes after their aborted plan to trap one of Nathaniel's captains. Seeing Arnie, Alexandra said, 'What's happening?'

'An assault on a section of the scrap wall as far as we can gather at the moment. It may just be them probing for weaknesses but it does seem a step up from their previous attacks. I'm sure Mikey will sort it out but we should get you to one of the armoured cars just in case things go badly.'

Beth said, 'I'd better get back to the bio-diesel plant and shut it down. It's too vulnerable to damage from explosion or even small arms fire and could be a big problem if they target it.'

Thomas said, 'I'll go with you, Beth.'

Alexandra looked alarmed and said, 'No, you come with Arnie and I.'

'I know the plant and it's probably the most use I can be in this situation,' replied Thomas.

'I could use his help,' said Beth. 'We will shut it down and try and disperse the stored diesel so it's less risk of all going up together.'

Alexandra wanted to insist but Arnie said, 'Time to move,' and the moment was gone.

Chapter Twenty-Seven

The attack on Mikey's town lasted for more than eight hours and it became apparent that Nathaniel had assembled a significant force with a couple of hundred or so men, armed with everything from automatic rifles to shotguns. They had the mortar but apparently, not very much ammunition for it as well as the two pick-ups with heavy machine guns mounted on them. The attack on the main gate had been a diversion drawing attention from the crew that had pulled heavy winch cables across rough ground to attach to the scrap wall which had been built to secure the community from raiders.

They had succeeded in demolishing a section of the wall, opening a way into the community that they had hoped to take advantage of with a massed attack. They may have had much more success, but the mortar crew were poorly trained and, attempting to cover an advance across open ground to the wall, dropped two rounds short amidst their own advancing men.

Although the mortars didn't actually cause more than a few light wounds, it did stall the attack and send the men back to cover, allowing Mikey's forces supported by Colonel Peters soldiers and the Lammermoor men the time they needed to establish a defence around the destroyed wall. The next attack met accurate fire that caused many casualties and although some of Nathaniel's men did get into the community, it was too few to do anything other than cause some havoc before they were hunted down and killed or captured.

Colonel Peters, himself in an armoured personnel carrier, led a counterattack that captured the mortar and its crew, and dispersed the surviving attackers who escaped with the remaining pick-up.

As night fell, Colonel Peters, Arnie and Mikey met to review reports on the attack.

'How many casualties, Mikey? We seem to have three injured, two are minor and the other will survive,' asked Colonel Peters.

'We weren't so lucky. Beth was killed and she will be a great loss to us. But it could have been a lot worse,' said Mikey.

'And from your men, Arnie?' Colonel Peters asked.

'One missing. Thomas who was with Beth at the bio-diesel facility, so we have to assume he was taken prisoner,' said Arnie. 'You were right about it being a vulnerable spot; it looks like a separate force got into the facility. As with Thomas, it looks like they have managed to take off with quite a bit of fuel. That says to me that it was a planned action rather than a lucky find.

'They would have needed some way of moving that amount of fuel. It looks they siphoned it from your drums probably to make it easier to manhandle to whatever transport they had waiting.'

Colonel Peters said, 'It seems that your fuel was at least one of Nathaniel's objectives in this assault. Perhaps on this occasion, Alexandra was wrong about women being the greatest prize for these bandits. Perhaps he was trading lives for fuel, and anything else including capturing women would have been a bonus.'

Chapter Twenty-Eight

Thomas slowly came to consciousness and immediately wished he hadn't as a wave of pain flooded his brain. It was so intense, he couldn't at first pin point which part of his body it came from. The pain began to subside enough for him to realise that he had a wound to his stomach, which had been roughly dressed. He was lying under a camouflage netting amongst boxes and crates of various sizes and descriptions.

His feet were tied and a boy, not yet a teenager, sat on a box holding a weapon which was pointed at him. Thomas focused on the boy as a wave of nausea began to make the space between the boxes pulsate. He squeezed his eyes shut hoping to control the nausea enough to be able to focus on the boy, but when he opened his eyes again, the boy was gone. He was wondering if he had been hallucinating when the boy returned this time followed by two men.

One of the men bent down and he felt an additional ping of pain and then an ecstatic relief as the painkiller the man had administered glided through his body. The man who had given the painkiller rose to his feet and said to the other man who was clearly in control. 'It should last for an hour or so.' He then left the room.

'Can you hear me?' A tall, thin man who remained said. He was dressed in combat fatigues of green and black but no insignia or rank.

Thomas murmured a yes, though his mouth was very dry and his tongue felt unwieldy.

'Sit him up, Nathan,' said the man to the boy who had been guarding him. The boy went to grab at Thomas' shoulders.

'Do it carefully, we don't want him passing out.'

Thomas, although grateful for the release from the pain he had been in, began to understand that his situation was ominous. He had not had any sense of warmth or friendship in the help he was being given by this man who obviously controlled his fate. Thomas worked with Nathan to prop himself up against a large packing box. 'Water, can I have some water?'

The man said, 'Fetch some water, Nathan,' and although the boy responded immediately, the look on his face told Thomas he felt these tasks were below his dignity.

The man had thin hair tied into a pony tail, probably in his late thirties or early forties. He sat on a box opposite Thomas and lit a cigarette. A moment later, Nathan was back with the water and the man held out his hand to take it from Nathan. He held it for a moment before passing it to Thomas, as he did he said, 'You have a stomach wound, I don't recommend you swallow this.'

Thomas took the cup and put it to his mouth and was grateful for the coolness in his mouth. He found it very hard not to swallow. Spitting the water out the set the cup on the floor at his side and looked at the casually smoking man. He asked, 'How bad is it?'

'You could live with surgery,' was the emotionless response.

Thomas was very alert to the implication that his fate was in the balance. 'Who are you?' He asked.

'My name is Nathaniel and this is my son, Nathan. You may have heard of me.' This was said in a conversational tone that only amplified the sense of threat coming from him.

Thomas sighed to himself and said, 'Yes, I have heard of you.' He added with a note of calm resignation, 'None of it good, I'm afraid.'

Nathaniel laughed. 'I'm glad you have a sense of humour, Thomas.'

'You know my name then,' said Thomas.

'Yes, we know a lot about our guest don't we, Nathan?'

Nathan nodded and took a crumpled sheet of paper from his pocket.

Thomas sighed inwardly as he recognised a letter he had been writing to Natalie.

Nathan said sarcastically, 'He's got lovely handwriting and writes so tenderly to his Natalie.'

'Nothing to be ashamed of in that, Nathan, but do we know where he is from?'

'Nothing in this to say where he is from, nor what he is doing so far from home,' replied Nathan.

'I'm from Jedburgh,' lied Thomas hoping to distract them away from his own community.

'That's unlikely don't you think, Nathan. I'm pretty sure Jedburgh is one of our many new ghost towns.'

'Shall I persuade him to tell the truth, Dad?'

'Now, now, Nathan, let's not be inhospitable to our guest. Perhaps he is trying to be noble and protect his Natalie from bad people like me and you. Is that right, Thomas?' Nathaniel smiled. 'Are you being noble and protecting your loved ones?'

Thomas persisted with his lie. 'I'm not lying. Jedburgh used to be a ghost town as you called it but refugees from the north east of England have established a community there and I joined them about a year ago. It's well defended, you won't find easy pickings to raid there.'

'Well, that's interesting, isn't it, Nathan. I suppose it is one of these tiresome new communities that Alexandra is so involved with.' Nathaniel paused but when Thomas did not take the bait, he continued, 'We are very interested in Alexandra and how she has managed to involve herself and that old rascal Colonel Peters in things that are not their business.'

Thomas said, 'I don't know anything. I was just told to pack my gear and come here to help with a bio-diesel plant.'

'Bio-diesel, what's that?' Nathan asked.

Thomas said, 'It's fuel made from plant or animal waste. It will work in old diesel engines, although it's pretty dirty stuff.'

'Interesting indeed. We found quite a bit of fuel in the place we found you. We knew they were making it. Our men had been observing this place with lots of pipes and tanks that smelt bad and seemed important.' Nathaniel was speaking to Nathan but turned his attention back to Thomas. 'Interesting, Thomas, that you would come from Jedburgh to help with such a very useful endeavour. However, what I need to know from you is what you, or more precisely, Alexandra and Colonel Peters are doing here?'

'We were just helping the people of Motherwell.' That produced an ugly snarl from Nathan, which made Thomas wonder how two people who shared a mother could be so different. He knew that Marina had two children with Nathaniel and was guessing that this Nathan was one of them.

'Very noble of you, I'm sure,' said Nathaniel.

'Shall I kill him now, Dad?'

Nathaniel stood up and with a warm smile placed a fatherly arm around Nathan's shoulders. 'Oh Nathan my boy, sometimes you have to show mercy to a defeated enemy. That would be the noble thing to do you know.' They both laughed at this until Nathaniel suddenly turned to Thomas all sense of mirth gone from his face. 'I want to know how many came with you and how they were armed.'

'About thirty,' lied Thomas. 'We had rifles, shotguns and some of Colonel Peter's men had automatic weapons. We brought some food in a lorry.' He tried only to give them what they probably already knew or could work out.

'Only thirty, my men must have exaggerated then, Thomas. How many are Colonel Peters' old soldiers?' Nathaniel snapped.

'Maybe half. The gossip amongst the men was that Alexandra wanted him to bring more but he refused,' said Thomas hoping that detail would gain him some credibility in Nathaniel's eyes.

'So who is in charge, the old soldier or the revolutionary in the red coat?'

'I'm not sure, they kind of both do, we get our orders from Alexandra, but Colonel Peters' men only listen to him.'

'Interesting, but we can't sit around chatting all day,' said Nathaniel and turned to leave.

Nathan asked, 'What do you want done with him?'

Nathaniel paused, lit a cigarette, and said, 'Oh dear, well, let me see. What would be the noble thing to do?'

Thomas tried to suppress the growing fear that he was going to be left to die of his wound, or maybe even die in the next few moments.

Still with his back to Thomas, Nathaniel said, 'Come on, Nathan, my boy. Advise your father what the noble, the honourable thing to do with our valiant enemy?'

Nathan looked a little confused for a moment and then said, 'Blow his brains out?'

'Good answer, not the traditional answer, but very modern and so practical. Well done, my boy.' Nathaniel stubbed out his cigarette with the toe of his boot and walked away.

Chapter Twenty-Nine

The hay barn of East Lowtown doubled as a meeting place for the people of the community. Today, it was decked out with greenery and flowers. Long trestle tables lined the space with an assortment of benches and chairs pressed into service to provide seating for all the guests. It was the day of Natalie's birthday.

That morning, Natalie had travelled the five or six miles to Stainton where she was to be honoured with a presentation by most of the community mothers in south east Scotland and a few who had travelled from further afield. Kenny had insisted that East Lowtown was far too small a place for the presentation and that she must travel. It was also the opportunity the people of East Lowtown needed for the "surprise" birthday party.

As she left the gates of East Lowtown, she found the whole community gathered and singing the happy birthday song. Embarrassed and delighted at the same time, she thanked them all by saying that she wanted no other present than to be allowed to return to their community and friendship as soon as possible.

A working car had been brought from Stainton the day before as East Lowtown possessed nothing finer than a tractor and a couple of decidedly agricultural pick-up trucks. Getting into the car, the door of which was very formally held open by a tense looking Kenny, she reflected it had been many years, even decades, since she had travelled in such comfort. Kenny kept her company in the backseat of the car, though he would play no part in the presentation, being an exclusively female event.

Kenny rattled on about the day's itinerary, even though he had already tried her patience by going over it several times in the last few days. The presentation would take most of the afternoon, but he expected them to be back in Lowtown by 6pm. They would be accompanied by an honour guard of community fathers led by Kenny, which no doubt, thought Natalie, would be the source of much of his excitement and nervousness.

Kenny was a young man and it was an honour and responsibility for him to be seen as leading so many of the new world's influential men. Natalie was glad for him. It would boost his confidence and his standing in East Lowtown as well as amongst the other communities.

Once Kenny had relaxed a little, she turned to him and said, 'Tell me of the raiders, Kenny, it has been sometime since we were last bothered by them.'

'Yes, they were heading to Jedburgh, quite a large band but very ill disciplined and poorly armed, thank goodness.'

'Was there fighting?' Natalie asked.

'Some; we managed to get ahead of them and stopped them without too much difficulty. There was a short fire fight but they were completely out-gunned and most quickly surrendered. A few ran off but we don't think too many got away. We sent runners to warn all the local farmsteads to be vigilant.'

'What did you do with the captured men?' Natalie asked with a slight sense of dread.

'We took all their weapons and herded them back towards Edinburgh. Then we let them go. Quite a few of our men wanted to slit their throats. Their blood was up after the fight and many had lost friends or family to raiders in the past. Others argued that letting them go would only mean they would cause trouble elsewhere. An argument which I can't help having sympathy with.'

Natalie said, 'You stopped the men from killing even though you lost family to raiders and have had to fight them for your life many times?'

'Yes,' he sighed. 'I have no love of raiders and they have hurt many of us.' He looked at Natalie first before saying, 'I know today, your birthday is also the day your Thomas was killed by Nathaniel.'

'Thank you for remembering Thomas. Even after forty years, I rather dread my birthday. However, my Thomas hated violence. He was the most forgiving and loving person I ever knew. Love and forgiveness are not easy in our world. Kenny, why did you stop the men killing those raiders?'

'Alexandra says that if we let hate rule our actions, then we will become what we hate. Her words were in my mind and they stopped me from killing or allowing our men to kill the captured raiders. I've have done it before you know. Killed prisoners I mean.'

'I know, and I don't judge you for it, but maybe it is time for us to allow love and forgiveness a bigger space in our lives. Alexandra's words are wise.'

Natalie could almost see the cogs turning as Kenny reflected quietly for a moment.

Kenny said, 'I knew those men were no real threat to the communities now. They were just a pathetic bunch of no hopers. They were mostly men expelled from the new communities of Fife who hadn't found much of a welcome amongst what's left of the Edinburgh gangs. I certainly didn't feel forgiveness for them, just hate. In a way, their weakness made my hate and desire to hurt them stronger rather than weaker. I reckon that's how people become bullies and it was then that Alexandra's words came into my head.'

Natalie smiled. It was the most mature thing she had ever heard Kenny say in the time that she had known him. She said, 'You acted well, Kenny. If the communities represent civilisation and rule of law, then we must try and carry that with us at all times and not shrug it off when it does not suit our immediate desires or goals. Being strong is a wonderful thing. We can defend ourselves better than we ever could, but strength is easily abused when it is used on those weaker than you. So you acted well, you used your strength well.'

'Thank you, Natalie,' said Kenny and then changed the subject. 'Are you looking forward to the presentation?'

'I think I am. There are so many women that I have met and admired amongst the community mothers. They do me a great honour.'

'You deserve it,' said Kenny simply.

'Why thank you, Kenny, and I hope you will give as much respect to Lowtown's next community mother.'

'I'm sure you have many more birthdays to come yet,' said Kenny thinking that she referred to the end of her life rather than the end of her time as a community mother.

'Hopefully,' she replied but not as a community mother.

'What do you mean?' Kenny asked with mixed suspicion and concern.

'I want you to know first, out of respect for you and your role as "father", but you must promise me that you will keep it to yourself. Just for a little while.' Seeing assent as well as curiosity in his eyes, she continued, 'I am going to announce my resignation.'

'When?' A startled Kenny said, who had no idea she was planning this and had assumed she would just continue until she died.

'Tonight at the surprise party,' she said in answer to his question but couldn't quite keep a smile from the corners of her mouth.

'Why…you crafty old bird,' it was out of his mouth before he realised he had spoken his thoughts aloud. She had surprised him twice in a matter of seconds once with her resignation and then with her knowledge of the "surprise" party. He wondered how long she had known and cringed at all his elaborate attempts to maintain the secret.

'Sorry, no offence, you aren't supposed to know about the party.' He shook his head and said, 'I should have known you would find out.'

'No offence taken, Kenny, I'm sorry it has come as a shock to you.'

'Alexandra told me never to underestimate you,' was his oblique reply.

'Did she indeed?'

'Yes, in fact it was when I called in at Jedburgh after dispersing those raiders. I was summoned to her rooms and she asked about the raiders, about Lowtown and then how you were keeping. I told her that you were well and that Lowtown was proud to have you as their mother.'

'Oh and what did Alexandra have to say to that?' She didn't even try to disguise her curiosity.

'I remember exactly what she said,' and he quoted Alexandra. "People always underestimate Natalie, Kenny. Other women especially. Something I have also been guilty of. So, Kenny, my boy, don't believe because she is old, she won't surprise you from time to time."

'Then she laughed, it did feel a bit like she was laughing at me. I felt about two inches tall in front of her and don't mind admitting I was glad to get out of her rooms.'

'Well, it's your turn to surprise me now, Kenny,' said Natalie.

'You mean because Alexandra spoke well of you,' said Kenny who was aware of the historic feud between the two women, although they had never spoken about it.

'No,' she said sternly but with a twinkle in her eye. 'I am surprised she thought so well of you that she saw fit to grant you a private audience.'

For a moment, Kenny thought he was being rebuked but then he saw that she was smiling and as she began to laugh, he joined her.

For the rest of their short journey, Kenny asked her for memories of her long life. He knew that she had survived the "death" and the collapse of the old world. He knew that she had helped establish several new communities and was the first ever community mother. He also knew that she had been partnered three times and had borne six children. He wanted to find something that was not on the public record of this remarkable women. Something that might bring to life the speech he was tasked with giving that evening.

As they neared Stainton, he knew that it was probably his last chance he would have to speak to her privately all day. He summoned up his courage and asked, 'Why have you and Alexandra not spoken for so long?'

'A man of course.' She laughed.

'A man, no, I can't believe that,' said an astounded Kenny.

'Alexandra was in love with Thomas but he chose me, and I blamed her for Thomas' death, unfairly, but I felt it strongly at the time of his death.'

'I wish I had known Thomas,' said Kenny.

'He would have liked you I think, but here we are. Are you ready to face the crowd?'

Chapter Thirty

It had already been a long day for Natalie. The journey to Stainton and the presentation from her fellow community mothers had all gone without a hitch and had seemed to be enjoyed by all. As she travelled home to East Lowtown, although tired, she relished the prospect of a smaller, more intimate party with her own community that she expected to be surprised with on her return. In the car with her were her three daughters. Her sons rode along with Kenny and her escort of community fathers from near and far.

She loved all her children but her daughters were a delight to her, each different but all strong in their own ways. She was very happy that they had all been with her at the presentation, and were now to join her in Lowtown for the evening. It was good that they all should hear that she planned to retire at the same time.

Her three partners had each given her the gift of a daughter, before they had perished in the journey from the old to the new world. Her sons were all the result of her first love, Thomas. The eldest was now older than Thomas when his life was ended so callously by Nathaniel. Each of her sons were fashioned so closely in Thomas' image that at times, it hurt to look at them.

'What are you thinking, Mother?' Daisy said, interrupting her mother's thoughts. She had named each of her daughters after plants that she loved. In addition to Daisy, there was Heather and Rose. Daisy was the oldest and was Thomas' child, though he never lived to see her.

'I was thinking of your father, Daisy, and how much your brothers look like him,' she replied honestly.

'You know, I have been asked if they are triplets, they look so much like each other,' said Daisy.

Heather joined the conversation. 'Well, when you know them, you can't confuse them. Only Tomas isn't a big pain in the ass, and that's only because he is a little pain in the ass.' She giggled.

Rose came to her brother's defence. 'Oh, Heather, you have always been mean to our brothers. I hope for our mother's sake that you don't start any arguments tonight.'

'Rose, you should know that I don't start arguments, I finish them,' replied Heather primly.

Daisy interrupted to head off a familiar family discussion. 'Did you enjoy the presentation, Mother? We were all so proud of you.'

'Not as proud as I am of you girls and your brothers,' replied Natalie. 'I did enjoy the presentation, it was lovely of people to think of giving me such an honour.'

'You deserve it, Mother,' said Heather. 'Your life, more than any other, represents the success of the new communities in defeating barbarism. You have helped to shape a new world that is safe and civilised.' Heather had recently followed in her mother's footsteps in becoming a community mother. Unlike Natalie, she had sought out the role as a politician seeks out a political office. Natalie admired her ambition and drive, but knew it also prevented her from hearing how grandiose she could sound at times.

'That's very kind of you, Heather, but you know all I ever wanted was to survive and bring up my children to be kind and decent people. I was no different to the vast majority of people who tried to pick up the pieces and make a new life as best we could.'

'You are far too modest, Mother,' exclaimed Daisy. 'Can you imagine Alexandra saying such a thing and yet you have been as important to the new world as she has been.'

'I thought Alexandra would say something at the presentation but she sat mute through the whole thing,' said Rose.

'What is it between you and Alexandra, Mother?' Heather asked bluntly even for her.

'What makes you think there is anything between us, as you put it,' responded Natalie with only a hint of irritation, but enough to be heard by her daughters. The irritation was in reality more tiredness than annoyance at the familiar if often unspoken question.

Looking at her elderly mother who rarely allowed irritation, let alone anger, into her voice, Heather wondered whether she had gone too far with her question. She was also aware of her sisters and their much more palpable annoyance with her at breaking the family taboo on the subject of Alexandra.

'Well, Mother, all we know is that you and Alexandra don't speak to each other and avoid each other whenever possible,' persisted Heather to the obvious annoyance of her sisters.

'What consequence is it that two elderly women have not spoken for a little while? I don't see anything for you to worry about, Heather,' said Natalie with a note of reproof that she hoped would be enough to steer her daughter from the subject of Alexandra.

However, Heather was not to be diverted and deliberately avoiding the eyes of her sisters, she once again persisted with her question, 'But, Mother, you must know that the gossip mongers in the communities come up with all kinds of stories about the two of you.'

Natalie had never really understood people's fascination with her relationship with Alexandra, but here it was written on the faces of her daughters. Heather was eager but the other two were just as intrigued.

Perhaps because she was contemplating change and ending in her life, she decided she would speak to her daughters of the relationship with Alexandra, but she let Heather's question hang for a few moments.

'Well, Heather, I can see your sisters also share your thirst for knowledge on this subject. Though they don't seem to be as parched as yourself,' that was said with a little more sarcasm than intended but she enjoyed Rose and Daisy's small smiles and Heather's frown.

There was an immediate hush in the car and Natalie also sensed that the driver had dropped a gear and slowed from very slow to a minimal speed.

'How to begin?' Natalie said as if to herself but into the silent expectation of the car. Looking out of the car window, she began to talk in a quiet but firm voice.

'I have loved Alexandra from the moment she took me into her arms from beneath a burnt out car at the old supermarket in Haddington. Before that day in Haddington, I was a young woman, a girl really, who survived the "death" but had lost her parents and the future she had been planning for. I felt I had lost everything, but that day taught me there was more to lose and it was Nathaniel and those he led who took it from me.

'I am so glad that you girls do not really know what it was like to be young and female in the years after the "death". It was not just that I had been raped by Nathaniel and others that followed him.' Natalie paused in her monologue to allow her daughters a moment to absorb the revelation of her abuse which she had so far protected them from. She raised her voice to still the incipient questions and condolence.

'Even had that not happened, I still wouldn't have been able to cope with being a woman amongst so many men. As Alexandra would say, I had not yet learnt the power of my femaleness.' Natalie laughed a little and looking at Heather in particular said to them all, 'I hope that is a power you have all learnt, and knowing it, can use it well.'

After a short pause, she again looked out of the window and continued with her story. 'As I said, I thought I had lost everything, but after being rescued and going to live in Stainton, I rediscovered family, and the warmth, support and security that comes from having trusted people in your life. More than anybody else, it was Alexandra who taught me to feel strong again. Although a little younger than me, it was her who taught me to be a woman in this new world.

'She was simply magnificent. Where other women covered themselves up and hid, even hiding behind men who abused them for the sake of protection from worse, Alexandra was confident, independent and resilient. Of course all the men desired her, not just because she was young and beautiful, but mostly it was that she emanated confidence and belief in herself and what she was becoming. For many years, we were inseparable like sisters not just best friends. We talked all the time and shared everything.

'I was absolutely in love with her, she was, in my eyes, perfect, and she could do no wrong.' Natalie smiled at her reflection in the window as she said, 'Though in retrospect, she frequently did, but was rarely caught in the wrong doing. We did have fun even though it was a hard world to live in.'

'Then we grew up I suppose. Alexandra's mother and our friend, Brenda, was taken from Stainton after a raid that nearly overwhelmed our little community. Of course, Alexandra led the men who went to search for her mother and Brenda. Amongst the men who followed Alexandra in her red coat out of the battered gates of Stainton was the man I was beginning to love, and who, though I didn't know it at the time, was in love with me. The journey those men made with Alexandra lasted for three months before they came back to Stainton.

'You understand that in those day only "raiders" were on the road for that length of time, most people cowered behind walls or hid away. They failed to find any sign of Marina or Brenda, but for Alexandra, that journey was the start of an even greater journey. In the time searching for her mother and our friend, Alexandra found the two loves of her life, one was a man and the other was an idea. The idea was what you all now live in, the "new world", an alliance of gender balanced democratic communities led by "community parents".'

Natalie paused and it was too much for her daughters to wait for her to continue.

'Who was the man, Mother? You must tell who the man was,' blurted out Daisy.

'The man was your and your brother's father,' said Natalie as she turned from the window to look at her daughters.

Taking in the surprised looks, she said, 'It's such a shame none of you got to know Thomas before he was killed. He was such a loving man.'

That Alexandra had been in loved with Thomas, who they knew only as legend, was a complete surprise to the three sisters. Natalie had never spoken so openly about her life and loves to them before and it made them all feel somewhat older and more adult that she was entrusting them with her story. They could feel the terms of their relationship with their mother shifting as she continued with her story.

'When Thomas chose me over Alexandra, our relationship changed. She became cold, even a little hostile towards me. I was no longer her confidant in all things. For years, it seemed to me that she was simply jealous, that I had what she wanted and she couldn't accept that. She was confident, respected and powerful; she was used to getting what she wanted from people. I thought she would come to terms with my and Thomas' relationship, especially after we married and your brothers came into the world.

'She didn't. Instead, our relationship settled into a cold and frosty respect. My role as a community mother brought us together on a regular basis as she sought support from Stainton and then Lowtown for what I came to think of as her "adventures". Alexandra's passion for and faith in the possibility of "a new world" was infectious and she had begun to have success in creating like-minded communities all along the east coast of Scotland. Her reputation travelled wide and she was treated with something approaching awe.

'As you know, she was never a community mother but there is not one community mother or father alive or dead that she did not support and mentor. We all came to rely on her to be the link between the new communities and the core of our mission to make surviving the wreckage of the old world more than just living from one day to the next. Many years passed and our relationship showed no sign of improving.

'I was busy raising children as well as supporting a community to overcome the collapse of civil order and infrastructure, so I have to admit that Alexandra was not a priority for me. I was sad about the coolness between us and missed the friendship, but annoyed at what seemed to me as pettiness in the not infrequent jibes and little digs in what communication we did have. Then not long after I discovered that I was pregnant again—with you, Daisy, Thomas and I travelled to Jedburgh for a celebration of the founding of that community.'

Natalie paused to order her thoughts, there was a lot to tell and they were already within a few miles of the gates to Lowtown. Smiling at the rapt attention on the face of her daughters, and the alertness in the set of the driver's shoulders as he steered the car on in its now painfully slow journey, she took up her story again.

'Well, as I said, Thomas and I had gone to Jedburgh and we had taken the boys with us. It was kind of holiday for us all. The day after the formal celebrations, I had slept late and Thomas had taken the boys to play at the river. Following the sound of their play, I noticed a splash of red in some scrubby trees overlooking the river. I knew it must be Alexandra in that already famous red coat, and the recognition made me pause.

'My encounters with her had become so frosty by then that I admit, I didn't relish the idea of meeting her. I watched her as I thought about what to do. Should I go by her, which was the direct route, or move further down the river before coming back to join them. Then it dawned on me that she was watching my family or at least the place where their noise was coming from. I was frozen to the spot as a dozen emotions and questions ran through me.

'Why was she hiding in the trees and watching my family at play? Did her enmity to me extend to them? Was she hoping to take Thomas from me? I had made up my mind to go and confront her when I felt a hand on my shoulder. Shocked and a bit afraid, I turned to find the man who is pretending not to listen whilst driving this car.'

The women all turned as one to stare at the cars very elderly driver to whom, until that moment, they had paid no attention.

'It's Arnie,' said Rose. 'Alexandra's bodyguard.'

Arnie lifted his fingers from the steering wheel to the brim of his broad hat in mock salute. Natalie could see his eyes smiling at her in the rear view mirror.

'Yes,' said Natalie. 'Although I always thought bodyguard was a poor description for the only man whose advice and support was accepted and even sought out by Alexandra.'

'But what is he doing here? I mean driving us now,' said the ever direct Heather?

'We shall ask him, but first, let me finish what I've started,' said Natalie.

'That day in Jedburgh, I'm not sure if our driver was there in his capacity as bodyguard or just watching out for a friend's well-being. Whichever, I am grateful that he was there and that he stopped me from confronting Alexandra. Arnie confided in me that Alexandra had never stopped loving Thomas. He took me aside and we sat under an old chestnut tree away from the river bank.

'He told me that Alexandra still loved me, as she loved Thomas, but the conflict in her over the loss of Thomas as a lover meant she struggled to express the feelings she had. Her personae within the communities was about strength and independence as a woman in the new world, being besotted by love for a man she couldn't have just didn't work for that personae. There was much gossip once about Alexandra being a virgin, which I knew to be rubbish, but Arnie said it was true in the sense that she had never taken a partner or shown an interest in men or women in the time that he had known her.

'In other words, since Thomas had chosen me over her. It was hard for me to really believe that she still cared for me given the ways she behaved.'

Arnie cleared his throat and keeping his eyes forward, he said, 'What I said then is as true now as it was then.'

Heather could not restrain herself, bursting into the conversation to confront Arnie. 'Why is it you that drives my mother today when the woman you have served all your life, and you say loves my mother, could not bring herself to speak today?'

'Your brother's asked me and I am honoured to do it,' said Arnie gently.

'I would have it no other way, Arnie,' said Natalie with a slight look of reproof at Heather.

'Thank you, Natalie. In truth, I was rather pleased that I wouldn't have to ride with the other men, the saddle doesn't suit me well these days. I think your sons were doing me a kindness as well as an honour.' He laughed.

Arnie turned, stiffly for he was even older than Natalie, and looked Heather in the eye for a moment before saying, 'Don't forget, young lady, that Alexandra is a woman just like you.'

Natalie looked at a slightly chastised Heather before continuing. 'Heather, my darling, you are a community mother now and you will no doubt learn, just as I had to, that in becoming a leader, you are judged by a different standard. Most people will expect more of you than they expect of themselves or their peers. That is right and as it should be. A very few community mothers are able to expose their private thoughts and feeling to this judgement, and simply except that they have very little if any private space in their lives.

'Most, however, must develop a public personae and live their private lives as much as possible behind the personae.

'Although Alexandra has never been a community mother, she is undoubtedly a leader and she has used the personae she developed to expertly communicate with tens of thousands and brought hope and purpose through that communication. On that day in Jedburgh, Arnie helped me understand the burden of other people's hopes and fears that Alexandra carried. He helped me to see that the woman who had been like a sister to me was still there behind the personae.'

Natalie paused to look at each of her daughters in turn for a moment. 'Do you understand? To be the woman in the red coat, the strong women who creates communities that work and defends them in battle, she could not also be the woman who cries at a lost love. The real Alexandra is of course as subject to the doubts, worries and personal faults that plague all of us. She would just never allow herself the luxury of expressing them openly.'

Looking at Heather but still speaking to them all, she went on. 'As a community mother, you learn that you often have to deny things to yourself if you are to fulfil the role successfully. To be the Alexandra you all know, she has had to do deny herself a great deal. Her love for Thomas was the first and last love of a man that she allowed herself. When he was killed, she felt his loss deeply, but she could not express it.

'At his funeral, she spoke of him as a community builder, but only a very few present, including myself, knew of her real feelings. I think she blamed me in part for his death, believing I could have held him back from the campaign to forge an alliance against Nathaniel with Colonel Peters. We decided who would join the campaign through a lottery, which seemed at the time the fairest way, and it did help to prevent tension within the community. In hindsight, I accept it was not a great way to select fighters.

'Thomas was brave but he was not really a fighter. So at the death of Thomas, in my grief, I could not help but secretly blame Alexandra and her "adventures" for my loss, and Alexandra blamed my "weakness" for putting him in harm's way when others would have served the cause better.'

No matter how slowly Arnie drove, the gates of East Lowtown finally came into view. Seeing the gates, Natalie brought her story to a close by saying, 'So now, my girls, you know what has kept Alexandra and I apart for so long. First, her love for my Thomas, and then her grief for him. A love and a grief that has been all the sharper because she never allowed herself to talk about it.'

Even Heather was silent as the car completed the last stretch of road to the gates of their mother's home. The whole community had turned out to welcome Natalie with much eager excitement for the celebration that was to come. Behind the car came men, some on horseback and some in small trucks. In all, a little over thirty community fathers as well as Natalie's three sons were formally led into East Lowtown by Kenny. Such a gathering was very rare in this new world and was a great day for Kenny, Natalie, and the community of East Lowtown.

The procession followed by the whole community continued through the streets of the small town to a large barn used as the main communal space. The town had been busy since Natalie left that morning—flowers and foliage completely covered the front of the barn except where it was covered by a banner that read "Happy Birthday Natalie". The wording of the banner had been a cause of much debate between two camps: one wanted "Happy Birthday Mother Natalie", the other wanted "Happy Birthday Granny Natalie".

Kenny in exasperation had forced the compromise on both camps.

Arnie brought the car to a halt in front of the barn and tuned to Natalie to say, 'It has been a delight to be with you on this day. Happy birthday, Natalie.'

'Thank you, Arnie. Your company and your discretion is as ever much appreciated, and I hope you will be joining us for whatever is being cooked up behind those doors,' she replied looking towards the barn.

'I'd be very happy to,' he said smiling as he added, 'Though if it's a ceilidh, you'll excuse me if I don't take the floor.'

'I'm sure you can still shame a few of the younger ones with your strip the willow.'

'Ah well, maybe not that, but perhaps I could be persuaded by one of your beautiful daughters to join them in a slow waltz.'

'No doubt they would be happy to do so, but it would be ungentlemanly of you not to offer the first dance to the birthday girl, would it not.'

Arnie laughed, but seeing the community fathers lining the path to the barn on either side of the car, he said, 'I think they are ready for you now, Natalie.' He left the car with the dexterity of a man half his age to open the passenger door. He stood as stiffly to attention as he had done once for generals and royalty.

Natalie was applauded by the lines of community fathers as she walked the short distance into the barn followed by her daughters. There was a time of shaking hands and greeting people as the barn filled with the bustle of people taking their places. Out of the corner of her eye, she could see a clearly nervous Kenny flitting about, making arrangements and probably undoing days of planning by the look on some faces.

However, a hush of expectation washed through the barn as she joined her family on the raised podium at the back of the barn. As she took her seat, all those who had found a seat in the barn rose to their feet and began to clap, which faded out into a chorus of the timeless happy birthday song with Kenny leading the hip hips. As the last "hurrah" sounded, the people stayed on their feet applauding with many shouting, "speech, speech".

Kenny called for order motioning with his hands for people to sit. Having obtained enough of a silence to be heard, he raised his voice to the assembled crowd.

'Friends, I am sure you will hear from Natalie shortly but first, let me say that this has been a great day for East Lowtown. We are so proud of our community, and most of all of our amazing community mother.' Kenny waited for the renewed applause to die down sufficiently before he continued.

'I would like to thank all those who made the journey to join us for Natalie's special day and to all those who have worked so hard to make it a special day. Now, I know that you can't wait for me to be quiet so that you can hear from Natalie,' said Kenny cutting off the inevitable heckles with, 'and so I ask our community mother and birthday girl to share some words with us.'

Natalie rose to the sound of applause and as she made her way to Kenny at the lectern and microphone, she reflected on how well he had cast off his nervousness and rose to the occasion. Reaching the lectern where the microphone was perched, it was apparent to her that she would disappear behind the lectern if she was to use it. She stood at its side and smiled at Kenny who flushed red as he fumbled to free the microphone and hand it to her.

'Thank you, Kenny,' she said into the microphone. 'And thank you all for being here to share my birthday.' She paused for a moment and then with a slight hint of sarcasm said, 'What a surprise!' She was rewarded with a rush of laughter.

'There have been many times on my journey through life when I was sure that I would not be privileged enough to make it to old age. Yet here I am, ninety years old; only a very few of the people that started with me on this journey are still here. I am grateful for my family, and glad that I have made new and younger friends on my journey so that I can share my last years with them here in Lowtown.

'As I look at you, I can see hope and joy in the future, but as I take the next steps of my journey, I know I will not forget how I came to be here and the many that have helped me on the way. I ask for nothing more as a birthday present from you all than that you take a moment with me now to remember those who are not here but who have shared our journey.'

Natalie bowed her head and closed her eyes and tried to imagine the faces of the people who she had loved and lost. The whole room followed her example, though some of the children took the opportunity to furtively peep about and chatter with their neighbours. Natalie became absorbed in memories, and had to wrench herself free as she realised she was in danger of losing track of time and turning her birthday into a wake.

She had not planned this, and now was wondering how long she should keep the people at remembering when a noise at the back of the hall claimed her attention. Opening her eyes, she saw that heads of the people at the long tables were turning one and all to look to the back of the hall. Natalie followed their gaze and saw an elderly woman in a red coat emerging from a small group of women that had made their way into the small door set into the now closed large barn gates. She knew instantly as did all the others that this was Alexandra.

She glanced quickly at Kenny, who in averting his eyes to avoid her, immediately raised her suspicion that this was planned. Alexandra was slowly walking along the aisle left between rows of tables straight towards Natalie, who to her annoyance, felt her heart rate rising. Her palms began to sweat and she hand to grip the microphone a little tighter.

Alexandra had got about half way to the podium and Natalie when people began to rise to their feet and applaud. Alexandra was as near to an old world celebrity that the new world could offer. For most, it was exciting and memorable just to see her.

Natalie looked on as the women in Alexandra's group stopped and joined the applause with Alexandra continuing to walk towards her. Natalie felt she ought to be angry with her, she was after all gate crashing her birthday party, but she wasn't. She had a strange feeling that the remembering she had initiated had summoned her into the barn.

As Alexandra reached the steps to the raised area on which Natalie and her family were seated, she raised a foot to the first step, but it was clear that the steps with no hand rail were going to be a problem for a women of her age. The applause began to die as people became aware of the little drama at the foot of the stage when as if from nowhere, Arnie (himself ninety-five years old) appeared and took a hand to help her balance as she climbed the few steps onto the raised platform.

As Alexandra took the last steps towards Natalie, there was complete silence in the hall. Many were aware that there was a tension between the two women and those more involved in community politics had heard gossip and whispers about the strain between them.

Stepping close to Natalie, who was smiling with puzzlement at this development, Alexandra whispered for Natalie's ears only, though many stained to catch the words.

'Natalie, I would like to say a few words on this occasion and beg your indulgence.'

For the briefest of moments, Natalie entertained the fantasy of denying Alexandra and publicly embarrassing her. Instead, she nodded her head and handed Alexandra the microphone. She took a step back offering her the stage.

Raising the microphone to her mouth, she said, 'Thank you, Natalie.' Turning to face the people assembled in the barn, she went on. 'Thank you all for such a wonderful welcome. Many amongst you will wonder why I am here and have so rudely interrupted the proceedings arranged to honour a good woman, a fine leader, and a wonderful example for you all.'

She paused almost daring anyone in the audience to react to her presence. However, people were gripped with the drama of the event, a party for a respected community mother and now the most well-known person in the new world making a speech.

She continued in a stern tone. 'It has come to my attention that on this joyful day, there is to be a sad parting.' Again, Alexandra paused to let the tension in the room work on what the parting she was referring to might be.

'A moment ago, Natalie asked you to remember those that have travelled the journey of life with us but are no longer here to share it. Natalie and I have shared a lot in our journey; we share many memories of those lost to us. We are old enough to have known the old world and survived its collapse. We have fought together to create a space in which friendship and community can grow.'

People began to applaud but Alexandra cut them off with a gesture of her hand.

Looking at Natalie, she said, 'I am not here for their applause but for your forgiveness.'

Some people in the barn took a moment longer than others to catch the change in the atmosphere as they all took in that Alexandra was asking for forgiveness from Natalie.

Indeed, Natalie was taking a moment to absorb what was happening and just stared at Alexandra with a puzzled smile.

Alexandra broke the silence by saying, 'I should have been a better friend to you, Natalie.'

The people in the barn were enthralled, as well as a little shocked and embarrassed as they witnessed something which seemed to be intensely personal between two very public figures in their lives.

Natalie came to her senses as she realised that this was real; this was her old friend asking for forgiveness, not a political speech by the great Alexandra of the red coat.

'Alexandra, you have always and will always be a dear friend to me. You are the woman that brought light into my life after I thought Nathaniel had thrown me into darkness forever.'

The excitement in the barn was palpable.

'It's true that you have always been a friend to me, but I have not always made the space for you in my life that a friend should have. I have not been strong enough to let you know that I loved you despite anything that might have come between us. I came today to let you know, before you step from this stage, that I have always loved you, dear Natalie.'

Natalie and the people in the barn were taken completely in surprise by the personal and almost pleading tone of Alexandra's speech. This was not the Alexandra they all knew and respected. As if she sensed the uneasiness in the minds of her listeners, Alexandra turned her attention back to the people in the barn.

'I said earlier that today is to be a day of partings as well as celebration,' she said resurrecting the personae that they all knew. 'I am going to add my own parting as, from this moment, I will no longer play a role in the public life of the communities. I am, for want of a better word, retiring.'

Alexandra allowed the excited chatter that greeted this announcement to rise and die down before she continued. 'If Natalie and you good people will make room for me, I would like to spend my last days here with you.' She turned to Natalie, but still holding the microphone, said, 'I will try to rediscover the friendship we once had.'

Natalie smiled and walked the few steps to Alexandra. She embraced her to cheers and stupendous applause.

As she released Alexandra from the embrace, she retrieved the microphone and quietening the community, which was on its feet and some literally on the tables, she spoke to them all in a quiet voice that easily commanded attention.

'Alexandra said she had heard that today was to be about partings as well as celebration. That is true, I had intended to announce to you all today that I was stepping down as your community mother.' She paused as people shouted "no", "stay" and chanted "we want Natalie". Eventually, she started to speak again. 'I am old. It is time for me to rest and you to choose another. However, as my last act as your community mother, I grant sanctuary to Alexandra in our community for the rest of her life.'

The barn exploded into another round of applause and stamping of feet as Natalie took Alexandra's hand and led her to the table where her stunned family and a beaming Kenny sat.

Sitting next to Kenny, she had to shout in his ear to make herself understood over the din made by the ecstatic crowd. 'It seems my secret somehow leaked, but no matter; it's over to your generation now, Kenny.'

The End

Milton Keynes UK
Ingram Content Group UK Ltd.
UKHW022032181123
432826UK00004B/64